THE BLOODY HERRING

THE BLOODY HERRING

*A Fantasy Historical Romance of the
First Decade of* Papa's Pride *by*

CLEA ORTIZ NEWCOME

*But Actually a Gilbert & Sullivan Fantasy
in Space Opera Framework by*

PHYLLIS ANN KARR

WILDSIDE PRESS

Published by Wildside Press LLC.
www.wildsidebooks.com

FOREWORD

Some have told me that the events of Ship Years 8 and 9 were far too terrible to use as underpinning for a light fantasy romance, and one that in any case can appeal chiefly to the hundred or so avid Savoyards in the ship's population. My response is that light treatment has been among humanity's most effective defense mechanisms for dealing with disaster, probably since our race became recognizably human back in Old Earth's paleolithic; and that Savoy enthusiasm is as precious in **Papa's Pride** *as any other artifact of our Old Earth heritage.*

In any case, these things lie more than half a century in our own past, and if half a century does not make them fair game for historical fantasy, what does? Is the past not the past, whether ten or ten thousand years ago, whether back on Old Earth or out here in our great colony starship of twenty-four pylons revolving around a vast central core?

While retaining the names of such entities as the Antique Terra Theater, which had not yet split into the Order-sponsored Old Earth Company and the Committee-sponsored Players to the Stars, with their respective screenplay arms Universal Aspirations and Pride Productions, I have fictionalized the names and other aspects of individuals actually involved in Chuck Wang's crime—the worst ever perpetrated and, we hope, ever to be perpetrated in **Papa's Pride**. *I have added some completely fictional people to the cast, omitted many historical figures entirely, and somewhat condensed, even rearranged, certain of the events. There were never any deliberate murders connected with Wang's outrage, at least as far as we know. Shipnet will make it very easy for interested readers to collate my tale with as much as we have of the truth.*

What I have striven to recreate as faithfully as possible are the conditions of "pylon fever" and the restless searching for family fulfillment that hothoused both Wang's crime and, arguably, the household conditions under which most of us have grown up: the reshaping of the old "Western World's" so-called nuclear family that makes that situation in **The Gondoliers,** when the characters all regard two husbands to three wives as a great problem, seem to everyone outside the Order of the Cosmic Christ such an especially quaint piece of museum morality. When we come to pylon fever and social ferment, however, we must deal more, almost, with theories than with hard data; and I believe my own theories to be based on the most plausible ones of our recognized ship social and medical historians.

It should go without saying that anything which may sound like an Old Earth racial slight or slur is purely an attempt to recreate the mindset of the Gilbertian characters within the fantasy. Papa Gadore had already disregarded "racial" and "national" distinctions, so perceived, in recruiting his great ship's complement; and the Committee's system of procreational lists has ensured the blending of genes beyond anything even Papa Gadore could ever have asked of chance and natural human promiscuity. Even I, who would never have existed if my parents had not defied genetic morality, who have been happily raised by a two-parent family living in sanctuary in the convent pylon, am forced to applaud genmorality in this regard.

Of course, the means by which my Dr. Chandra Falcon incubates and enters her patient's fantasy world—thanks to data allegedly obtained in my fictionalized "last download from Old Earth," are completely my own invention. Pylon 19 has no such devices. As far as anyone not actually employed in that pylon knows.

—Clea Ortiz Newcome
Loneman's Haven, pylon 13, May 11, S.Y. 63

CHAPTER 1

THE LAST DOWNLOAD FROM EARTH

He almost looked like he was asleep. He was actually in coma.

Dr. Chandra Falcon gazed down at him, rubbing her even chin. Robert Lozinski, 23. Among the brightest stars in the musical comedy and operetta firmament of Antique Terra's repertory company. Specializing in such roles as Ali Hakim, Papageno, and Ko-Ko of Titipu. The only time Chandra had really talked to him for any length of time, he had been pre-miniscing about when he would be old enough naturally to play Sir Joseph Porter and the Duke of Plaza-Toro. (Aging make-up, like almost everything else, was precious in *Papa's Pride*.) His friendly rival in the company, Steve Davis, who at fifteen years older was playing those very roles, had quipped that Bob had better enjoy the ones that could be interpreted as juvenile while he could, and why not go for Peter Pan while he still had his youth? Bob had said something about a good role, but…and that was all Chandra had heard before moving along to a different part of the reception. Two thousand colonists and about half a thousand mingling sisters and brothers of the O.C.C. might be a pinpoint population compared to your average small village on the Old Earth they'd left behind, but it was still too many people for anybody to interact intimately with everybody.

She had enjoyed Bob Lozinski's work in any number of plays, though, since Liftaway, watching him grow up from young adolescent roles (when she hadn't been much older, herself) to the ones he presently enjoyed. As she'd watched Steve Davis mature from ones Lozinski was playing now to the inescapably older-gentleman ones.

And now Steve Davis was dead and Bob Lozinski in a coma, following the same backstage accident during a rehearsal for *The Yeomen of the Guard*.

"Deuces," said Sister Harriet, "doesn't think it was an accident."

"What, then? A practical joke that went wrong?"

"Murder. And attempted murder."

"Murder and attempted murder?" nurse Misaki Lang wanted to know. "Who? And why? Bob himself? Could that be why he went into this coma? Couldn't cope with the guilt? Or the knowledge of Steve's having tried something? Stars know we can't find any physical reason for Bob's coma."

Chandra Falcon said, "I'm going out and have a talk with Deuces Osborne. Maybe a good, long talk."

* * * *

Deuteronomy Osborne, called "Deuces," had been in his twenties at Liftaway, eight years ago. Now in his thirties going on fifties, a lank and craggy hawk of a man, after falling away young from a Bible Belt upbringing, he had jumped at the chance to sign on with Papa Al Gadore as a member of ship security. Osborne's specialty was sniffing out conspiracies. Not that there had been many to sniff out the first several years, or that they had ever been either large or very serious. Usually two or three colonists at most, more often than not kids plotting to raid the ration baskets before distribution, or sneak marijuana seeds out of the flora ark in the core and raise a little of the stuff in some hidden patch in one of the forest pylons.

But as the voyage lengthened, the downloads from Old Earth grew weaker and stranger, and it became more and more obvious habitable planets were so few and far between in the galaxy that finding one might take several generations—that, in fact, everybody now in *Papa's Pride,* and very likely their grandchildren, might live and die in the pylons and core without ever setting foot on a new earth or seeing a real atmosphere sky rather than a simulated one, something like what Old Earth had sometimes called "cabin fever" set in. *Papa's Pride* took to calling it "pylon fever," and for some years it was a very real, if slippery, problem. Among other symptoms, conspiracies started getting worse. Two or three actually managed to plant marijuana, and several groups learned how to cook up worse stuff in midnight kitchens. Drying addicts out, whether in the hospital or either of the O.C.C. pylons, wasn't pretty. But every life was precious in *Papa's Pride*, and worth salvaging when and if at all possible.

Less harmful—some already called it even beneficial—was the experimenting with family groups of multiple mommies and daddies. This had actually begun on Old Earth, but pylon fever gave it a big boost in *Papa's Pride*. Things got pretty wild in the colony pylons. The Order of the Cosmic Christ might actually have had a lot more to alternately castigate and ignore in those last few years before the Coup than after genetic morality became colony law.

Chandra Falcon had been seventeen at Liftaway, and completed her formal education in the ship, progressing in leaps and bounds as long as the downloads continued from Old Earth. They grew incredibly more sophisticated as time dilation advanced Old Earth civilization and knowledge lifetimes to the ship's months, until suddenly they stopped altogether. And *Papa's Pride* could never know if this was because it had finally gotten out of range, or because human civilization on Old Earth was no more, or both.

By then, Chandra Falcon was formally educated to a fare-thee-well, both mentally and physically, with doctorates in liberal arts, physical medicine, and mental hygiene, as well as black belts of various degrees in several martial arts. But her informal education would never stop. There was already a suspended animation pod in the deep sleep pylon with her name on it: she was a ship's treasure, to be stored at sixty for revival whenever the ship finally made planetfall and needed her brain and expertise in setting up a permanent colony.

Sister Mary Harriet Sanford had already seen her personal half-century mark at Liftaway; but procreational age didn't count for the thousand aboard who belonged to the Order of the Cosmic Christ, any more than for the papal nuncio and the clerical members of his small staff: part of Pope John Paul IV's price for helping finance the construction of *Papa's Pride*. Sister Harriet had begun the voyage as one of the nuns strictly cloistered in the convent pylon, but by about five years into the journey had, Chandra believed, been among the earliest to start experiencing pylon fever—Harriet herself put it down to a late midlife crisis—when she supplicated for and received transfer to the sisterhood, which mingled freely with the colonists in public areas of the pylons and core. As a sister,

Harriet had plunged into Antique Terra's theater work, which was seen as an essential in keeping up morale. She specialized in directing light comedy, musicals, and operettas—the same shows Bob Lozinski was and Steve Davis had been such hits in.

Misaki Lang had been twelve at Liftaway. Now, at twenty, she was one of the best practical nurses in pylon 19, medical research and hospital. She had been assigned to Bob Lozinski at Dr. Falcon's personal request. If any nurse's input could help the doctor diagnose the reason for this coma, it was Misaki Lang. If Misaki suggested it might be conscience unable to cope with guilt—either Bob's own or Steve's—that might be worth looking into. Only... how?

* * * *

Deuteronomy Osborne, who didn't really like the nickname "Deuces," but put up with it because he didn't really like the mouthful of his christened name, either, and preferred "Deuces"—if not by much—to such alternatives as "Deuter" and "Ozzie," was in the nearest waiting garden. In a classic Old Earth movie, he would probably have been smoking. Clean air being precious in *Papa's Pride,* smoking was prohibited except for virtual tobacco in virtual recreation booths, and a very few areas set aside for the thirty or so colonists who still practiced the amalgamation of beliefs and customs they had put together as recreated Native American religion, and who alone in the ship had the legal right to use any of their precious growing soil for actual tobacco. So Deuces was simply pacing, glancing only often enough at the oxygen-producing plants and soul-soothing aquariums all around him to avoid pacing into them.

"How's the kid?" were his first words the minute Chandra came in.

"Still in coma. I understand you don't think it was an accident."

"Nup." The tall man shook his head. "Like they usta say back on Old Earth, Doc, something's about t' go down. Something big. Either Lozinski's in on it, or he knows who is, an' what it is. And, lemme tell you, if this one's as big as I think it is, it's something we *all* oughta know about yesterday."

"All right," she agreed, half humoring him and half respectful because, even if Deuces Osborne sniffed conspiracies in every insul-tube, enough of his hunches played out to make him a security man worth listening to. "Let's start with what you already know, and how."

"Okay. First off. About half, two-thirds the Antique Terra folks are O.C.C., live in their own pylons—monastery an' convent—just come over to the uptown pylon to put on their shows an' suchlike. They're okay. We don't have t' worry about them. The Order polices its own. But Lozinski's in one uh those cozy little households, colony foursome with Pete Schultz, Barbara Cripps and Judi Oshita. Who are also with Antique Terra. Who also just happened to be backstage when that so-called accident occurred."

Chandra almost asked Osborne who his spy had been this time, but she knew by now it was better to let him tell it his own way. He'd pause when question time came.

"And Steve Davis," he went on. "Davis was sniffin' things out for me. I had him tryin' t' move himself in with Lozinski's household, scope out what they've been up to. He figured they were about t' let him in, advanced age be damned. Last word I had from him, he was gonna meet me at Ishmael's Downtown between rehearsal an' supper. Said he had a really big can uh beans to spill, was hopin' to bring either Schultz or Lozinski or both of 'em along, figured at least one uv 'em was ready to help him spill 'em. So. That's where I'm waiting for 'em—Schultz and Davis—when the news hits shipnet there's been some kind uh accident at the Antique Terra." He paused long enough to signal her question time.

She asked, "But you don't know who, exactly, is planning to do what, exactly. Unless that 'accident' was it."

"Nope. That accident wasn't it. I still don't know what it really is. Just wish I did. One uh those housemates does—Lozinski, Schultz, Cripps, Oshita... Maybe all four." The security man shook his prematurely graying head. "Whatever it is, it's somethin' big. Somethin' that could maybe threaten this whole damn ship."

"Something big enough to...commit murder about?"

"Could be," said Deuces Osborne. "People are gettin' funny in *Papa's Pride* these days. In case you haven't noticed. Puttin' their values in funny places. Everything for fun and games, anything for a laugh, never mind what kind uv a laugh, or who's the ones laughing."

"And you haven't questioned them yet—Schultz, Cripps, and Oshita?" If he had, he'd have summed up what they'd told him, even if he thought it was only lies and evasions.

"Hey. When th' news hit shipnet—you know how it is, rumors at first and then as soon as anyone in power really knows anything hard, they cover it up—I lit out for the uptown pylon right away, figuring t' find out what I could first hand and asap. Schultz could've been on his way to meet me, after all—I could've missed him in the insul-tubes. By th' time I got uptown to the Antique Terra, medical already had th' two casualties packed off to you friendly folks here in pylon nineteen, and Oshita and Cripps had packed themselves off t' Lord knows where. Closest guess I heard, privacy pod somewhere t' comfort each other…you know…an' there's privacy pods all over every pylon in this blessed ship an' the core besides."

"Except the two C.C. pylons," Chandra pointed out.

"So they tell us," Osborne replied noncommittally.

* * * *

Chandra had already heard what little Sister Harriet could tell her about the accident, which dovetailed with Osborne's scanty data. As the show's director, Sister Harriet had been out front, concentrating on what the audience would see. The late Steve Davis as Sir Richard Cholmondeley, the Liuetenant of the Tower of London, where the operetta was set; Bob Lozinski as Jack Point the jester, and Pete Schultz as Wilfred Shadbolt the head jailor were all in the wings offstage left, exactly where they were supposed to be, waiting for their next cue to go on, when the accident—a large falling ladder—had happened. Barbara Cripps as Dame Carruthers the Tower housekeeper and Judi Oshita as her niece Kate should have been in the wings offstage right, with most of the chorus: what they'd been doing offstage left with the three men at the fatal moment, Sister Harriet couldn't say. In the first stunned flurry, she hadn't asked; and by the time she thought of it, Cripps and Oshita had vanished.

Only two people had been onstage at the time: the romantic leads, tenor and soprano, both members of the Cosmic Christ. According to the script, a shot from an arquebus was supposed to interrupt their tender scene. The arquebus was a medieval weapon, and nobody in *Papa's Pride,* or for that matter back on Old Earth at the time of Liftaway, had ever heard one fired, so the company's backstage crew were using the same sound effect as for a standard loud gunshot. At first Sister Harriet thought they had tried something different this time, and made a quick mental note to tell them, "Too soon—wait for 'I spake but to try thee—' and tone it down some, we don't want the audience thinking the ship's shielding just failed and let a chunk of space debris crash through."

But it turned out not to have been the planned sound effect. It had been that heavy ladder falling, catching Steve Davis right on the temple and, they'd thought, knocking Bob Lozinski out, too. Sister Harriet had been genuinely surprised when the scans showed Lozinski with no sign of concussion, leaving his coma a mystery.

"If I'd only cast Steve as Point," Sister Harriet kept repeating. "He wanted Jack Point—he'd played it back in ship years three to five—there isn't any reason Point shouldn't have a few gray hairs—but I wanted to try it with a younger man this time...especially after giving Bunthorne to Steve last year—they'd both read for it, Steve and Bob...if Steve had just been standing a little farther back—the lieutenant goes on a few minutes before Point and Shadbolt—he might've still been alive."

"And whoever else you had playing his role might've died instead," Chandra tried pointing out.

"Maybe...maybe not..." The sister gave a shaky smile. "It's really futile, after all, the 'might have been' game."

* * * *

All that had been before Chandra's chat with Osborne. Now, Chandra having shared with the nurse and Antique Terra director what Deuteronomy Osborne had had to say, Misaki told Sister Harriet, "So you see, if Deuces is right, it wouldn't have made any difference what part you'd had Steve playing."

Sister Harriet sighed. "At least he would have gone out in a role he really liked. He didn't enjoy playing the lieutenant nearly as much."

"Maybe not the role," said Chandra, "but he was still doing the *kind* of work he liked, and that's maybe the best any of us can hope for at the moment of death."

"Unless it's going into deep sleep as a future colony treasure," Misaki remarked.

"Even if," Chandra replied. "Even if deep sleep and revival works, a person still has to die sometime, sooner or later. Meanwhile. If there's anything solid beneath Osborne's theory, and if it's even half as big as he's afraid, we'd better do everything we can to find out what it is.... I think it might be time to risk trying that last download from Old Earth."

"'That last download'?" asked Sister Harriet. At almost the same instant, Misaki said, "Dr. Falcon, are you sure?"

* * * *

As nearly as they understood it, it was a refinement on the old method of sharing virtual realities, but whether for recreational, or therapeutic, or psychoanalytic purposes, or some combination of all three, they hadn't entirely figured out. By the time Old Earth uploaded this one to them, thought patterns back there seemed to have morphed and fluxed almost beyond recognition.

Of course, for two or more participants to share a virtual reality had already been popular before Liftaway, and was standard recreational procedure in the uptown and downtown getaway pods of *Papa's Pride*: the hope of keeping morale balanced was worth the power it took to run the equipment. But these were preprogrammed virtual realities, chiefly from computer files of Old Earth sites and sights: the Louvre, Bayreuth, the Grand Canyon. Also specific historical recreations of the Crystal Palace, the original ancient Grecian Olympics, the Battle of Gettysburg, and so on. And of course it was popular for people to create their own made-up worlds and share them with other people...once they were created and filed. What the last download from Old Earth seemed to provide was a modification allowing new auto-fictional reality to be molded from one user's mind, then one or more other people to experience and actually lend input while it was actually being created—a sort of simulation of that elusive wisp, the shared sleep-dream. It had been a philosophical and scientific daydream for so long, it was only surprising they had taken so much time developing it, back on Old Earth where power supplies were less strictly conserved.

The modifications of the virtual reality equipment in *Papa's Pride* looked feasible, and Dr. Falcon thought they had effected them well enough. And the directions for building the virtual re-ality from one person's brain and opening it for another brain's input seemed as nearly straightforward as anything could seem in downloads from Old Earth by this time, when the language at the uploading end had morphed and fluxed even more, perhaps, than the thought patterns, and the people uploading had had to translate into the language that had become almost as archaic as Linear B to the people back on Old Earth.

Chandra had even tested it, once, with Dr. Omar Tarkindar, who had been her lover for a brief time before his laying to sleep with premature symptoms of Riker's syndrome. They had shared a visit to the Mahabharata, and it had worked quite well. But they had had no motive beyond testing the process, seeing how well it worked for them. Chandra had not had the equipment out since. Power was too precious in *Papa's Pride*.

She had thought about it, wondered if it might offer enough potential for boosting morale over and beyond what the standard virtual realities provided to be worth the risk of magnifying and spreading grimmer kinds of fantasizing…but time was precious, too, even on a long, long journey through galactic light-years, and the pair of virtual-sensory kits with their specially modified mo-dems had stayed unused in a box in medical research storage.

Dr. Chandra Falcon led the way to get them out now.

CHAPTER 2

BUILDING A FANTASY

"This really should have his conscious input," Chandra mused. Too bad that getting him back to consciousness was one of their goals. "The next best thing, I suppose, will be to adapt some sort of guided meditation technique."

"Why don't *you* built a world to start with," Misaki wanted to know, "and bring him into yours."

"I already considered that. Whether our first goal is to bring him out of coma or find out what he knows, I think our likeliest starting point is in his imagination rather than mine. I'd also like some kind of non-threatening world, I think. As non-threatening as possible."

"He likes light theater of all kinds," Sister Harriet suggested, "but Gilbert and Sullivan has always been his first love."

"Sounds like an idea." Chandra nodded. "But—your present show, the one in rehearsal when all this happened—that's the grim one of the series, isn't it? Heavier mood, unhappy ending?"

Harriet nodded. "For Jack Point, at least. The character Bob was playing."

"I want to aim for the lighter mood of the others. We can try playing music from *H.M.S. Pinafore* or *The Pirates of Penzance*."

"How about *Pineapple Poll?*" the director suggested. "A ballet made up of bits from all the operas, a sort of Gilbert and Sullivan sampler."

"Worth a try." No need to ask whether shipnet had it. Shipnet had everything available to Old Earth's internet at the time of Liftaway and everything downloaded over the years they could still get reliable downloads. Text, graphics, and sound, even virtual 3-D.

"What kind of input do you plan to supply in this world?" asked Misaki.

Chandra smiled. "For one thing, I plan to use Dr. Charles 'Chuck' Falcon."

"Charles?" Harriet repeated. "Chuck?"

"My own virtual version of my 'inner male.' The one I've developed over the years for virtual mountain climbing, Olympic competitions, things like that."

"You don't think Dr. Chandra Falcon is good enough?" Misaki seemed to be bristling a little. Too many classic Old Earth movies from male-supremacy eras.

"I think Dr. Chandra might be *too* good. In some ways. Think about it. Deuces Osborne, Steve Davis, Pete Schultz, Bob Lozinski...seems to be building into a ring of males, informants as well as investigators. If Osborne had been expecting either of the women of that household to meet him in Ishmael's Downtown... But as things stand, go in as myself, and I might scare Lozinski off, look like Mata Hari or Delilah to him. No, I think this calls for a little 'male bonding' to have the best chances of opening him up. Let's see... I think I should be dressed like a hiker, Victorian style...tweed knickers and leather knapsack, wasn't it? That kind of gear."

"Why the knapsack?" asked Harriet. "Just a prop?"

"A little more than that." Chandra thought back, not only over her Mahabharata adventure with Omar, but also over climbing the Himalayas and so on in the uptown booths. "For virtual supplies. This could turn out to be a lot like any virtual adventure of the more gardenhouse variety. And I'd like to have a virtual copy of the Gilbert and Sullivan librettos along, tucked away where whoever I meet—'in there'—won't notice it. If his world itself is grounded in G. and S., they probably won't have any reference copies of those librettos, not as we'd recognize them. To Lozinski and his virtual characters, whatever isn't the living actuality of Gilbert and Sullivan's world, will be history-book stuff."

Serious though the situation was, Chandra found herself looking forward to it.

* * * *

Music. A light, infectious medly breaking over and over into the well-loved tunes. In glorious synesthesia, the notes as bunches of round, phosphorescent grapes when the melody was smooth, jagged splinters of brilliance when the tune burst into staccato. During the quick tempos, dozens of cross-winds like a concatenation of miniature tornadoes buffeted her free-falling body. While during the sweet-flowing interludes she drifted softly, as though through a giant crystal decanter filled with thick, perfumed syrup. During one slow, vaguely familiar melody, she floated down upon a pear swollen to the size of a grand piano. "Pear-shaped tones," she thought almost dreamily, slicing her hand through the mushy surface and scooping out a lump of soft pulp. Even as she sucked its sweet juice, a new burst of march tempo shook her up to the top of the fluid again—as if Lozinski's virtual dream were welcoming her in...'her' no longer...

The fluid churned ever faster, glints of colored light shooting through it, bubbles forming, fizzing upwards, bursting around Dr. Charles Falcon. The invisible yet tangible orchestra crescendoed towards its grand finale, building louder and faster into a frenzied climax. Chunks of sharp-faceted arpeggios slammed against his skin, needle-sharded bubbles burst inside his ears, nose, armpits...

A great, shattering crash, as if a pair of cymbals had smashed together on the decanter of churning liquid. He felt himself draining out with the champagne, coming to rest on a sandy surface through which the fluid drained from around him, while the thunder of the cymbals echoed gradually into silence.

* * * *

After a while, he rolled over onto his back and blinked a few times at the haze-shrouded sun. Then he stood and took a thorough look around. He was on a coastline of high, rocky cliffs and craggy, moss-encrusted boulders. Above was a sky scudding gray with piles of cloud; below, a white-cresting ocean that foamed over the rocks in weird silence for a few moments until the sound effects—temporarily exhausted by that last musical crescendo?—caught up again with the visuals.

Chuck Falcon turned to face inland. Gray, matted grass that might be green under a sunnier sky; straggling fields marked with rough stone fences; in one pasture a few brown sheep grazing around a ring-shaped stone set up on end. A few fields further, a small graveyard with tangles of twisted black gorse growing up around leaning tombstones. Beyond that, a castle, massive, black, menacing. Not exactly the light, cheeky umwelt he had aimed for.

But, yes, there were castles in the Gilbert and Sullivan world. And the castle was a fairly common symbol, worn deep in the human consciousness. So that one was the logical place to start looking for Bob Lozinski. Dr. Falcon hitched his backpack and started hiking across the fields.

For about fifty yards he strode over spongy grass. For another thirty or forty he followed the hint of a groove through hip-high prickles of gorse. Arriving at last at the stone fence around the sheep pasture, he put one hand on top and vaulted over. (Even Chandra Falcon could have done it—perhaps more easily than Chuck Falcon. If he was more muscular, with greater upper body strength, she carried less weight and was equally athletic.) He landed lightly; the sheep looked up at the slight jarring, and calmly returned to their grazing.

As he neared the standing, doughnut-shaped stone, he paused, sensing the presence of another person in the field. He took a closer look at the stone. On the lower edge of the center hole, he saw a brownish tangle that might have been some strange plant growth, or a small animal with long, shaggy fur, or the back of a human head.

Someone, he guessed, was lying on the other side of the stone, using the lower edge of its center hole for a pillow. He turned toward the stone, walking softly enough not to disturb a sleeper, but firmly enough to avoid the appearance of stealth.

When he was about three meters from the stone, the bunch of brown hair shook itself and rolled over, bringing a face into view— a woman's face, dirty and piquant, with broad forehead, wide green eyes, and a small pointed chin, resting now on the stone.

She studied him for a moment, solemnly, then wriggled up through the doughnut-stone's hole. The effect was almost like the slow materialization from the head and shoulders down of a supernatural being. There were fairies in Gilbert and Sullivan. But this young woman was in rags, one shoulder left bare by the ripping of a sleeve, the skin of her arms and legs covered with dirt and scratches, her waist-length reddish hair tangled thick with twigs and wilted wildflowers. Hardly the attire of a fairy, no matter how elfin her face!

"Good afternoon," Chuck Falcon began, taking a step forward.

She remained for a moment leaning against the stone, ignoring his offer of friendship, staring at him with such a blank expression that he could not be sure she really saw him. Then suddenly, with a wild laugh, she ducked behind the stone, poked her head out through the hole again, smiled up rakishly at him, and said, "When the foxgloves drip dark nectar, we'll have time enough then for my lady's own dinner-party."

He stepped back and rubbed his chin, considering. He had rather expected to recognize Bob Lozinski right away, but in the Mahabharata world Omar had appeared as Yudhisthira and Chandra as Draupadi. And it might be as normal to switch genders in this application of virtual reality as in the commoner varieties. Wasn't Chandra herself appearing as Chuck?

The woman had started to sing:

"The cat and the dog and the little puppee
Sat down in a—

"Are you a gentleman?" she asked, breaking into speech. "Or do you go to church on Tuesday morning with a great black hat on your head and a basket of charity suppers in your hand?" She plucked a daisy from her hair and began meditatively eating it, gazing at Chuck Falcon from her upside-down angle.

He leaned over and gently took her arm. "There's a storm coming up. I think you'd better come with me to find shelter."

A flicker of understanding seemed to come into her face, and with it a look of terror. "No!" she cried, jumping up and spinning away from his touch. "You want to go there!" She pointed one thin finger at the castle looming a few fields away, just beyond the graveyard.

"Do you know of a better place to find shelter?" He was careful to keep his voice quiet.

"Don't go there! You mustn't go there!" She darted around the carved stone, across the field, and clambered up the fence.

He began walking toward her softly, trying not to startle her.

Her mood had changed again. As the first few raindrops fell, she straddled the fence, gazed up at the lowering sky, and remarked, "There's always a storm. It's the way of the world. There was a mermaid once, loved a high-born squire, but he gave her a pearl comb and left her to weep alone when the moon was high and green. Whisht!" Then, looking down at Chuck Falcon, who had almost reached the fence, she repeated, "Don't go there! Never go there! They're all mad in there, quite mad."

With that, she slipped off the fence to the other side. By the time he reached it and looked over, she had already disappeared among a jumble of large boulders that covered the slope below. Apparently she had taken shelter beneath some of the great stones. The rain was coming fast and heavy now, and he decided his best course would be to get to the castle as he'd originally planned.

As he turned back, he heard the madwoman's song filtering through the rain:

> *"The cat and the dog and the little puppee*
> *Sat down in a sieve on the sands of the sea.*
> *The sand was so green and the sea was so gray*
> *That the three brave explorers were all rinsed away!"*

CHAPTER 3

THE MAP

In a bookshelf-lined chamber deep within the castle, a young man in Regency attire picked up a dagger with an ornate Florentine handle and a blade of Spanish steel gleaming blue in the firelight. Feeling through the cloth of his waistcoat, he placed the dagger's well-sharpened point in the furrow between the two ribs he judged most immediately over his heart. He then leaned back in his armchair, waiting for the courage to drive home.

After a few minutes, with a sigh and a shudder, he lifted the dagger away, tossed it on the small table beside his chair, and rubbed one fingertip over the frayed threads in his waistcoat. Someone, he sensed, might be coming—someone who could possibly help. He took another drink from his goblet and picked up his book once more.

* * * *

Chuck found a footpath of sorts on the other side of the sheep pasture, but already it was a channel of mud, and he kept as much as possible to the slippery grass and weeds beside it. The trail led straight through the small graveyard. He wondered whether relevant clues might be found on the tombstones, but those nearest the path were lichened over, the inscriptions all but obliterated; and he did not stop to investigate the monuments farther away. The castle should be at least equally fruitful in clues, as well as drier.

There was neither moat nor drawbridge. He mounted about a dozen cracked stone steps to a Gothic arch, and found the massive oak door standing two feet ajar. Was someone trying to draw him inside? Drenched as he was, before entering he lifted the heavy iron knocker and let it fall several times. Its echoes gave the impression of long hallways and empty chambers. The knocker was shaped like a herring, and when he took his hand from it, his fingers were smeared with a brownish-red stain, like rust or dried blood.

He rinsed the stain off by rubbing his hands in the falling rain. Then, no one having answered his knock, he pushed open the door, stepped inside, and pushed it almost shut again, listening to its squeaks and being careful to leave it ajar as he had found it. Stumbling on a loose piece of masonry in the hall, he moved the chunk into place to prevent the door from closing all the way.

With little light seeping in from the murky day, and no kindled lamps on the walls, it might as well have been night in the vestibule. He dug his virtual flashlight from his virtual backpack, glad of the waterproofed canvas that kept the pack's inside safe from the virtual rain. Virtuality could be very realistic. Aiming the beam of light around the vestibule, he located and lit a number of candles in wall sconces.

The walls were covered with medium-large pictures in gilt frames. He examined them by the light of the candles, using his flashlight whenever he wanted a closer look at some detail. The pictures were theatrical costume designs, unexpectedly airy and colorful in this gloomy hall.

He looked over several costumed figures—English village girls, Peers of the Realm, fairy-tale princes and princesses, gaudily melodramatic pirate captain, quaintly old-fashioned London bobby, Japanese costumes with exaggerated fans on suspiciously non-Oriental-looking people, a pair of gondoliers posed in imitation of Siamese twins, a vaguely Wagnerian fairy queen…all Gilbert and Sullivan characters. Of course.

And here was the picture of a thin, sallow-faced fellow in velvet knee breeches, his hair wildly bouffant and an oversized lily in one hand. Bunthorne, from the operetta *Patience*. Steve Davis had played that part in Antique Terra's repertory the first couple of years after Liftaway and again in the revival two years ago. When Lozinski also had tried for the part.

This time around, in Antique Terra's *Yeomen of the Guard*, Lozinski had the part he'd wanted. The part both he and Davis had wanted. The late Steve Davis, who—according to Deuteronomy Osborne, had had bigger things on his mind. Had Bob Lozinski?

Just as Chuck headed for the archway leading to the rest of the castle, he saw a picture of the woman he had met in the sheep pasture. Yes, there was no doubt: the same ragged garments, the same tangle of red-brown hair, the same piquant face with its abstracted yet curiously alert eyes. But which operetta did she come from? Dr. Falcon couldn't quite remember. One Antique Terra hadn't done yet?

He entered a long hallway, came to its end, found another, climbed up a flight of stairs, emerged in yet another hallway. Ever keeping a mental map of the way he had come, he followed the same procedure in each hallway—turn off the flashlight and try to spot a line of light seeping out from underneath one of the doors. At last, in the fourth passageway, along the bottom crack of the sixth door, he found such a line. Softly he turned the large gilt doorknob and went in, to find himself in a library, surrounded by the oiled spines of leather-bound books which gleamed in the light of candles and fire.

In a cushioned, highbacked armchair near the stone fireplace sat a smallish, black-haired young man in knee-breeches and a cutaway, swallowtail coat.

Glancing up at Chuck Falcon, the youth gave an exclamation of pleasure, closed his book and put it down between a half-drunk goblet of milk and a fancy dagger on a small table. Then he rose to greet his unexpected visitor. "Your servant, sir! Delighted to make your acquaintance! Mother of pearl, man, you're drenched! Beastly weather in these parts—come over to the fire and dry yourself."

He poked it up with a fire-iron and threw another log on the blaze. Chuck needed no further urging. The worst of the excess rainwater had dripped off in the passageways, but the warmth of the fire was still gratifying. He slung off his backpack and turned first his face, then his back, to the flickering heat.

His host straightened, looked at him, and hesitated a moment, still holding the poker uncertainly in his hand. Then, thrusting it back into its stand beside the fireplace, he went on, "Sherry? No—no, I think brandy, to take off the chill."

"Brandy will be fine, thanks." Studying the young man's face, pale and haggard-eyed as it was, Chuck wondered if he had found Bob Lozinski.

* * * *

While his host was pouring the brandy, Chuck Falcon picked up the book the young man had been reading. It was a collection of poems by Swinburne and Morris, with a calling card inserted as a bookmark. The card was printed with the name "Sir Despard Murgatroyd, Baronet," but the "Despard" was lined through and the name "Ruthven" printed neatly above it. In small Gothic letters beneath the name was printed, "Villain-at-Large. Abductions, Burglaries, Assassinations, & Other Assorted Criminal Activities." In the lower right-hand corner was the simple address, "Ruddigore Castle." Yes, all this sounded like Gilbert and Sullivan's way of looking at things. But which operetta?

Chuck's host turned with a snifter of brandy in each hand, and saw him reading the card. Noticing a slight blush spread through the young man's cheeks, Chuck replaced the card, having kept his finger between the pages where he'd found it, and laid the book back on the table. "Sir Ruthven?" he asked conversationally, accepting his snifter.

"Rivven," replied the baronet, correcting his pronunciation. "We usually utter it with the elision. Not a pleasant name in any case, is it? But I regret our lack of a formal introduction…"

"Falcon. Dr. Charles Falcon—call me 'Chuck.' I'm a stranger to these parts."

"Dr. Falcon." Sir Ruthven bowed, then lifted his own snifter of brandy. "Your servant, sir. To a mutually profitable acquaintance-ship."

Apparently, going by the half-emptied goblet of milk, Sir Ruthven was a social rather than a serious drinker. Now, after one (admittedly generous) swallow of brandy, he seemed to relax a little. "May I inquire, Doctor Falcon, what induces you to seek our peculiarly grim corner of the country?"

Well, why not start with something obvious? "I'm hoping to look up a fellow named Bunthorne."

"Bunthorne? Not Reginald Bunthorne, the fleshly poet?"

Remembering the skinny character in the costume design, Chuck smiled. "Well, I'd hardly have called him 'fleshly,' but I believe he is a poet."

"It refers to his style. Wait, I have his book here somewhere."

While Sir Ruthven was searching the crowded bookshelves, Chuck took the opportunity to re-examine the volume his host had been reading. Opening it to the place marked, he noticed in the margin of the right-hand page a small, elegant pointing hand drawn in ink. He followed the pointing finger and read the lines:

> *"From too much love of living,*
> *From hope and fear set free,*
> *We thank with brief thanksgiving*
> *Whatever gods may be*
> *That no life lives for ever;*
> *That dead men rise up never;*
> *That even the weariest river*
> *Winds somewhere safe to sea."*

"Ah, here it is!" came Sir Ruthven's voice. Again Chuck replaced the volume of Swinburne and Morris on the table, as the baronet brought a slim leather-backed book to the fireplace. *"Heart-Foam and Other Poems.* Actually, he did not publish the title poem; but he inscribed it in holograph on the flyleaf of each and every copy:

> *"Oh, to be wafted away*
> *From this black Aceldama of sorrow,*
> *Where the dust of an earthy to-day*
> *Is the earth of a dusty to-morrow!"*

Sir Ruthven's taste in poetry—assuming Sir Ruthven was Bob Lozinski—disturbed Dr. Falcon. But all he said for the time being was, "Very nice."

"You really think so? Well, but you're in the wrong part of the country entirely to find Mr. Bunthorne. He resides in Suffolk."

"I see. Maybe you could show me a map?"

"A map? Nothing easier!" Crossing the library to an oakwood writing-desk, Sir Ruthven lowered its top and rummaged through the pigeonholes until he found a rolled piece of paper. Unrolling it on the desk, he weighted down one edge with a blown-glass paperweight, looked around for something to hold down the other edge, and chose the heavy-handled Florentine dagger that had been resting on the table with his book and milk.

Chuck squinted down at the map, memorizing it. As nearly as he could remember from Chandra's schooling, both the early part of it back on Old Earth and the advanced degrees earned in *Papa's Pride,* it showed a fairly accurate representation of southern England, with Penzance, Portsmouth, and London clearly marked about where he thought they should be. But the size of southern England seemed to be exaggerated, and the size of the surrounding bodies of water and land shrunk, so that in the heart of a scaled-down eastern Europe Chuck quickly saw a bright gold area labeled "Pfenning Halbpfennig" in large letters, and above it to the northwest a tiny drawing of a fortress labeled "Castle Adamant." More operettas he wasn't familiar with. At the top of a miniaturized Italy he found Venice; and just off the coast of a squashed Spain he noticed an island named Barataria—that was for *The Gondoliers,* which Chandra had seen. Beyond Barataria was another island, named Utopia—that rang no bell—and beyond that, with no regard for the American continents or the Pacific Ocean, was Japan, its principal metropolis captioned Titipu.

"Here is Ruddigore Castle, where I regret to say we are now." Sir Ruthven pointed to an ill-starred location near the western tip of Cornwall. "And here," he went on, moving his finger across the map past London to a site near the eastern coast, "is Castle Bunthorne." Returning his finger to Ruddigore Castle, he traced a line along the southern Cornish coast. "Now, I think your best plan would be to travel overland to Penzance. If you tell the Pirates you're an orphan, they'll gladly smuggle you to Portsmouth. From there you can probably find passage on the *Pinafore* to Ploverleigh, here—and one of the villagers will be honored to drive you the ten miles further inland to Castle Bunthorne."

"Thanks. This is a great help." Though Chuck preferred to stick near Sir Ruthven. Considering that the secondary sharer of this kind of virtual world ought to meet the primary sharer quite early, if the madwoman hadn't been Lozinski, it logically almost had to be the baronet. "Of course, I don't much feel like starting out in a storm."

"That's understood." Sir Ruthven lifted the dagger from the map's edge and shifted his fingers nervously from handle to blade and back. "You'll dine with me, of course, and—stay the night. I'll...I'll ring for my man to air out a room for you."

The baronet started toward the bell-pull, and Chuck bent over the map again, holding its unweighted edge down with his hand.

The next instant he felt a sharp point at his back.

"I...apologize for this with all my heart," said Sir Ruthven. "I assure you, I bear you no personal ill-will whatsoever. Quite the contrary. But..."

* * * *

Chuck was not alarmed for himself; nor, with his assorted black belts, was his attacker in any particular danger. Suddenly ducking forward, he threw his left elbow around in a back hook that connected with the baronet's hand and sent the dagger clattering across the floor. Continuing the movement, he straightened his arm, caught Sir Ruthven's forearm near the wrist, and spun his own body around to face the pale and shaken baronet.

Sir Ruthven dropped to his knees and buried his face in his free hand. Chuck released his other arm and said in a firm but quiet voice, "All right, now suppose you tell me why you tried it."

"I'm...awfully glad you did that." Pulling himself together Sir Ruthven got to his feet again. "It was expected of me—I think you read my card?—but you can hardly imagine how grateful I am to be foiled. I trust this won't prevent you from stopping to dine with me?"

"Leaving now would be the farthest thing from my mind." Chuck returned to the fireplace, pulled up a second armchair, and sat. The baronet followed his lead, sinking again into his own faded plush chair. Chuck warily relaxed.

"I expect you'll want a room with a lock?" asked Sir Ruthven.

"No." Chuck saw that his host would doubtless have his own complete set of keys. "I'll want a room with an inside bolt and some heavy furniture I can move against the door."

"An excellent precaution. I congratulate you heartily and will see to it that your wishes are fulfilled."

Both sat silent for a few moments, the baronet staring into the fire, Chuck sneaking glances at his haunted profile. After a short time Sir Ruthven said diffidently, "You know, I...I'm a rather better poet than Mr. Bunthorne, myself."

"Oh?" Chuck tapped his fingers together meditatively. "I'd like to hear your stuff."

"It's all in manuscript, of course. I haven't published." The baronet rose and pulled a bound notebook from the shelves. After some self-conscious riffling through the pages, he nodded and began to read, wandering around the room as he did so:

> *"Oh, painful is the honeybee's mistake,*
> *Who stings the careless hand that meant no harm.*
> *And painful is the martyr's fiery stake,*
> *Who senses, at the climax, some alarm.*
> *And painful is the lobster's bubbling lake,*
> *Who's dropped in by the cook's relentless arm.*
> *But to their endings let us now cry truce—*
> *These creatures did not live without some use."*

Sir Ruthven had wandered behind his guest's chair during the last few lines, his footfalls ceasing as he reached the final couplet. Now, when his voice also stopped, Chuck felt a surge of alarm.

Jumping up, he turned and saw the baronet huddled on the floor, his book still in one hand, his other hand closing around the Florentine dagger, which Chuck had neglected to retrieve from where it had fallen. Without a glance at the other man, whom he apparently believed still watching the fire, Sir Ruthven turned the blade toward his own chest.

Chuck pushed over his chair. As Sir Ruthven turned at the crash, Chuck sprang upon him and wrestled away the dagger. This time he carried it to the fireplace and dropped it deliberately into the flames. For a while, at least, it would be too hot for any more mischief.

Sir Ruthven was definitely suicidal, as Chuck had already feared from his taste in poetry. And he might be more dangerous as a would-be suicide than as a would-be murderer.

If he was Lozinski, and succeeded in killing himself, what would happen to whatever he knew about…whatever Deuteronomy Osborne suspected was about to "go down"?

That his whole virtual-reality world would vanish went without saying.

CHAPTER 4

PHILOSOPHY IN THE KITCHEN

"All right," said Dr. Charles Falcon, "now suppose you tell me why you tried to do it."

"I should have thought my reasons not only obvious, but laudable." For the second time, Sir Ruthven gathered himself up from the floor and returned across the room to drop into his armchair. "I quite appreciate your motivations for foiling my attempt on your life, but I'm dashed if I can see why you foiled my attempt on my own!"

"Let's just say you promised me dinner."

"True. There is that." Nodding as if that settled the whole question, Sir Ruthven drained off the rest of his milk like an old imbiber. "But I have been remiss in my duties as host. No doubt you wish to dine as soon as possible." He stood up briskly and started for the door. "I'm not entirely sure what the larder affords today, but I believe there's half a joint, or a promising leg of mutton if you'd prefer—"

"I'd prefer," said Chuck, noticing that his host had said nothing more about having a servant on hand, "to do the cooking myself."

Sir Ruthven stopped and looked back at him, momentarily puzzled. Then his face cleared. "Ah! Do you expect me to poison you, or myself, or both?" Picking up a lighted candle, he opened the door. "Allow me to show you to the kitchen, then. I'm quite safe for the moment." He playfully lofted the candlestick an inch or two. "I really have no desire to set either of us aflame."

Chuck blew out the candles in the room, hefted his backpack, and followed the baronet out of the library, through numerous corridors, and down numerous stairways, continuing to keep a mental map of the building. If its floorplan did any changing, he wanted to know.

Four corridors and five stairways later, having reached the level below the door through which Chuck had entered the castle, they arrived in the kitchen, a cavernous, high-beamed vault complete with banked fire in huge fireplace, stone oven, festoons of onions and sausages (but no garlic in sight—Dr. Falcon thought she remembered from a lit class somewhere that Polidori's "Lord Ruthven" had been the popular Victorian vampire before Bram Stoker's Dracula), larder, buttery, salt closet, and—the one false note in an otherwise convincing layout—a sideroom which Sir Ruthven referred to as a "galley" and which apparently existed here only because Bob Lozinski had a vague idea that a galley should be here, without knowing exactly what it was.

"Assuming you will find my company *de trop,* I'll leave you now, to await the outcome of your culinary endeavors." Sir Ruthven began to bow himself out, but Chuck stopped him.

"You're assuming too much, my friend."

The younger man blinked. "You prefer to chance having me here to slip nightshade or belladonna into the soup when you're not looking?"

"Better that then have you trying to do away with yourself again once you're out of my sight."

Setting his candlestick down on a table, the baronet quietly opened a drawer and brought out a coil of thick satin cord, the kind used for old-fashioned bell pulls and drapery ties. "Best bind me," he said pleasantly, handing it to his guest. "I've forgot where I last hid the belladonna, but there's any number of cleavers and such about the place."

Chuck decided to adopt the suggestion. It would put them both more at their ease, mentally at least. "Rather odd gear for a kitchen," he remarked, accepting the strong but luxurious cord.

"One never knows where and when one may need a length of rope in this beastly castle. I find it best to guard against such emergencies as the present." Sir Ruthven settled down in a heavy, high-backed wooden chair and held out his crossed wrists. "I had a namesake once who contrived to behead himself," he went on cheerfully. "Made a very neat job of it, too."

"Must have been quite a trick. Hardly the kind of thing anyone can practice ahead of time."

"Even if one could succeed in cutting it only half off, that would be something."

Dr. Falcon had only a first degree black belt in hojojutsu—the ancient martial art of binding an attacker or prisoner securely, artistically, and non-injuriously—but the cord seemed more frictive than satin might prove in actual reality, and Sir Ruthven both cooperated and watched with what resembled professional interest, even expressing the hope that someday, when it was quite convenient for them both, Dr. Falcon might give him a formal lesson or two.

The baronet secured artistically, non-injuriously and as comfortably as possible, both hands still in front, Chuck turned his attention to dinner. It was amazing how hungry a person could get in virtual reality, and how satisfying virtual food could seem: in virtual reality, as opposed to life out in the reality of *Papa's Pride,* any kind of food was programmable in any amount. Not only had Sir Ruthven's brandy been good, but his larder seemed stocked with solid, well-flavored groceries. Suicidally inclined he might be, but at least not indifferent to creature comforts.

Chuck found a vegetable brush, rolled up his sleeves, and set to scrubbing potatoes for a quick ragout version of shepherd's pie.

"I really would be interested to know," said Sir Ruthven, appearing perfectly at his ease, now that doing harm was beyond his power, "why you prevented me from terminating a useless existence—alluding, of course, to my own, not to yours."

"Negative thinking, sir. Your existence is far from useless."

"In the deleterious sense, perhaps not. My loss would no doubt be a distinct gain to society at large." The baronet shook his head and tsked. "Ah, Dr. Falcon, you have done society at large a grave disservice."

Chuck decided to try a hint of what he suspected. "The reverse is true. I've saved society at large. If you ceased to exist, so would society."

For an instant the baronet looked puzzled, as if trying to remember something. Then he smiled broadly. "Ah, a philosophical discussion!" He let out his breath and probably would have stretched out if the cord had not held him upright in the chair. "That society would cease to exist in so far as it touches myself is obvious; but that it would be a cessation to avoid is highly debatable."

"I'm talking literally." Chuck cubed the potatoes for quick boiling. "If you died, so would the world as you know it—people, rocks, grass, everything—gone. Not just as they touch you. As they touch one another."

"'No man is an island?' Come now! Surely you're attempting to carry the analogy of 'the death of every man diminishes myself' rather too far! In my case, the world would feel amply compensated for the diminishment."

"You may think you're being very humble," Chuck said, tempering his short sermon with a grin, "but insinuating that the whole world is going to notice your particular demise is the most egocentric statement I've ever heard."

"That's it exactly!" The baronet appeared delighted. "I congratulate you, doctor—you've caught my character to a 'T.' At some season when it's convenient for both of us, you must allow me to shake your hand."

"But as it happens, your egocentricity is justified. I *did* mean it literally, about the world dying with you." Locating a piped-in water supply, Chuck filled a small bronze kettle and added the potatoes.

"Ah," said Sir Ruthven. "The famous theory called…well, I forget the name. 'I (the cogitator) am the only thing that exists, and all things else are merely my imagination.' But I refute this theory for three reasons, namely: First. If the world were entirely my own imagination, I would certainly imagine it a good deal more favorable to myself. Second. If this theory were true, I would, by definition, be God. But one of the attributes of God, again by definition, is omniscience; suggesting that if I were God, I should at least entertain some suspicion of the fact. Third. Granting this theory to be true, it should be impossible for me to destroy myself by any means—poison, dagger, noose, cliffs—all, being mere effusions of my own mind, should prove utterly ineffective against the only true reality, myself. But if you truly believed this to be the case, you would have no need to try to dissuade me from making the attempt."

Chuck hung the potatoes on an iron hook over the fire to boil.

Maybe the most direct therapy—the full truth—might both effect a cure and gain the information they wanted—if Osborne was right, desperately needed—with no further loss of time and no further danger to anyone.

"Does the name Robert Lozinski mean anything to you?" said Dr. Falcon.

The baronet took a moment to adjust to what clearly seemed to him a sudden change of subject. "No…no, I think not. Should it?"

"It very definitely should." Chuck found a flitch of bacon and began cutting it.

Sir Ruthven pondered a moment or two, apparently humoring his guest. "Robert was more or less my own chosen pseudo-forename for some years, but Lozinski…a foreign name, is it not? Japanese?"

"Polish."

"Polish! There you have it—yet a fourth refutation of the famous theory (whatever it is called). If all things existed only in my own imagination, it should be impossible to surprise me with any new scrap of knowledge."

Having chopped enough bacon, Chuck began on some leeks. "I could refute every one of your arguments, but I'm talking facts, not philosophy. I'm not trying to tell you that you're God, or that the world around us is all there is anywhere. Because there's a world outside us big enough to swallow us down and never even belch— a whole universe that'll go on existing without knowing whether we're alive or dead."

"I notice you've begun using the first-person plural, Dr. Falcon. Are you including yourself with me in the putative creative mind, now?"

Dr. Falcon thought, Am I wrong? *Is* this Bob Lozinski? Still, having come this far, what did he have to lose? "I'm telling you that you're no one named Ruthven Murgatroyd. Your name is Robert Lozinski, and at this moment you are lying unconscious, in a deep coma."

Sir Ruthven looked startled. Then he smiled. "Am I comfortable?"

"Physically, as comfortable as good nursing can make you." Yes, the virtual-reality equipment both of them were wearing "out there" really was pretty comfortable.

The baronet made an elaborately visible attempt to shift his position. (Not even the best hojojutsu could eliminate all physical annoyance.) "You've no idea what a relief it is to learn that. Might I ask how you know all this?"

Chuck put the bacon and leeks in the bottom of an iron saucepan and set it on a rack above the fire. "I've come here from that big world outside."

Sir Ruthven cocked an eyebrow. "Some gentleman of science come inside my own brain to visit me?"

"Stripped of technical language, you might think of it that way." Chuck's own thought was, He's intelligent, but I'm not getting through to him.

"I'll resist the temptation to ask for the technical language, at least until we've dined on—why, I suppose we must call the contents of my larder literally food for thought!" The baronet leaned back and chuckled. "At least it's a novel presentation of the theory of…whatever it is called. With all due apologies, Dr. Falcon, I hope that your culinary art is more substantial than your philosophy."

Forcing a grin, Chuck began to carve the cold roast beef. He had lost the first round, but that worried him less on his own account than on Lozinski's. Well, all he could do for the present was learn as much as he could of the young man actually before him, and meanwhile finish cooking dinner. Apropos of both projects, he remembered his earlier suspicion on failing to spot garlic among the kitchen stores. "My culinary art would be all the better for a little garlic," he said with another grin. "Got any around?"

"Garlic?" Sir Ruthven glanced around at the spices and condiments in his line of sight, then closed his eyes and frowned. "Try that cupboard," he said after a moment, pointing one forefinger. "The third shelf down."

Chuck tried the cupboard. On the third shelf down, among jars and canisters of rice, dried peas, and other staples, he found a dozen heads of garlic. He broke off two or three cloves, returned, and chopped them fine before the baronet's unperturbed gaze.

At least he wouldn't have to worry about a bite in the neck. But he wished he had some way of knowing for sure whether those heads of garlic had been on that shelf before Sir Ruthven turned his mind to the problem.

CHAPTER 5

ENCOUNTER ON THE CLIFFS

Chuck took care not only of cooking the meal, but also of laying the table in the dining-room immediately upstairs and of selecting the wine—a bottle labeled "Pommery '74." By now he had decided that his host's earlier statement about a servant on the premises had been a mere pretext to make the half-hearted attempt on his life. Either that, or Lozinski had somehow quietly written the servant out of the virtual script.

On being released for the meal, Sir Ruthven seemed deeply moved to find himself trusted with a table knife. "True," he observed, "it is far from sharp, but, for all that, a sudden lunge at the face—"

"Would probably do less damage with a table knife than with a fork," Chuck replied. "And I'm not going to make you eat with your fingers."

He abandoned his earlier design of sleeping in a room with an inside bolt. He had no intention of leaving his host alone to make another suicide attempt. To help ensure them both a good night's rest, he mixed a harmless sleeping compound from the virtual med-kit in his knapsack into the baronet's after-dinner brandy. "How very clever of you!" was Sir Ruthven's comment on learning he had just been drugged. "Not quite necessary...I rarely make the attempt at night...the more unpleasant aspects of the next life look a little too strong by night. Still, deuced clever of you..." Then the drug took effect.

After carrying his host upstairs and finding a suitable bedroom, Chuck left him long enough for a brief trip back to the library. A quick check of the reasonably well arranged shelves did nothing to disprove the theory of the Gilbert and Sullivan libretti being unavailable as such in a virtual scenario based on them. Good thing he had that virtual copy in his knapsack. Reasoning that sitting Sir Ruthven down with a ponderous tome which required at least two hands to manage, and instructing him to read aloud, would keep him out of mischief while Chuck fixed breakfast in the morning—any cessation in the reading voice would alert him to trouble at once—he selected more or less at random what looked by title to be the least weighty—in subject matter, at least—of the large leatherbound folios.

Next morning, Sir Ruthven agreed that the idea was excellent in principle, but could not suppress a smile at Chuck's choice of folios. "*The Merrie Jestes of Hugh Ambrose*—I fear we shall both regret this, doctor!"

He was right. Long before the bacon and eggs were ready, Chuck had resolved that next time he would stick to light and frolicsome reading matter, like the *Roman Martyrology*.

Despite Hugh Ambrose and his Merrie Jestes, the baronet seemed in a comparatively cheerful mood. "I have decided to misdirect you today," he informed Chuck happily. "So if you hope to reach Penzance, you'll do best to ignore what I tell you and ask your way of the virtuous countryfolk instead."

"Thanks for the warning, but you're going with me."

Having just taken a bite of toast, Sir Ruthven swallowed it before replying. "You honor me, but if you expect me to prove a trustworthy guide—"

"Not at all. I'll still ask the way of your virtuous countryfolk. But you're still coming with me."

"Do you presume to order me about in my own ancestral hall, sir?"

"Yes."

The baronet's sudden show of wrath subsided as quickly as it had appeared. "I do it on compulsion. Well, it seems a fine day for an outing, and I daresay it'll do me good to get away from the gloomy old pile for a while." Helping himself to more eggs and bacon, as if to fortify himself for the day's exercise, he went on, "You'll want me to accompany you all the way to Penzance, I take it?"

"All the way to Castle Bunthorne, if necessary."

Sir Ruthven looked at him in surprise, then calmly spread marmalade on another piece of toast. "You'll probably regret it," he said, in a voice that implied, "But *I* won't."

* * * *

"Fortunate weather for traveling," Sir Ruthven remarked an hour later, as they strode along on the pleasantly springy turf beside muddy footpaths, with a cloudless sky arching above. "And so you still believe me to be this Lozinski, and feel compelled to prevent my destroying the entire world along with my own expendable existence?"

"Well, actually," Chuck found himself admitting, "I'm only about eighty-seven percent sure. Keep concentrating on good weather, and maybe we can test it out."

"Whereas if I am not he, then I am merely a fragment of his imagination, whoever he is. Hardly flattering, that. The surest test for you, of course, would be to give me a compassionate push over the nearest cliff."

"No."

"Well, Dr. Falcon, I don't know whether you're mad or merely a merry wag, but it should prove diverting to help you search for the mind who, by your theory, controls..." His voice trailed off. They had just rounded a turn in the path, and in front of them, balanced full-length on her stomach, atop a long boulder, was the same young woman Chuck had encountered yesterday in the sheep pasture.

"Meg!" whispered the baronet.

"Oh, the brave bold poppies! See! See them fly away on their wings, all red and gossamer with their great black and gold lips dripping sweet, sweet power?" Half rising on one arm, she pointed past the men into the distance, energetic for an instant and then suddenly languorous again.

"Meg!" said the baronet once more, advancing a step.

"Meg—beg. Keg—leg. Beg—badge—Madge. Daft Madge!" As if she had settled the matter to her own satisfaction, she chuckled and slid more snugly in among the rocks, wagging an admonishing finger at him. "Daft Madge—Poor Peg. What things are you, so brown and blue?"

Dr. Falcon wondered what she was seeing when she looked at them with those wide, green, glazing eyes.

"Margaret!" The baronet was halfway to her perch in the boulders overlooking the sea. Dr. Falcon stayed uninvolved and in the background, studying the scene as dispassionately as possible.

Sir Ruthven came a few steps closer to the woman, holding out his arms beseechingly. "Margaret—don't you know me?"

She stared down at him. Her eyes seemed almost to focus. Then suddenly she sprang to her feet on the boulders. "Don't come! Don't come!"

He stopped dead in his tracks, but kept on talking, persuading. "Come down, then. I won't hurt you, Meg. You know I won't hurt you. Come down!"

"Hush! Don't you hear it? Oh, the bright purple wind in the waves, in the waves…" She began to sway back and forth, perilously poised on the rocks above the sea.

"Margaret, be careful! Meg, Meg, come down!"

She looked at him again. "Don't come any nearer. There's blood beneath your fingernails." Smiling mischievously, she lifted one bare foot from the rock and began to sway again.

Sir Ruthven dashed forward, clearly hoping to catch her before she fell. She watched him for a few steps, chuckled, and delicately stepped off the boulder into space and disappeared from their sight.

"Margaret!" screamed the baronet, falling to his knees and burying his face in his hands.

Chuck sprang forward at last, hardly sure whether he or the baronet were the more alarmed. If he had been wrong—if Margaret were Lozinski… Chuck clambered up the boulders and looked over the cliff's edge, half-expecting that at any second Lozinski's virtual world and everything in it might collapse around him. And if that happened…was Chandra Falcon's own mental health quite safe?

He let out a sigh of relief. A wide ledge ran along the face of the cliff wall, slanting down gradually to join the beach. Margaret had landed safely, about eight feet below Chuck's vantage point, and was skipping down to the sands.

Chuck turned back to the baronet, who knelt weeping in the grass. "She's safe. There's a ledge."

"Thank God!"

"Hmmm." Chuck rubbed his chin, noticing that here in virtual reality, Chandra's inner man was growing beard stubble. Should've remembered to use the virtual, battery-powered razor in his knapsack this morning. "You're a native of these parts?"

Still kneeling, Sir Ruthven nodded.

"And you didn't remember that ledge was there?"

"What are you hinting at, doctor?"

"Only that whoever is building this world in his mind—genders can fluctuate 'in here,' but 'out there' we know it's a 'him'—could have put a ledge right where it was needed at an instant's notice."

"Please, Dr. Falcon. Is this a time for jesting?" Sir Ruthven eyed his fingernails wearily. "I have never felt less like a god than at this moment.

"Egocentric again."

"Sir?" The younger man looked up in pained aggrievement, but Dr. Falcon, having decided it was time for the emotional equivalent of a slap across the face, went on,

"You assumed I was talking about you. I could as easily have meant *her.* "

"I stand corrected." As if to suit the action to the words, Sir Ruthven rose and dusted off his knees. "But I fear," he added, shaking his head, "that if this world were a creation of poor Margaret's brain, it would have even less of sense and justice than it has."

He turned and began walking along a path that cut inland, between the fields. Chuck caught up with him in a few long strides and then moderated his pace, his own brain working the while.

He knew, now, where these two characters came from. It had been easy enough to check last night in his virtual copy of the librettos, simply by scanning the cast lists. And there really was very little connection, in their own operetta, between Sir Ruthven and Mad Margaret.

There was obviously a connection in Bob Lozinski's virtual fantasy.

CHAPTER 6

THE PIRATES OF PENZANCE

They had walked in an almost straight line overland for almost an hour before Sir Ruthven, apparently remembering his earlier resolve to misguide his companion, began making a circle. Chuck humored him a quarter of an hour longer, until a sturdy peasant turned up opportunely to point out the true direction. Once on a road, Chuck found plenty of old-fashioned milestones to keep them going right.

It was twilight when they arrived on the southern coast, the hike across the western tip of Lozinski's virtual Cornwall having taken a summer's day of weather as pleasant as in any programmed pylon of *Papa's Pride*.

"Tremorden Castle." Sir Ruthven pointed to an old pile, almost as grim as Ruddigore Castle, on the cliffs above them to the right. A few paces farther along, they came in sight of Mount's Bay, opening out below them to the left, lights beginning to show in the tiny black shapes of houses that spread from the landward edge of the darkening beach up the sloping shore. Sir Ruthven pointed again. "Penzance."

Chuck would not have been surprised to find the pirates keeping house respectably in the heart of town, but Sir Ruthven led him down a narrow, almost invisible smugglers' path between Tremorden Castle and the small city. As they came in sight of another, much smaller bay, its waters and the ship riding thereon fast merging into the general darkness, a stout but shadowy figure stepped out in front of them.

"Friend or foe?" It seemed to be a woman's voice, deep contralto and slightly hoarse.

"Friends," said the baronet.

"Give the password."

"I have given it often." Sir Ruthven pronounced the last word as if it were a homonym of "orphan."

"Murgatroyd!" The pirate sentinel flung both arms round the baronet, then fired a pistol into the air, apparently to alert the rest of the band. A cheer rose from the beach below, where Chuck glimpsed torches being lighted.

"Who's the other one?" asked the pirate.

"Quite all right, Ruth. He's an orphan also. Allow me to present Dr. Charles Falcon. Dr. Falcon, Mrs. Ruth Cripps, piratical maid of all work *par excellence*."

Thrusting her pistol back into her belt, the piratical maid seized Chuck's extended hand and shook it heartily, at the same time clapping him on the back with her other hand. "Welcome aboard, Dr. Falcon! Any orphan is an honorary member of our band. Come on now, watch your step."

Familiar with the trail, Ruth bounded down ahead of them with surprising agility for her bulk. Sir Ruthven followed more slowly with Chuck, who inquired, "How did they know she fired that shot as a salute instead of a warning or to kill an intruder?"

"They never fire at intruders under such circumstances—the pistol would give the sentinel an unfair advantage. They grapple instead."

"Suppose the intruder is the weaker party?"

"It's assumed that anyone who comes forcing his way here is stronger than whomever he hopes to find. If he *should* prove the weaker, of course, the sentry takes him down and feeds him."

"They must get raided fairly often."

"Every time an enemy comes here. By the way, don't let it slip that you're not an orphan. You're probably much stronger than any of them, so they would have no scruples about attacking you."

"Thanks for the tip, but it's okay. I really *am* an orphan." At least, *Chuck* Falcon was. *Chandra* Falcon had a mother still living in Gadore neighborhood, pylon 8.

"I do wish you hadn't told me that. I'd hoped I was telling a terrible story." The baronet sighed. "But perhaps it's as well. I would rather hate to see any of the dear fellows injured."

* * * *

The fact that the piratical maid of all work shared a surname with one of the Antique Terra players who had been in the same backstage area when Steve Davis died had not escaped Dr. Falcon; but it could be coincidence. The cast list for *H.M.S. Pinafore* attached the name "Mrs. Cripps" to Little Buttercup, though nobody ever called her that in the show itself. Lozinski might have assigned it to pirate Ruth also, as part of his virtual world-building. Chuck would have tried probing Sir Ruthven about Ruth's surname, but they reached the bottom too quickly.

How far were real people Lozinski knew in the ship turning up as characters in his virtual fantasy? How important might it be to know whether or not the real Barbara Cripps had become piratical Ruth "in here," and how much might it have to do with whatever Deuteronomy Osborne suspected? Dr. Falcon looked forward to getting a closer look at Ruth by the light of the cheery picnic fire the pirates had kindled on the beach.

Somewhat to his surprise, he found a closer look impossible to get. At one moment or other during a pleasant evening of balladeering and storytelling, the flames lit up every other pirate's face—black beards, bristling whiskers, eye-patches and scars superimposed as if for a costume party on mild faces with round cheeks and ingenuous eyes—but Ruth was always half in shadow, the flickering light doing more to distort than reveal her features. The few times Chuck should have been able to see part of her face clearly, what he saw seemed slightly blurred, like a movie a fraction out of focus.

The pirate king, a tall English gentleman of the bluff-and-hearty school, with long, curling black hair and frown-lines that appeared to have been etched in with dark pencil—less precious in virtual fantasy than out in *Papa's Pride* proper—agreed readily to take the visitors to Portsmouth next day. "We were planning an attack on Tremorden Castle tonight, but that can wait."

"I trust you will not be too much inconvenienced?" asked the baronet.

"No, no. Little matter of a bloody vendetta—stern revenge, just though technically illegal retribution, all that sort of thing. Necessary to keep up our reputation, y'know."

"I quite understand. If you'd prefer to keep to your schedule," said Sir Ruthven half-heartedly, "we might accompany you. I really ought to learn a bit more about how such things are done."

"Never worry about it, lad. It's like tobacco—comes to you in a moment when the time comes; and we'll be the better for a bit of sleep before the morning tide." The pirate king gave his mustache a picturesque twirl, but Chuck guessed he was secretly just as glad of the excuse to postpone his vendetta for a few days. "There's poor young Frederic, though," the chief pirate went on. "Been a little lower lately than usual. I'd take it as a great favor if you'd see what you can do to cheer him up."

Sir Ruthven eagerly sought out a beardless youth who had so far been sitting moodily eating an orange and tossing little chunks of peel into the flames. Frederic—the pirates' apprentice, bound to them by mistake; his father had meant for him to be apprenticed to a pilot, but Ruth (now the piratical maid of all work), who was then Frederic's nurse, and for some reason in charge of drawing up the articles of indenture, had misunderstood the word "pilot" for "pirate." As far as Chuck could see, Sir Ruthven's efforts to "cheer Frederic up" were taking the form of mutual commiserations on the far side of the fire; but the two appeared safe enough, enjoying a fit of Byronic gloom together in the midst of the Victorian-parlor roystering of the other pirates.

"Every baronet of Ruddigore is, *ipso facto* and *ex officio,* an honorary member of our bloodthirsty band," the pirate king confided, pouring Chuck a mug of sherry. "Sir Roderic, uncle of the present bart., gave me my own start in the trade, as you might say. Well, well, maybe we'll find a nice Cunarder to scuttle on our way out, give him a little experience. One with an unorphaned crew."

"Have you ever considered," Chuck inquired, "if you took a ship that wasn't manned by orphans and scuttled her with her crew, the grief you'd cause the bereaved parents?"

"By Jove, you're right, lad!" The pirate king blinked, drained off his sherry, refilled his mug, and eyed Chuck with renewed interest. "You think like one of us, man—bloodthirsty but not altogether heartless. I don't suppose I could persuade you to throw in your lot with us?"

Chuck grinned and shook his head. "Sorry, captain, not this time out. Pressing engagements elsewhere."

"Pity." After several puffs on his pipe, the pirate king went on, "Maybe it's just as well for us, though. Perhaps you've heard we never attack a weaker party than ourselves? Now, unless I mistake you, you're a man who could take on any two and, in certain cases, any three of us at once. With you on our side, devilish little chance we'd have of ever finding anybody at all to attack."

Yes, Chandra thought, my inner man really is quite a fine figure of a male, isn't he?

* * * *

The pirates' ship, the *Divine Emollient,* weighed anchor at dawn and rode out on a fresh tide, with a favorable wind. The sun rose in a clear blue sky, a few small whitecaps danced on the waves, the Jolly Roger flapped merrily overhead, and Chuck realized he was dangerously near hoping his mission would be a long one. At least in virtual time; for Osborne's sake, they should maybe hope it was short "out there."

Chuck leaned on the rail of the poop deck, inhaling the salt air and watching the crew at work. If they were incompetent at piracy, at least they were good at sailing and singing.

> *"Come, friends, who plough the sea!*
> *First-class navigation,*
> *Each man at his station—*
> *This is the way that we-eee*
> *Go about our piracee!"*

The cheerful bustle on shipdeck made him think of *H.M.S. Pinafore*, which made him think of the scene in which Ralph Rackstraw announces his intention of committing suicide, and his crewmates, dolefully singing their grief, do all in their compassionate power to help him, by loading the pistol and passing it up to him. Humorous in its proper stage context, the image was disquieting here. Sir Ruthven had said earlier that he rarely attempted suicide at night through fear of the less pleasant aspects of the other world. Might it follow that a bright, sunny, invigorating morning would inspire him with the boldest ideas of self-destruction?

Dr. Falcon looked down, searching the decks below. Sir Ruthven was still chumming with Frederic. They stood together at the afterdeck rail, throwing bread crumbs to the gulls that were flapping along almost batlike behind the ship, diving occasionally into her wake for the tidbits. A peaceful enough picture; but if the baronet should suddenly feel moved to put a pistol to his head or jump over the side, the pirate apprentice would probably prove very cooperative. Chuck decided to lose no time joining them.

He was halfway down when a long, sharp, intense, tremendous roll of staticky thunder split the air—shaking vessel and ocean alike. The pirates were in instant confusion, shouting and running from port to starboard and vice versa, scanning the horizon in varying degrees of hope and timidity, looking for the enemy ship which was nowhere to be seen. The pirate king, trailing a string of picturesque oaths, came running around the corner of the cabin and almost careened into Chuck.

"What is it?" Chuck demanded. "Any chance some of our own guns went off by accident?"

The pirate king shook his head. "Samuel, Frederic, and myself are the only men aboard who know how to load the blasted things, and Samuel's not working at all today—his birthday. Stand by to repel boar-r-ders!" he shouted, brushing past Chuck to rally his men against the invisible foe.

Chuck sprinted, reaching the after-rail in seconds. At least Lozinski's virtual world had not winked out—but a sudden fog was coming up over the sea on all sides…

He found Sir Ruthven staggering, supported by Frederic and Ruth. "What happened here?" Dr. Falcon demanded, pushing Frederic aside almost brusquely in order to take hold of Sir Ruthven himself.

"Ah, Dr. Falcon!" Reeling, the baronet attempted a weak smile. "Absurd, really—seems to be a touch of…of *mal-de-mere,* I suppose. I say, I never asked—are you a medical doctor or a D.D.?"

His eyes closed, he swayed in Chuck's grip, and the fog became several degrees darker. Ruth shuddered and untied the knot that held her workaday shawl about her shoulders. "It seemed to begin at the time of that incredible thunder," said Frederic.

"Shock, I daresay," murmured Sir Ruthven. "Set up a reaction, no doubt…bit of vertigo, I suppose. Dreadfully embarrassing, never seasick before…"

"Lord bless us!" ejaculated Ruth, staring up into the fog, which was so dense and black now that they could barely see the ship around them. The piratical maid took off her shawl and wrapped it around the baronet.

If...whatever...hadn't happened within Lozinski's virtual world, it must have been something "out there." Chuck spoke low, trying to impress the baronet with his own sense of urgency. "Sir Ruthven! You remember what I've been trying to tell you?"

"What? Ah, you mean..." Sir Ruthven shook his head, clearly trying to go along with what he must consider a diversionary tactic. "That theory...self as center...the self as...stranger with a Japanese name? Odd sort of moment to bring it up."

"No. It's the vital moment to bring it up. Something's happened in the outer world—"

"Ah, the thunder?" Sir Ruthven smiled hazily.

"I'm going back out there and see what the hell's happening."

The baronet nodded. "I assume you'll...be flying upward through the air? Forgive me if I do not see you off."

He reeled again and fell to the deck. The fog grew several degrees darker yet. Kneeling beside Sir Ruthven, Dr. Falcon squinted around, trying to see Ruth or Frederic, calling them and getting no answer. The ship was preternaturally quiet, and the deck boards seemed to be melting, fusing with the atmosphere.

"Lozinski!" Chuck bent and spoke the name like a command. The baronet's eyelids fluttered—in recognition of his name, or in mere acknowledgment of the sound? "Listen to me," Chuck went on. "If you want to suicide, this is your chance—all you've got to do is let go. But if you care about the people around you—the pirates, Frederic, Margaret, all the others—if you care about your whole world here—then you'd damn well better hang on! I don't know if something's happened to you 'out there' or if it's some... something else wrong, but if it's some outer threat, for God's sake, fight it!"

Sir Ruthven frowned up. "Do you presume to command me, Dr. Falcon?"

"Damn right I presume to command you!"

"Very good. I do it on compulsion."

Dr. Falcon helped the baronet sit up and wrap Ruth's shawl more closely around his shoulders. The fog was still darkening, but now, to his relief, he again heard the voices of Ruth, Frederic, and the rest of the pirates. Good. All he had to do now was remember how he himself got back "out there"…

"Oh, I say, Dr. Falcon, when shall we two meet again?"

"If I don't make it back aboard the *Divine Emollient,* I'll try to meet you in Portsmouth."

A helmet, that's right. He was in a virtual suit…all he had to do was lift off the helmet with its goggles and earphones…

CHAPTER 7

INTERLUDE

The virtual helmet came off. Other hands than Chandra Falcon's had lifted it from her head. She looked around the medical lab.

Misaki Lang was at the keyboard, typing and joysticking desperately.

"What happened?" Chandra demanded.

"Doc!" Misaki exclaimed joyfully, without turning around, and "Oh, thank God!" Sister Harriet echoed, holding the virtual helmet she had just lifted from Chandra's head.

"What's going on?"

Before either Misaki or Sister Harriet could answer Chandra's question, Deuteronomy Osborne burst into the room. "It's gone down," he said. "And it's big. Damn! It's big."

White-lipped, Sister Harriet told Chandra, "Shipnet's crashed."

"Shipnet's...crashed? My God!"

"It still used to happen, back on Old Earth, sometimes." Harriet was shaking. Not uncontrollably, but continually. "But there were so many systems all over the planet, so many back-ups...we sort of figured, there'd always be ways to fix it—clean it up—replace the lost data—"

"We'll do it here," Misaki said, still at the keyboard.

"Yeah?" Deuces made it a challenge.

"Yes! Think Papa Al Gadore would've taken off without back-ups of the ship's own?"

"Enough?" Sister Harriet asked weakly.

"For starters," Misaki replied, "I switched our own pylon's computers out of shipnet at the first glimpse of the death symbol."

Deuces shook his head. "First glimpse, already too late."

"That might have been true back on Old Earth," said Dr. Falcon. The scope of it was sinking in. Shipnet, their entire store of knowledge brought from the home planet plus everything they'd learned and gathered in eight years through the galaxy…the controls that maintained climate, growing conditions, gravity… life itself! in 24 pylons and the gigantic core…their very ability to get—even to communicate—from pylon to core to pylon via comps and insul-tubes…the steering that kept them on trajectory, the shielding that turned aside space debris, guarding *Papa's Pride* from collisions… "Here," she reassured herself as much as everyone else, "acting at the first glimpse should keep most of the infection out."

"I'd feel happier," said Sister Harriet, "if we could have inoculations against these kinds of viruses."

Misaki said hotly, "Who'd ever have thought anybody would play the computer virus trick in *Papa's Pride?* That's like signing a death warrant on the whole ship and everyone in it!"

"Probably th' last little piece uv Old Earth anywhere in the universe," said Osborne. "Outside the blame memory uh God."

"It…it probably…" Sister Harriet shook her head and tried again. "Whoever did this…probably thought of it as just a…just a practical joke."

"Yeah?" Osborne snarled. "Like t' 'practical joke' *them.*"

"Thank God you're safe, anyway, Dr. Falcon," said Misaki. "Who knows what it could've done to your brain?"

"Who knows what it's doing to poor Bob's?" As if she'd just been reminded, Sister Harriet made to lift the virtual helmet off Lozinski's head.

"Leave it," snapped Dr. Falcon.

Osborne gave an approving grunt and Sister Harriet looked aghast, but Dr. Falcon went on:

"When you brought me out—thanks, by the way, I'd just been groping for the helmet—it looked like a dark fog settling over his virtual world. Nothing they couldn't survive. It might be more dangerous to jolt him out of it now, all at once, than to leave him in."

Sister Harriet began, "But you—"

"I'm the secondary one 'in there.' Bob Lozinski is the primary builder of that little world. Now. Inertia should be keeping the ship turning, keeping up our gravity, for quite a while. That gives us some time. We'll have to isolate every computer we can reach— meaning in this pylon, terminal by terminal, give it an individual cleansweep, then filter data back into it from the others. Using a double virgin-fine set of filters."

Osborne seemed to relax a little. "Yeah. And if they're handlin' it like that in the rest uh th' pylons an' th' core, then mebbe, just maybe, we can get through this, after all."

"If we thought of it," said Chandra Falcon, "you can be sure so did Papa Gadore's brain trust. Probably beat us to it. Misaki, start with the computers here in this lab. As soon as they're cleaned, I'm going back 'in.'"

Deuteronomy Osborne said, "Why bother, Doc? If this kid is even partly responsible, he deserves everythin' that can go wrong to him 'in there.' Call it th' pangs uh bad conscience."

"And if he isn't?" she replied. "If Steve Davis was going to bring him along to Ishmael's Downtown to warn you about this? Does Bob Lozinski still deserve it in that case?"

CHAPTER 8

THE ROOK AND PIGEON

Sir Ruthven was definitely puzzled. Naturally, he did not believe the claims of Dr. Falcon to have come from some world 'outside' the known universe. Hence, the doctor's disappearance must have been some sleight-of-body, some conjuror's legerdemain. The good doctor was, of course, hiding somewhere aboard the *Divine Emollient,* perhaps to test whether the baronet would continue to Portsmouth as planned.

Still, when they had passed through the pirate king's cabin to the guest quarters designed for captive ladies and prisoners of high degree held for ransom (although the pirates had never yet taken any) and Sir Ruthven realized that Mrs. Cripps and Frederic also found the fog to have penetrated even here, filling the ship's interior as thoroughly as the air outside—then the baronet determined to follow the instructions of his strange friend as well as he could. Despite the stabbing pains in his head, fingers, and elsewhere—a curious symptom of seasickness—and the blandishments of his piratical nurses to encourage a nap, he held off the stupor that tried to engulf him. For several hours he drank Mrs. Cripps' tea and played chess with the pirate apprentice. Only when the atmosphere in the cabin cleared, to his eyes as well as theirs, did he sleep. And even then, although he believed none of Dr. Falcon's philosophical jesting, it was with a sense of relief verging on surprise that he awoke in the morning.

Dr. Falcon had never again showed his face aboard the ship. The pirates were amazed and perplexed, but they held their course throughout the night. On Sir Ruthven's insistence, they held it throughout the day as well, hoping that their second passenger, who had seemingly played the incomprehensible trick of stowing away after he was already on board in the capacity of privileged passenger, would come out like a rat from hiding once they lay in Portsmouth harbor.

He did not—not, at least, as far as anyone could see; but Sir Ruthven had the pirates put him ashore. Why, exactly, he chose to wait in Portsmouth for an enigmatic acquaintance of two days who might merely be making a fool of him, the baronet could not say. But he seldom had the chance to travel, and the prospect of a week or so in Portsmouth—he had never before been so far east—followed, perhaps, by a leisurely overland return west, was far more appealing than an immediate homecoming to his lonely ancestral hall.

For safety in port, the pirates flew the Union Jack instead of the Jolly Roger; but they wore their customary picturesque costumes ashore. No one noticed. The town was in a festive mood. Portsmouth had turned out with bells, salutes, and parades to welcome the lord high ambassador of Japan and his charming young wife, who had just arrived in her majesty's ship *Pinafore,* and fancy dress was the order of the day. The pirates passed for honest revelers as they mingled with the rest of the crowd to get a glimpse of the ample ambassador and his diminutive lady.

Had the thing been possible, Sir Ruthven would have thought he recognized the lord high ambassador, a surprisingly tall Japanese of surprisingly portly girth beneath his loose silken kimono, as an old acquaintance. It was of course not possible, for the baronet had never been out of England and by all reports his excellency the ambassador had never before been out of Japan. Still, it was astonishing how little difference there was, after all, between a Japanese face and an English one. (Ah, well, two eyes, so—nose in the middle, mouth beneath.) It was also very unsettling how the ambassador' dainty little wife seemed to pick out Sir Ruthven's face from the crowd and aim a wink directly at him.

Escaping from the press, Sir Ruthven dined with his piratical friends at a reputable inn and then saw them off again to catch the evening tide. Still the mysterious Dr. Falcon had failed to make his reappearance. Sir Ruthven watched with a lonely heart as the pirates rowed back to their ship. Then he turned and made his way once again into the town.

In the respectable streets the citizens were already setting lighted candles in their windows, illuminating the town in honor of the lord high ambassador. Sir Ruthven reflected that, as a titled gentleman, he might have been able to obtain an invitation to the ambassador's reception, had he known he would be in Portsmouth for the event. He was not sure, however, that he would have found the reception pleasurable, or even less lonely than his present circumstances.

Reaching an eminence, he watched night fall over the harbor, where the *Pinafore,* brightly lit, lay prominent among the vessels at anchor, while the *Divine Emollient* could still be glimpsed by its faint lights far beyond as it put back out to sea. At last the baronet left the respectable illuminated streets and made his way down to the disreputable nether regions of the town, the waterfront stews where rats of both species, rodent and human, went back and forth between unsavory ships and worse taverns.

Today was drawing to a close, and yesterday he had done nothing more criminal than cheating Frederic at chess. Yesterday, of course, he had been seriously, if rather absurdly, incommoded—he still felt stabbing pains in his head from time to time—and some small allowances could be made for periods of illness. But after not doing very much the day before yesterday, and accomplishing nothing more drastic than an abortive attempt the day before that, he really must look for some desperate deed to perpetrate today.

He entered a derelict establishment that, by the remains of the weather-stained sign, might once have been called the Rook and Pigeon, the interior of which bore some resemblance to a tavern. By the light of a few begrimed lanterns three or four tables could be seen, with chairs in various stages of dilapidation distributed unevenly round them. The occupants of the Rook and Pigeon were an elderly tapster, a young woman with costume less tattered but more revealing than poor Mad Margaret's, and half a dozen other dark-clad and dark-visaged persons seated at table. Everything, from tables to customers, appeared to be covered with several layers of dust and dirt; and everything that could move of its own power turned to look at Sir Ruthven when he entered.

Most of the inmates turned away again, scowling, after a moment or two; but a few pairs of eyes were constantly gazing at him from one part of the tavern or another. Rather nervously, he made his way to an empty table in the room's farthest corner and sat on a semi-broken chair. The young woman approached, seeming to walk with her hips and bosom rather than her legs. She perched above him, her torso incredibly skewed round and one hand on her hip, and inquired, in a voice at once bored and sultry, wot was his pleasure.

Trying to avert his eyes from her bodice, which by Sir Isaac Newton's law should have fallen from her shoulders momentarily, the baronet requested milk.

"Milk?" the young woman repeated incredulously.

Gazing as if in fascination at a peculiarly ugly face with only one good eye, which seemed to be watching him half surreptitiously from across the room, the baronet repeated his pleasure. "Milk…one—large—glass of milk…if you please."

A laugh went up round the room, without, however, enlivening it. "Mothers' milk, you want, maybe?" the young woman persisted, doing remarkable things in the way of causing her bosom to heave. "Mothers' milk is gin to most of 'em wot come in here."

Another laugh went round, the identical tone of snigger echoed in half a dozen different throats. Sir Ruthven judged it time to assert himself. "Cow's milk or goat's, warm or chilled, sweet or buttermilk," he stipulated, striking his palm on the table. "One large glass, mug, or tumblerful. I suppose money paid for milk is as good as that paid for another beverage?"

The tavern maid shrugged, as if daring Newton's law to do its worst with her bodice. "Well, I'll see wot I can do. Might be a while, mind, and I don't promise results. Best give us a bob first."

A shilling seemed an excessive price for a glass of milk, and Sir Ruthven had the uneasy feeling he was being gulled. Nevertheless, he tossed the coin to her, mentally justifying the expense as a kind of bribe to remove her from his immediate vicinity. After giving the coin a bite that would hardly have been countenanced in polite society, she betook herself off, to the baronet's immense relief, and left him to examine his palm for any splinters he might have picked up when he struck the tabletop.

The one-eyed seafaring man on the other side of the room seemed still to be watching him.

Sir Ruthven's table was uneven, and each of the four legs of his chair seemed to be shorter than the other three. The stub of a candle, half concealed, like the crater of a volcano, in its own congealed and dusty drippings, squatted on the scarred and stained tabletop; but the baronet did not quite dare disturb the atmosphere of the place again in order to ask a light for the dead wick. At the only table which boasted a burning candle, a pair of unshaven domino-players appeared to be cheating one another with grunting satisfaction. The rest of the room had settled back from its ripple of supercilious mirth into a sort of ooze of malevolent lethargy.

The one-eyed man was still watching Sir Ruthven—not sporadically, like the others, but steadily. His face, though grotesque in its ugliness and largely covered by black whiskers, seemed cleaner and better-combed than the other faces in the room, and beneath his nondescript greatcoat Sir Ruthven thought he glimpsed the uniform of a bluejacket.

The baronet continued searching his palm for splinters. Although it was useless in the bad light, it provided him occupation for his eyes and thus a measure of privacy. He could not shake off the sensation that this adventure was not working out quite as it should—in this place he was more likely to end as victim than perpetrator of a desperate crime. Moreover, he began to suspect the one-eyed sailor of being some spy or secret officer of the law. The thought had its measure of consolation; but if the man had power to stop any violence the thugs might attempt upon Sir Ruthven, he could equally well stop any violence Sir Ruthven might attempt upon the thugs…and it was the baronet in whom the one-eyed man seemed most interested.

Sir Ruthven thought of calling for a pack of cards when the serving-maid brought his milk, cheating at a game or two of patience, and escaping from this place. But cheating at patience could be done more safely, and no doubt with cleaner cards, in the haven of a respectable inn. Nor did it seem a particularly desperate crime…although merely remaining in the Rook and Pigeon for any length of time might, in itself, be desperate enough. Perhaps if he left now, having caused the serving-maid to run a fool's errand? Unfortunately, having paid an exorbitant price in advance, Sir Ruthven could not work out the situation so that anyone would be cheated except himself were he to leave now.

He tried for a more comfortable position, causing the uneven legs of his chair to click, which drew all eyes in his direction again for a moment. A friend—even a sympathetic acquaintance—would be a Godsend in this place. If not the strange Dr. Falcon, at least some person of solid respectability and a cheerful, mild, healthy countenance…

The one-eyed man rose and started walking toward Sir Ruthven's table. The uneasy twinges that had troubled the baronet's head since yesterday's inexplicable thunder and the unusual *mal de mer* that followed chose this moment to converge furiously in the middle of his brainpan. For a few moments he bent over, breathing painfully, closing his eyes in fear of seeing the fog again, and more than half expecting to be, while in this helpless state, either stabbed or arrested by the one-eyed sailor.

But the fit passed; and, straightening again in his chair, Sir Ruthven saw that the one-eyed man had veered aside to the row of kegs that served the publican as a countertop. More surprising, a new patron stood in the doorway—a tallish, middle-aged gentleman with a cheerful, benevolent countenance and a clerical collar.

CHAPTER 9

THE MESSAGE

The gentleman in clerical attire glanced—fastidiously but not censoriously—round the unwholesome interior of the Rook and Pigeon. Then, evincing no uneasiness, he picked his way to Sir Ruthven's table. "Pardon me," he said with a bow, "but I believe we have a mutual acquaintance, do we not?"

The baronet jumped up and returned the bow. "Indeed, now that you mention it, I am sure we do." Who the mutual acquaintance might be, or how the clerical gentleman had come to recognize the acquaintance of an acquaintance by sight, were questions Sir Ruthven had no immediate desire to press. The newcomer seemed the answer to his fond prayer for a friendly face; and, if they had not the honor of a mutual acquaintance, no doubt some other two gentlemen, somewhere in Portsmouth tonight, did. The baronet offered his name and right hand.

"Daly," responded the reverend gentleman, drawing off his glove in order to accept the proffered handshake. "Dr. Barrington Daly, at your service, Sir Ruthven."

They settled themselves at the table, Dr. Daly first dusting off his chair with his pocket handkerchief.

"You must forgive my surprise," said Sir Ruthven, still wondering who their mutual acquaintance might be, "but—if you'll pardon the question…that is, it does seem a trifle…unexpected… to meet with a friend of…that is, with a friend of his here."

"An errand of mercy to an unfortunate great-aunt of Sir Joseph's second cousin once removed—or is it the second cousin of his aunt, thrice removed?—no matter. Her modest abode is located in an humble though respectable quarter, but in returning from the good lady's residence I seem to have missed my way by a street or two. Insufficient familiarity with the town."

"Remarkable coincidence!" said Sir Ruthven, thinking, I wonder if this Sir Joseph could be our mutual acquaintance? "I hope you found the lady well?"

"Recovering from a slight cold, but otherwise quite well. Ah, my dear young lady!" Dr. Daly went on, hailing the tavern maid.

"Milk's off," she said, sidling back to their table.

"*Is* it? Dear, dear, what a pity." Casting a reverendly appreciative glance at the young woman, the cleric smiled and winked. "Never mind, my dear, I'm sure we can do very nicely with a pot of good, strong tea and two cups."

Somewhat to Sir Ruthven's surprise, the serving-maid did not argue, the other patrons of the place did not laugh, and in a very short time the pot of tea, complete with two cracked cups, two chipped saucers, sugar-bowl, and a small plate of biscuits appeared on their table, at a price only slightly extravagant. The teapot dripped when it poured, the cups hummed through their cracks when filled, and the tea left a slippery new brown film on the layers of old stain in their once-white interiors; but the tea was strong and steaming, the caked sugar yielded quickly to an assault with the dented spoons, the biscuits had once been almost crisp, and Sir Ruthven felt such a surge of envious admiration that, had it seemed respectful, he would have asked the secret of the clergyman's mystic power.

By the time the tea arrived, they had managed to get the conversation around to philosophy. Through over-meditation on the seeds Dr. Falcon had planted in his mind, Sir Ruthven had by now remembered a term for the idea of self as the sole thing in existence. "Dr. Daly. What is your opinion of the notion of solipsism?"

"I have no particular quarrel with it," replied the vicar (it was by now established that Dr. Daly was vicar of the village of Ploverleigh) as he poured the tea. "No quarrel, that is, provided that mine is the mind granted to be in existence, and not yours. But the great difficulty, you see, lies in proving or disproving it. As: if yours is the mind, who am I that you should listen to me; and if the mind is mine, whom have I to convince one way or the other, except myself?"

"And if the mind is truly alone," added Sir Ruthven, "it might be preferable not to know it."

"Exactly so. 'That way lies madness.' Although, of course, a mind alone in a universe of its own creation must be its own criterion of madness or sanity." The vicar sipped his tea. "Slightly weak. Just half a spoonful more would have made all the difference. Yes, solipsism is an interesting idea, but I prefer abstractions which are more susceptible of demonstration."

"But if the mind were not completely alone in the universe…if it had, for instance, manufactured its own small universe, and if a being from the greater universe beyond were to visit it…"

Dr. Daly blinked. "My dear Sir Ruthven! Is that your own idea?"

"No," confessed the baronet, "Dr. Falcon first mentioned it to me." He was very careful how he brought up the name. Dr. Falcon might, after all, be their mutual acquaintance.

"I should like the meet the chap. His must be a mind of no common order. May I rely on you for an introduction, should the opportunity arise?"

"Certainly. But I fear he is rather elusive." Sir Ruthven hesitated a moment, then decided to take the plunge. Leaning forward and lowering his voice, he went on, "The fact is, Dr. Daly, he claims to have come from this outside universe."

Again the vicar blinked. "Does he seem to have any ulterior motive in making this extraordinary claim?"

"No…that is, he seems to have one or two, but I can't quite make them out."

"Great genius," murmured Dr. Daly, "leads sometimes, alas, to madness."

Sir Ruthven shook his head. He thought of telling his new friend the whole story, from the sudden appearance of Dr. Falcon in Ruddigore Castle during a thunderstorm to his far more baffling disappearance from the deck of the *Divine Emollient;* and he thought, alternatively, of attempting to pass Dr. Falcon off as something of a practical joker.

"Whose mind does he claim to be the one that created this…this smaller universe, I suppose you'd say, as we know it?" inquired the vicar. "Not his own mind, surely?"

Sir Ruthven felt himself blushing. He thought, briefly, of telling a lie, but instead tried to pass the truth off as a kind of jest. "No, as a matter of fact, he claims it's my mind."

"Yours! If it were not presumptuous in one who never saw the man, I should be tempted to put you on your guard against the ultimate flatterer."

"Except that it isn't precisely flattering, you see." Again the baronet hesitated. For two days, Dr. Falcon had been the only person he saw, and himself—as far as he knew—the only person Dr. Falcon saw, excluding poor Mad Margaret. It was not inconceivable that Sir Ruthven had himself gone mad…that the friendly pirates had only pretended to converse with his invisible companion in order to humor him. The idea was something less than bearable, and Sir Ruthven decided to unburden himself. "He claims, you see, that I am not really myself, but another being from this outer universe of his—in which I wear, as it seems, some sort of foreign name—and I have somehow retreated into a world of my own imagining."

"What? And left all your memories behind in this hypothetical universe outside?"

"So it would appear."

"But what, my dear sir, would that make the rest of us, then?"

As Sir Ruthven searched for a tactful answer, a fight broke out between the domino players at the next table. In such close quarters, the quarrel quickly spread, and for a time it seemed that even the baronet and vicar must be drawn willy-nilly into the general melee. Their table actually went over, to the negligible loss of the plate of biscuits, the teapot only being saved because Dr. Daly snatched it up and stood with it, back against the wall, as if ready to baptize his first assailant with hot tea.

During this donnybrook, someone bumped against the baronet. Preparing to defend himself, Sir Ruthven half turned, and found the one-eyed seafaring man with the ugly countenance, whom he had almost forgotten during his chat with the vicar, nudging up against him. Instead of attacking, the man winked his single eye and groped for Sir Ruthven's hand, slipping something into it.

He then pushed away through the fracas and out the door. Sir Ruthven, investigating furtively, found it was a wad of crumpled paper that had been given him. Fearing to be jostled again and lose it, he slipped it into his waistcoat pocket.

"If this is a world of your creation," remarked the vicar whimsically, "you would do well to stop the present riot."

Even as Dr. Daly spoke, the tavernkeeper and the serving-maid, each armed with a short whip in one hand and a shillelagh in the other, obviously prepared for this sort of thing, charged into the fray and quelled the ardor of the combatants.

The tables being righted and the teacups and plate of biscuits replaced, Dr. Daly went on, "How long ago does this Dr. Falcon claim you retreated into a universe of your own creation?"

"Why…I…hardly know. I don't believe I ever asked him that. Why?"

"Because it hardly seems likely that you could have not only forgot all your memories of that other life *in toto,* but manufactured a complete set of memories for this imagined life as well. I assume you do enjoy some memories of your childhood and early manhood?"

"As many as most people, I suppose." The earliest ones were not particularly enjoyable. "But if I could have manufactured a complete world in all its details, most of which details I know nothing about, I could probably have manufactured a past history for myself out of whole cloth."

"Have a care, Sir Ruthven. You sound half in danger of taking all this in earnest."

Sir Ruthven rubbed one finger across the wad of paper, a tiny bulge in his pocket. "Merely playing the devil's advocate, nothing more. But tell me, Dr. Daly, were you here in Portsmouth troubled yesterday morning at about…um…eight o'clock with a sudden, peculiarly dense fog?"

"A few minutes before eight, actually. Immediately after the single, loud crackling thunder-stroke. I remember pulling out my pocket watch to note the time of that curious cascade of sound, and even as I read it the fog rolled in between the watch's face and my own. Extraordinary atmospheric phenomenon. Where were you at the time?"

"In a vessel just standing out from Penzance."

"Really? As widespread as that? I half expect the next papers from London will bring news of its occurring there also, along with various speculations of the most noted meteorologists. About what time did the fog clear off in Penzance?"

"Why…I…I'm not quite sure." Sir Ruthven had been by then too outworn to care for anything beyond the fact that, the fog being cleared, it should at last be safe for him to sleep.

"It cleared about noon here. I wonder if it could have reached as far as Ploverleigh?… But do you mean to say that this Dr. Falcon somehow wove yesterday's fog into his rather bizarre hypothesis?"

The baronet managed a laugh. "Not at all. Merely a change of subject…. You in Ploverleigh are near neighbors of the poet Mr. Bunthorne, are you not?"

"Ah, yes. The 'fleshly poet.' I fear I can hardly approve of his verses, of course. Still, I'm sorry for his misfortune."

"His misfortune?"

"Oh, hadn't you heard?" said the vicar. "I should have thought a few paragraphs would have got into the papers, even as far as Cornwall. It seems Mr. Bunthorne's castle has been besieged and captured from under him by a band of pretty bluestockings under the leadership of an Hungarian princess."

"Remarkable!"

"Yes, it has caused a bit of excitement in the neighborhood. By the way, Sir Ruthven, forgive me for inquiring, but what was it that nautical fellow slipped you just now?"

"Why, I—really haven't the least idea. Practical joke of some kind, I daresay—I never set eyes on him in my life before today." Sir Ruthven was not entirely sure of that last statement, however.

"I thought as much, or I would not have asked. If it is a practical joke, best have a look at it at once and be sure it isn't a dangerous one."

Sir Ruthven was suddenly puzzled as to why he had failed to investigate the thing at once with Dr. Daly, unless it was that the manner of the one-eyed sailor had suggested confidentiality. Relieved of the burden of keeping a secret which was no secret after all, the baronet fished out the wad of paper and began uncrumpling it gingerly, half expecting to find either some exotic spider or the black spot of pirate lore.

Instead, the paper contained a hand-printed message cryptic in its simplicity: "Nr. 47, Etched Moon Street, 11:30."

"An invitation of some sort, I imagine." The baronet pushed the note across the table. "What do you make of it?"

The vicar studied it by the light of the guttering candle. "I passed the street in question earlier this afternoon. It looked disreputable, but reasonably safe—by daylight. If you choose to pursue the matter, I suggest you interpret the time as a.m. rather than p.m."

"Yes, but my difficulty is that I fancy the hour meant must be tonight. I don't suppose I could persuade you to accompany me, doctor?"

Dr. Daly shook his head and smiled. "I make it my strict rule to be abed by half-past ten. Indeed, I was hoping to persuade you to accompany me back to my inn for supper?"

With a profound sense of relief at quitting the Rook and Pigeon, Sir Ruthven accompanied Dr. Daly to the inn, and engaged a room there for himself for the night. They spent a pleasant hour and a half, including supper and a few rubbers of whist. When the vicar had gone to his room, however, the baronet reluctantly donned his cloak again and slunk away to nr. 47, Etched Moon Street.

CHAPTER 10

PIPE DREAM

Somewhat to Sir Ruthven's surprise, he found Etched Moon Street within three quarters of an hour, arriving at the place shortly before the appointed time, without having been robbed or garroted on the way.

He wondered whether to look upon nr. 47 as a refuge from the dangers of the street, or *vice versa*. It was a grim derelict of a building, compressed between two others with facades equally uninviting on a street that had apparently begun a half-hearted effort to turn from a residential neighborhood into a row of shops, perished in the attempt, and been left unburied to rot. *Rigor mortis* had long since worn off, and decomposition seemed to be in about its middle stages, but the *risus sardonicus* was still plainly visible along the length of the street, at least by cloudy moonlight. Half the street lamps were broken.

Nerving himself, Sir Ruthven rapped at the door of nr. 47. It was opened by a stooping individual of masculine attire but indeterminate gender and age, whose deep swarthiness appeared to have been put on with burnt cork, and who communicated through shrugs and grunts in preference to articulate sounds. This person seemed to have been expecting the baronet. With a contortion that must have been meant for a bow, he took his cloak and conducted him up two narrow, squealing flights of stairs upon which cobwebs encroached quite industriously, through a heavy door with splintering wood but—surprisingly—well-oiled hinges, and into an antechamber filled with the smells of incense and stranger odors. Almost shapeless in the light of a brace of candles, the dusty refuse of an Arabian Nights pantomime lined the walls. A doorway curtained with ropes of glinting beads led to the inner chamber. From between these crystalline draperies curled languid wisps of smoke.

The swarthy person conducted Sir Ruthven, with a series of gesticulations like ill-rehearsed Oriental bows, into the inner chamber. Here the light was even worse, coming from a single candle in a wall sconce and several glowing sticks of incense. The incense, while it increased the density of the atmosphere, did not cover a more sinister aroma. Cushions and low divans with broken legs strewed the floor, and some of the cushions were partially concealed by dark shadows that gradually resolved themselves, beneath the baronet's scrutiny, into human forms. The room held at least two occupants already, one lying prone on a divan, the other slumped on cushions, with his head and shoulders at a strange angle against the wall.

For a moment Sir Ruthven wondered if he had come to an establishment specializing in murder or the disposal of corpses on a business footing. Then the prone figure stirred with a low moan and the slumped figure moved his arm, a momentary spot of radiance showing he had taken a puff on a long-stemmed pipe. The baronet understood the true nature of nr. 47, Etched Moon Street.

At first queasy, he soon adjusted with a deep sense of relief. Less than half an hour remained of a day in which he had done very little to justify his continued existence. His arrival in an opium den at this moment seemed nothing short of providential, and rather than wondering why the one-eyed sailor had directed him here, he blessed the man as a benefactor. Paying for the pipe which the swarthy person offered him, he settled as comfortably as possible on the greasy silk cushions and prepared to puff himself into a state of comparatively pleasant criminality.

Unhandily, he had never before now indulged in so much as a pipe of innocent tobacco, and the first inhalation of poppy fumes brought on a fit of coughing. Recovering, Sir Ruthven found that the hitherto-slumped figure had detached itself from cushions and wall to settle by his side. It was the one-eyed seafaring man from the Rook and Pigeon.

"Don't swallow the foul stuff, mate," muttered the sailor. "Just pretend."

Faced with the practical problem of teaching himself the skill of smoking, Sir Ruthven had neither inclination nor motivation to teach himself the skill of *pretending* to smoke. "Why did you direct me here, if not to indulge?"

"For a witness. T' help us clear out this here ugly nest o' vultures."

"I see nothing particularly repulsive in it," said Sir Ruthven. Indeed, it seemed a relatively harmless way of getting in his crime.

"Wasting lives, ruining health, eating away mind and money— you call that pretty, mate?"

"All the resources you have mentioned," said the baronet uneasily, "are mine to waste or ruin as I see fit."

"The first time or two, mebbe, it's your own choice...but the stuff gets its hold on you, ye see, like leprosy. And ye don't think places like this survive on special customers like you, m'lad?"

There was a great deal in what the one-eyed man said. Nevertheless, it must be barely a quarter to midnight by now, and a grim misdeed—which in itself would harm no one but the evildoer—was close at hand. Moreover, since this sojourn was bound to overlap well into the early hours of the morning, it could be made to serve for tomorrow's duty as well as today's. "I conceive I'll be a much better witness for you," said the baronet, "if I can testify as to the actual noxious effects of the stuff they sell here, than if I can state only that I was given a pipe with some slowly burning substance of indeterminate nature in the bowl. Now I beg you to leave me in peace until tomorrow morning."

"Smoke that stuff, mate, and I can't promise to get you out of the penalty for it."

"Nor can you get me out of the penalty for *not* smoking it!" Sir Ruthven began to grow angry, in part because he knew the one-eyed man to be—in the general sense of things—right and because, although curious and somewhat eager, he was also afraid and more than half inclined to avoid the experiences that lay immediately ahead. "I promise you I will play your witness in the morning and take the penalty, man," he went on. "Now kindly return the favor by allowing me the dubious pleasure of tasting to the full what it is you wish me to testify about."

The seaman shrugged and retreated into the shadows. Sir Ruthven took advantage of his anger to puff determinedly at the opium. After several more fits of coughing and a strong seizure of nausea, he found the fumes gradually overriding the acute discomfort.

Inhaling more deeply, he watched the single candle burning on the far wall. Slowly, like a flower blowing, the wax peeled down and away in clear petals, while the flame enlarged, growing at the same time more and more translucent, diffusing its softened radiance throughout the chamber. Now the baronet's cushions were nesting inside a great, square-cut ruby, glowing gently from within, with wisps of brilliance crisping along its facets. Looking again at the heart of the ruby, Sir Ruthven saw that the candle's wick was a small black man with puffed-out orange cheeks, blowing the ruby up like a balloon.

The facets swelled outward and upward, the edges softened and disappeared, and the baronet was in the stately pleasure dome of Kubla Khan. Houris, looking much like winged hourglasses (from which, no doubt, they had taken their names, or *vice versa*) whirled about him; lights—the sounds of festivity made visible—sparkled and danced at the far side of the dome. Sir Ruthven began making his way through the houris, toward the safety of the colored lights, and found himself on the cliffs overlooking the sacred river.

He stood poised high above the torrent, looking down through the yeasty caverns to the line of swift-flowing lace, too far below for its sound to reach him. He extended his right hand to the opposite bank, and saw that instead of a smoking pipe, he now held a fistful of tiny beads that trickled like sand between his fingers into the chasm below.

He tried to close his hand more tightly, but the beads held his fingers apart even as they slipped through. He tried to pull back his arm, so that the globules would fall to the parquet floor rather than into the gulf, but instead of bringing his hand towards the rest of his body, the effort seemed to bring the rest of his body towards his hand, until his toes were at the very edge of the precipice. He gave up and turned his attention to the grains he was losing irretrievably.

They were not beads after all, he saw with shock, but persons— human figures squirming out of his fist, clinging for a few seconds to his fingers, then falling or jumping. Some seemed to let go reluctantly, others wriggled out laughing and dragging companions with them.

Size ceased to have any relevance. These were full-grown people who fell out of the baronet's hand—at least they became full-grown as they left his fingers, before he lost sight of them; yet he himself had become no larger (and he was not that large a man to begin with) nor was he more than dimly aware of the incongruity of his being able to carry a throng of friends and strangers in his palm.

He watched Dr. Falcon fall out of his hand, arm in arm with the one-eyed seafaring man…then a number of barely-remembered acquaintances, the tavern wench from the Rook and Pigeon, Ruth Cripps embracing the Hungarian princess, more strangers, Dr. Daly the vicar of Ploverleigh, the lord high ambassador of Japan, the fleshly poet Mr. Bunthorne, and so on until poor Mad Margaret slipped out from between his thumb and forefinger, perched there a moment staring upwards, and finally rolled over backwards with a laugh. He tried to catch her with his left hand, but she was too large and fell too fast. Now only one being was left in his hand—he could feel the person, and squeezed tighter yet, covering his right hand with his left—*"O God! Can I not save* one *from the pitiless wave?"* His chest constricted, his blood beat painfully against the skin, breathing became difficult, but still he pressed down on his fist—until suddenly the pressure popped open around him and he was free again.

Looking down, he saw that the last person in his palm had been himself.

Not a self he recognized clearly on second examination—a very young self, strangely attired and with lighter hair and eyes—but himself none the less.

He clung for a while to his own thumb, then dropped off like all the others and fell into the foaming river far below—a river that drowned without killing and dashed the body apart limb from limb without disconnecting it, like words divided at the end of a line of print. Possibly because this was a sacred river, its water holy. As the initial horror waned, Sir Ruthven began to take a perverse comfort in being drowned and dashed apart.…

Is all *that we say or seem but a dream within a dream?…*

Many visions later, he stood on a speckled plain, looking at a line of trees. He knew by some racial memory that the trees had been planted in an immense circle, yet all he could see appeared to be in a perfectly straight line from horizon to horizon—the circle was that vast—and he was too far away to see the nearest trees clearly. He walked toward them, his purple shadow, cast by a scarlet sun, shrinking and extending over the ground in front of him, and after an interminable period of suspended time he reached them.

The trees were human beings, standing with their feet planted ankle-deep in the soil. Their arms were raised at easy angles, and their fingers had grown into leafy, fruit-laden branches. All except Dr. Falcon, whose fingers had as yet only a few, stunted twigs and withered leaves, and who kept pulling first one root-covered foot and then the other from the ground.

Sir Ruthven heard voices discussing the doctor—"Bad investment, that one." "Have to transplant him." "No, better use the wood for desks and chairs." "What kind of fruit did they plant him for, anyway?" The baronet could not tell whether it was the other tree-people talking, or some unseen gardeners too large to be visible. He felt he should assist his friend out of the soil; but Dr. Falcon's face now wore a fierce, angry expression. Sir Ruthven backed away without attempting to speak to him, then turned and ran along the line of trees.

One of them extended an arm-branch and stopped him. He saw to his horror that it was the one-eyed sailor, branches laden with small packages of powder. "Take one, mate," said the sailor, waving his boughs an inch from the baronet's nose.

Sir Ruthven heard footsteps behind him, thudding forward mushily. He did not know whether it was the gardeners coming to plant him along with the others, or whether it was Dr. Falcon, self-uprooted and pursuing him for unknown purposes; and he feared to look. Hurling himself against the sailor's branch, he tried to break free.

The sailor pulled back with a cry as of pain, and fell with a heavy thud.

CHAPTER 11

THE RETURN OF DR. FALCON

The strains of "We Sail the Ocean Blue" dropped Chuck Falcon aboard a ship in harbor. He guessed the ship to be the *Pinafore* and the harbor Portsmouth; but instead of bustling with melodious activity on a bright morning, the deck lay deserted in the moonlight.

Not even the *Pinafore* should be lying here at anchor without at least a skeleton crew, but no watch was in sight. Chuck was just as glad. Gazing across the bay at the lights of the town, he pondered how to get ashore. He could easily swim the distance, even weighted with his knapsack. But though the knapsack was waterproof, his clothes were not, and a dripping wet stranger would be more conspicuous than a dry one on the streets of Portsmouth, some of which seemed to be heavily illuminated and populated. He might appropriate a lifeboat, but that seemed too much like theft, even in a virtual fantasy world.

The notes of a mandolin drifted down to him. Looking up, he made out a white-clad sailor comfortably enmeshed in the rigging, thrumming out a melancholy tune. As he listened, the sailor began singing of a maiden fair to see. Coming to the end of a rallentando, the singer paused as if in expectation. Chuck echoed the last line of the lyric in his inner male's bass-baritone. It seemed somehow expected of him. The sailor glanced down for a moment and looked pleased before returning his gaze to the moon and continuing the tenor aria. Twice more he came to a pause, and twice more Chuck obligingly supplied the refrain. At length, finishing the song, the sailor slung his mandolin over one shoulder and descended from the rigging.

"Ralph Rackstraw, I believe?" said Chuck.

"Your servant, sir," responded Rackstraw, with a tug at his fore-lock. "But where did you spring from, my kindly chorus? Are you a dream?"

"That's right, I'm a dream." The excuse seemed ready-made. "Watch your step there. You're really asleep in the rigging, you know."

"Strange. I'm usually the smartest topman in the fleet, though I say it who shouldn't. But I knew at once you must be a dream. That speaks well for my alertness, even in sleep. We wouldn't have a stowaway from Portsmouth this long before embarking, and I know we had none aboard from our last port of call."

"Which was?"

Rackstraw blinked. "Don't you know?"

"I'm only a dream, not a seer. In fact," Chuck went on, warming to his fabrication, "since I just came into existence tonight, I can't be expected to know any past history."

"Logical enough," agreed the sailor. "A figment of the heat-oppress-ed brain. Our last port was Titipu."

"Titipu? Titipu, Japan?"

"Of course, where else? It's hardly a good British name. But how, knowing none of the past, did you know Titipu's in Japan?"

Chuck had been startled by the idea of a vessel sailing from Japan to England without, apparently, stopping at any port between. But that was thinking in terms of classroom Old Earth geography. Going by the map he had examined in Ruddigore Castle, it might be entirely possible for a ship to make the crossing nonstop. "I passed a map on my way up, as I was materializing in your dream," he explained. "What were you doing in Japan?"

Rackstraw pulled an Oriental fan from his jacket and executed a sort of graceful but unlikely salaam. Doc wondered if it were some salute they had devised or if the sailor, convinced he was dream-ing, was acting accordingly. "It was our august mission to collect the new lord high ambassador of that quaint country and transport him to his duties in our own great nation."

"I see. And would the town be lighted up in honor of his ar-rival?"

"Naturally. We took him ashore this afternoon, amid suitable pomp. Our gallant captain and his beautiful daughter are at the reception for the ambassador." Rackstraw heaved a heavy sigh. "Most of the crew are on shore leave in honor of the occasion."

Again Chuck gazed at the lights on shore. The pirate ship should have had time to reach Portsmouth by now, and Lozinski's virtual world seemed to have righted itself; *ergo,* there was a good chance that Sir Ruthven was awaiting him somewhere in town. "Well, what would you say to rowing me ashore, Rackstraw?"

The sailor looked startled. "But you're *my* dream. Why should you wish to go ashore?"

"Sightseeing. Besides, you'll be waking up eventually, and I'll have to find another sleeper."

"I take your point. And so you flit around from dreamer to dreamer? Aye, you'll have a wider choice of berths ashore than aboard…. Well, it won't really be leaving my post, since I'm asleep at it."

In the act of lowering one of the boats, however, Rackstraw suddenly paused. "You may find me a weary oarsman, being asleep and all. Why don't you just take the boat and row yourself? Since you haven't really taken it, it'll hardly matter."

Rackstraw might have to face a few awkward questions if a boat that should have been on the ship was found tied to the dock instead. "One reason people dream," Chuck explained, thinking quickly, "is to work out their frustrations of the day. Dreaming you've rowed ashore and back will help you release your pent-up emotions."

"Ah!" said the sailor, and when the boat was lowered he rowed with a will, obviously having a good store of pent-up emotions to release. "You seem a very educational dream," he remarked as he left Chuck on the dock. "I shall miss your company."

* * * *

The time was 11:23 by the first clock Chuck passed. Following the areas of brightest illumination, he came to some kind of large public building, whether town hall, embassy, or mayor's residence he could not say. It appeared that Lozinski had no very clear idea of what sort of public buildings a city like this would have in which to host a reception for a newly-arrived ambassador. The edifice was colonnaded in the pseudo-classical style, and all the stone pillars were festooned with flowers and Japanese lanterns.

By luck, the affair looked like a costume ball. Walking up boldly, Chuck informed the servant at the door that he was Lord Mentone. Calmly accepting the newcomer's hiking clothes and knapsack as a costume, the doorman announced him; and, clad in his freshly-invented title, Lord Mentone began working his way through the crowd of guests, gathering introductions. Several costumed gentle-folk who had been near enough the door to hear him announced began trying to curry his favor at once—a few even claimed prior acquaintance—and although Chuck moved from group to group with no waste of time, he found himself rarely without someone at his elbow who was willing and eager to point out the celebrities of the evening to him.

He was figuring out that many of these creations were people Bob Lozinski knew in *Papa's Pride*, wearing virtual costume in his fantasy world—the masked ball could be a symbol within a symbol. But in how far did this virtual population, both those with exterior originals and those without, have their own individual ex-istences—hopes, fear, ambitions, and all the rest? Was there was a subtle balance between the two conditions? Even on Old Earth, sci-ence practice and fiction had wrestled with these questions already for generations before Liftaway; the more regularly tailored virtual recreations of the ship continued to fuel the debate. Dr. Chandra Falcon believed that all these virtual people, with or without living prototypes "out there," had their own conscious existences and, within the limits of their world, a measure of self-determination. At the same time, their world and to some extent their moods, ac-tions, and freedom of will seemed to depend on the state of their world-builder, something the way that atmospheric and weather conditions had affected even the most self-sufficient spirits by the testimonies of Old Earth scientists.

Tonight the guests at the ambassador's reception seemed to be in a peculiarly giddy mood, with the sensation of unreality run-ning high. While not an orgy, the affair had as nearly decadent an atmosphere as was possible without becoming actually destruc-tive. Someone costumed as a chess knight balanced astraddle an imromptu maypole trying to snip silhouette pictures in one of the Japanese lanterns. The lord and lady mayor of Portsmouth, clad like the king and queen of hearts, were playing London Bridge on the dais with the lord high ambassador, his lady, and a couple of aldermen got up as American Indians—interesting, when the geography of this world seemed to omit the entire North and South American continents from between Europe and Japan. The captain of the *Pinafore,* in his regular dress uniform, and an Arabian caliph were trying to feed each other sherbets while standing back to back. Every few moments some individual or small group would break suddenly into a wild, frenzied dance—always careful, however, to confine the contortions to a small area—and at the card tables the players were enjoying a complicated game that used cards, dice, chessmen, and knucklebones, many of the rules of which seemed to be improvised on the spot. As Chuck paused briefly to listen to an argument about whether the ace should count as highest or lowest card, someone pelted him with a handful of rose petals, which were being used as gambling counters.

Dr. Falcon feared that some mood of Bob Lozinski's was acting as an intoxicant on the people here. Yet Rackstraw, while possibly over-credulous, had seemed sober enough, as had everyone Chuck passed in the streets on his way here. Lozinski's mood, then, had either spread over his interior world in the last few moments, just as the fog had covered his ocean yesterday (virtual time); or, like weather conditions back on Old Earth, it was acting primarily on folk already receptive to an unusual mood. Whether the basic influence was one of hilarity or depression Chuck could not yet tell, and that was his background worry. His foreground worry was that he could not spot Sir Ruthven anywhere among the guests.

Pausing at an open window to get a breath of fresh air and decide where to search next, still hoping that Lozinski's probable alter ego was somewhere in Portsmouth, Chuck noticed, through all the noise in the room, one set of footsteps that seemed to be approaching him. Turning, he found himself face to face with Captain Corcoran of the *Pinafore.*

Corcoran had wiped his face clean of all traces of his recent parlor stunt with the caliph and the sherbet, and appeared to have thrown off to some extent the prevailing giddiness of the assembly. "I trust you will pardon my rudeness," he began, after clearing his throat, "in not waiting for an introduction; but the fact of the matter is that I *have* been introduced to Lord Mentone, sir, and you are not he."

Having just invented the title, as he thought, for the occasion, Chuck was momentarily taken aback. Maybe the word had been floating through Lozinski's mind and Chuck had unconsciously tuned it in? He parried Corcoran's accusation with an excuse borrowed from Corcoran's own operetta: "You're partly right, sir. I wasn't Lord Mentone yesterday. But we just discovered that he and I had accidentally been mixed up in babyhood. We resumed our rightful places only this afternoon."

Corcoran nodded. Chuck reckoned that the thing must not have happened yet aboard the *Pinafore,* but already the Captain took such matters in stride. "Ah, yes. Quite so. There was a similar case described only last year in the *Times*—Vollaire and West, I believe. Hope you left the late Lord Mentone reasonably well off?"

"Not badly. In fact," Chuck went on, having a bit of fun with his lie, "I would've preferred staying my old self, but—" He shrugged. "—duty, you know."

"Quite true. It 'doth make slaves of us all'—or is that honor? Well, much of a muchness. Since you are his lordship now, I wonder if I might prevail on you for the favor I would have asked of him if he were still, so to speak, you?"

"I'm rather busy tonight," Chuck began.

"Oh, this won't take an hour." Corcoran waved his hand. "The fact is, I've just received intelligence that a crewman of mine is eloping tonight with one of the admirable women who provided the refreshments for this reception."

"Well?"

Corcoran looked surprised at Chuck's calm acceptance of the statement. "Well, bother it, sir, we can't have it, can we? She's a respectable widow."

Chuck considered how best to excuse himself before getting drawn into this new subplot. "They're both of age, aren't they?"

"I doubt it," said a deep, stately voice behind him. Chuck turned to look at the lord high ambassador of Japan, who was almost as tall as Chuck Falcon himself, probably weighed twice Chuck's 93 kilos (all muscle; as Chandra, she weighed 50 kilos, equally athletic and well distributed) and had not a single Oriental feature in his face, which was broad and basically jovial, though forced into a stern and dignified expression. "The woman looked scarcely forty-three," he went on, "though of course I only saw her in the dark, with the light behind her, and did not consider her of sufficient rank to warrant closer inspection."

"In fact, Mrs. Cripps is very young for her age," replied Corcoran, with a touch of choler. "But in our land, your excellency, women come of age considerably before fifty."

"That is well," said the ambassador's wife, coming up at Chuck's other shoulder, "but it's a pity the men come of age so long before they reach years of discretion."

Chuck looked down at the lady. Pretty and petite, the top of her Japanese hairdo barely reached his chest, and her features, unlike her husband's, actually had a slight Oriental cast. Chuck remembered that Pooh-Bah, the lord high almost everything, who was almost certainly the ambassador, married one of the three little maids from school at the end of *The Mikado*.

Chuck turned again to Captain Corcoran. "Did I understand you to say that Mrs. Cripps is mixed up in this affair?"

"Indeed, Lord Mentone. An excellent woman. Of course you know her? I've only learned of the thing myself. Had I learned earlier, I would have been searching for them even now."

Thinking of Ruth Cripps, the piratical maid-of-all-work, and Barbara Cripps the member of the household that also included Bob Lozinski, Chuck said, "Then you can count me in."

"For a reasonable insult," said the lord high ambassador, holding out his hand, "I could provide you with information that might make your search less tedious."

"Go on, love!" said his wife. "How could you have learned anything of the matter? You must not try to retail secrets you know nothing about, my own."

The ambassador flipped open his fan and cleared his throat, staring down at his wife. "You should make some attempt, my dove, even in your artless way, to remember your dignity. Moreover, your statement just now was not the sort of insult to which I referred."

"By 'insult' he means a bribe," Corcoran confided privately to Chuck. "Being able to name a primordial amoeba amongst his ancestors, his excellency suffers from a severe case of family pride, and seeks therapeutic remedy by demeaning himself through any means available, preferably those that simultaneously enrich him." The captain slipped a five-pound note into the ambassador's free hand. The ambassador sniffed and put the bill into his pocket, from which he withdrew a small, crumpled wad of paper. "I found it," he said, with another glance at his wife, "on the floor beside the refreshment table, shortly after the person you are about to seek had replenished the plate of sandwiches. Obviously, it had been dropped by mischance and left by oversight. I believe it would have merited a heavier insult, but we will let that pass."

Corcoran uncrumpled the paper, read it, and handed it to Chuck. In blunt, block letters, it said: "Nr. 47, Etched Moon St., midnight."

"We'd better find the place in less than no time," said Corcoran. "I believe it's after midnight now."

Chuck could not be sure, but he thought an angry expression flickered across the face of the ambassador's lady.

CHAPTER 12

ECHOES OF MURDER

Of course, Dr. Charles Falcon was a complete stranger to the town. Captain Corcoran was familiar with Portsmouth, but not, it seemed, familiar enough. Once or twice the captain came close to using stronger language than "Bother it!" as he swore some old landmark had been removed overnight and replaced with a row of shabby shops. The people they met in the streets were either too drunk or too lost themselves to give coherent directions. Nor did Chuck like what the moon was doing—it seemed to be progressing through the sky at an even speed, but it sometimes appeared full, sometimes gibbous, and sometimes crescent. Once, during this last phase, he watched a cloud that was drifting across it shear into two sections as neatly as wheat beneath a sharp sickle. Corcoran did not seem to notice anything peculiar in the moon's behavior, and Chuck did not point it out to him.

It was after one a.m. when they finally found Etched Moon Street and approached nr. 47. The door had a knocker, but the ring was gone, leaving only the gargoyle head screwed into the wood.

"We must be firm, but polite," Corcoran observed, rapping loudly with his knuckles.

Hearing no sound within, Chuck joined Corcoran on the top step and they knocked again. A third application of their fists to the door brought a sleepy protest from an upper window in a neighboring house, but no response from nr. 47.

At last the door swung silently inward, while whoever opened it apparently crouched behind it in order to stay hidden from the newcomers. Chuck was about to wrench the door forward for a look at the porter, when a man's scream came from the floors above, followed by a woman's scream.

Corcoran took the rickety stairs three at a time, with Chuck right behind, glancing back over his shoulder to cover their rear. The first flight brought them to a dusty landing where they could hear the woman's sobs coming from still higher up. "Little Buttercup!" exclaimed the captain, and led the way up the second flight. Their whole ascent had taken less than a minute.

At the top of the second flight they glanced around briefly at a sort of long hallway furnished with pseudo-Oriental trappings in the worst taste. The sobs came from behind a bead curtain at the far end. Through this the two men charged, into a smoky, ill-lit opium den.

The woman, tall and portly, was leaning against the wall near the doorway, dabbing her eyes with the corner of her shawl, but doing nothing to stifle her sobs. "Mrs. Cripps!" said Corcoran, halting at once to comfort her.

Chuck had never gotten a really clear look at the face of Ruth Cripps, but something in this woman's bearing told him at once she was not the piratical maid-of-all-work. He pushed past Corcoran and the new Cripps and hurried toward the slight figure standing in the middle of the room.

His toe struck something yielding. He looked down to see a prone shape on the floor. He did not like the dark pool, barely visible in the murky light, which seemed to be spreading out beneath its head. Crouching, he turned the body over.

It was a dark-bearded man with one good eye that stared whichever way the head was turned, while the other eye remained screwed up as it must have been in life. The corpse was still warm.

"I—I fear he's dead," said Sir Ruthven. Chuck looked up. The baronet had taken a pace or two forward. In Sir Ruthven's right hand was a bludgeon, dripping blood.

Turning it delicately, as if hating to handle it with even the tips of his fingers—although they, too, were already wet with blood— Sir Ruthven handed the weapon to Chuck. "You seem to be haloed, Dr. Falcon," he said with an attempted smile. "Like the good lady. Does poor Steve's blood look like liquid gold to you?" He shook his head, pulled out his handkerchief, and began trying to wipe his hand. "Forgive me… I seem to be somewhat…hazy yet. Unforgivable. But he warned me, he…"

The baronet slumped to the floor. The room's last occupant, a man lying on a low divan, stirred, snorted, and fell back into torpor, too deep in opium trance to show any awareness of whatever was going on around him.

* * * *

Corcoran and Little Buttercup confirmed what Chuck had already guessed: the dead man was Dick Deadeye. More to the point, Deadeye could have been Lozinski's virtual version of Steve Davis, and what had happened here tonight, a symbolic reenactment of Davis' death. Chuck regretted not having witnessed it.

Sir Ruthven, recovering more fully from his experiment with opium, insisted on binding himself over to justice. He also insisted it must be done properly, and refused to stir from the building where the victim lay until some representative of the local force came to collect him. Corcoran promised to send round the first officer he met as he escorted Mrs. Cripps to her home. Dr. Falcon would have preferred the good woman to remain at hand and answer questions—her hysteria did not sound quite genuine to him—but both the captain and the baronet insisted she be allowed to depart.

Whoever had opened the door to Chuck and Corcoran had long since disappeared, along with any other staff that might have been on the premises. Carrying the still-drugged derelict over one shoulder, and followed by the baronet, Chuck descended to the ground floor, where he found a small, neat kitchen adjoining a small, neat bedroom. He deposited the derelict on the bed and began preparing coffee and scrambled eggs.

"He warned me," Sir Ruthven repeated. "Poor fellow! He tried to warn me not to inhale the beastly stuff."

"Steve Davis?" Chuck kept his voice as casual as circumstances allowed.

"Who?"

"Davis—Steve Davis. The dead man upstairs. You called him Steve, didn't you?"

Sir Ruthven shook his head. "If I did, I suppose I must have been thinking of 'stevedore.' Inaccurate, of course, but I fear I was still half in trance. Though not too far gone to realize that was not the name his captain gave him.... Deadeye, was it not?"

"And you never met him before?"

"I never saw the man until this evening—never heard his name until…poor Deadeye! He came to me for assistance."

"What kind of assistance?" said Chuck.

The baronet glanced up at him and back down again. "He…wished my testimony on a certain matter…not guessing what testimony I would shortly give about…his own death."

"And what testimony is that?"

Sir Ruthven smiled ruefully. Not guiltily—ruefully. "I had thought it rather obvious."

"Not so obvious as it looks, is it? You didn't kill him, did you, Lozinski? You may have stood there with a bloody bludgeon, but you weren't the one who had used it."

"I do wish you wouldn't use that name, doctor. Not at a serious time like the present." The baronet put his hands on the back of his neck, closed his eyes, and drew a deep breath. "Of course I killed him. Not, perhaps, in quite my right mind, but I am guilty, none the less."

"Unfortunately," said Chuck, "unless you make up your right mind to tell what really happened, the jury is probably going to believe that."

"I know," Sir Ruthven said miserably, yet with a touch of pride. "I know."

The police officer arrived about the time the eggs were cooked. "Sergeant Edwards, Portsmouth police," he introduced himself, tipping his hat with his truncheon. "Very sorry to intrude on you here, but would either of you be the gentleman desiring arrest?"

"'Desiring' is rather strong," replied Sir Ruthven, "but I think you must be referring to me."

The sergeant shook his head. "A gentleman like you, sir? Are you sure there isn't some mistake?"

"It is because I *am* a gentleman that I am giving myself up!" the baronet exclaimed a trifle testily.

"You look hungry, sergeant," said Chuck. "Come on, sit down and join us."

"Only on condition we none of us mention this sorry business during supper, sir," replied the policeman. "Consorting with the criminal element otherwise, you know. Might be misconstrued—prejudicial to the case. Not that I've anything against the criminal element, myself," he hastened to add, sitting down and heaping his plate. "Many a heart amongst 'em beats as true and fair as any in Belgrave Square. Brothers under the skin, you know—all brothers under the skin. I say, could you please pass the pepper?"

Chuck passed him the pepper. "Agreeing with your sentiments in general, sergeant, I'd still call it a good idea to be sure who your criminals are before you label them."

"Right you are, sir. I don't suppose there's a few drops of milk for the coffee? Of course, if a man comes up to me and says, 'I am a criminal,' then what choice do I have but to believe him? Especially when the man's a nob—the word of a gentleman, you know, sir. Speaking in generalities, of course."

"'Hath not a murderer eyes?'" the baronet misquoted the bard a little.

"Exactly, sir." Sighing, Edwards shoveled a forkful of egg into his mouth and swallowed it down. "'Hath not a thief hands, organs, and so on?' Ah, it's a painful business, friends, a painful business all round."

"Speaking in generalities, of course," said Sir Ruthven.

"Speaking in generalities, of course." Sighing again, the policeman took a drink of coffee. "'If you bash them, do they not bleed?'"

"Now you're coming dangerously near specifics," Sir Ruthven said with a slight shudder.

"Speaking in generalities," said Chuck, "haven't you ever had cases of false confession, sergeant?"

Edwards considered the question. "Without descending into specifics, sir, I may say we've had one or two in our time."

"From which it follows," Chuck suggested, "that true culprits are not likely to come forward with unsolicited confessions."

Edwards took a solemn swallow of coffee. "If I thought you meant that remark to apply to any particular case, sir, I should not have listened to it. However," he went on, ostensibly in a sort of stage aside to Chuck, "I think I noticed a prone gentleman in the next room, in no state to confess to anything, and not so much of a nob, neither, by the looks of him. Now I'll need to be going shortly to have a look at the unfortunate victim—upstairs, is he?—and if I were not to find anyone else here on my return, I still wouldn't have to go back empty-handed, if you take my meaning, sir."

"I am hurt, deeply hurt, by the suggestion," said Sir Ruthven. "Is there not one single law for the peasant and the peer?"

CHAPTER 13

CHARLES FALCON'S MAIDEN BRIEF

Lozinski seemed determined to chastise himself as quickly as possible, perhaps in order to keep Dr. Falcon from breaking through Sir Ruthven's surface awareness and communicating with the higher consciousness in time. When the party arrived at the Portsmouth gaol, Sergeant Edwards and Sir Ruthven bearing Deadeye's sheet-covered body on an improvised stretcher and Chuck carrying the slumbering derelict over his shoulder, they found a trial (Edwards referred to it as a 'hearing') already set up in the station room, with twelve jurymen in nightshirts—there was that much artistic verisimilitude, and they were all males, as no doubt befit the period—yawning in their box and grumbling that they should demand overtime pay. A portly usher, more stoic, leaned on his staff working a newspaper crossword puzzle. A single bewigged barrister sat at his table shuffling note cards as if they were playing cards.

Seeing the new arrivals, this last individual rose and approached them. "Barre, sir," he began briskly. "Bailey Barre, esquire, at your service. Counsel for the crown."

"Then I don't quite see how you can be at *my* service, Mr. Barre," replied Sir Ruthven, smiling and extending his hand, "but I thank you for the sentiment."

Barre coughed. "Not necessarily mere sentiment, sir. Under the circumstances, I am prepared to act in this unique case as counsel for the defense also and simultaneously."

"Sorry," said Chuck, to whom Bailey Barre, esq., looked like a shady young opportunist, "but he's already got a lawyer."

Sir Ruthven looked around in surprise, and, since there was no other possible counsel for the defense for him to see, settled his glance on Chuck. "I didn't know you were qualified to approach the bar, Dr. Falcon."

"I am in this jurisdiction." It was close enough to the truth. Dr. Falcon was a qualified psychiatrist, practicing in the jurisdiction of the mind.

"Nonsense," said Barre. "You can't plead without a wig, sir." Sidling a little nearer, he touched his own wig and went on in a lower voice, "Of course, since only one of us can speak at a time, we may be able, for a very reasonable consideration, to work out an arrangement..."

"Not to worry, doctor," murmured Sergeant Edwards in Chuck's other ear. "I'll soon fetch you a wig."

Waiting only long enough to receive Chuck's thanks, the policeman disappeared. Barre, disgruntled, retreated to his table and began laying out note cards in what appeared to be an intricate solitaire. While a couple of police officers took charge of the corpse and the derelict, Chuck and Sir Ruthven settled themselves at the small table reserved for the defense.

"I owe you a large debt, Dr. Falcon," said the baronet. "I expect Mr. Barre would have asked an exorbitant fee, and, really, it seems hardly worth the expense."

"The best way you can show me your gratitude," said Chuck, "is by telling me what really happened this evening. If I'm going to act as your counsel, I'll have to be briefed."

Sir Ruthven sighed and leaned forward, burying his face in his hands. "I am sorry, doctor. I had assumed you understood the hopelessness of our case when you took it upon yourself. I suppose I ought to be in the dock," he went on, brightening slightly as he raised his head and looked around the improvised courtroom. "I wonder where it is. I say! Isn't that his excellency the Japanese ambassador and his lady?"

Chuck turned his head in the direction of the other's gaze. Pooh-Bah's form was unmistakable, sitting among the very small audience near the back of the room. His diminutive wife, snuggled at his side and daintily tapping her folded fan against her softly pointed chin, seemed to be trying to catch Chuck's eye—or was it Sir Ruthven's? Before he could determine which, the judge was ushered into court with all due solemnity.

Having the court's full attention, more by virtue of the cere-mony surrounding his entrance than by any commanding qualities in his appearance, his honor leaned partway over his rostrum and introduced himself with a long ditty which began:

"I am the very model of a modern judge upon the bench:
I understand James Joyce, the tarot pack, and medieval
   French..."

Chuck leaned over and whispered to Sir Ruthven, who was about to join everyone else in the chorus, "Is this sort of thing usual in courts of law?"

"I'm not quite sure," confessed the baronet. "This is the first time I've been in a court of law in any capacity. But I believe it's a type of song more usually employed by military men—major-generals and such."

By the time the judge had finished his song with an admission that, while on every other theme but this his learning was untaint-ed-oh, the law's a thing with which he was entirely unacquainted-oh, Sergeant Edwards had returned with a wig for Dr. Falcon and the process was ready to get underway.

Despite Chuck's efforts, it went badly for the defense. Captain Corcoran had found his way here in time to be put on the stand by Bailey Barre, esq., as a witness for the prosecution. He identi-fied the corpse as that of his late able seaman, Richard Deadeye, and told the court, truthfully but with an apologetic glance at Dr. Falcon and Sir Ruthven, all that he had seen at nr. 47, Etched Moon Street. His evidence did not sit favorably with the usher or the audience, who seemed the only impartial members of the court to be paying much attention to the proceedings. The jurors were dozing in their box and the judge was writing something on a sheet of pale violet paper.

Dr. Falcon moved for a recess to summon Mrs. Cripps, other-wise known as Little Buttercup, as a witness, but the jurors shouted him down, being eager to get back to their beds (which were more comfortable than the jurybox), and the judge, waving his violet stationery in the air to dry the ink, denied the motion on grounds that the good woman was probably still suffering from hysteria and in no condition to give reliable evidence. Sir Ruthven, apparently asking nothing more of life than that he be allowed to continue sitting at his table instead of standing in the dock (wherever it was), leaned back and looked on with quiet interest. The judge folded his billet and lit a stick of scented wax to seal it.

The derelict was somehow sobered up sufficiently to take the witness stand, testify that his name was Solomon Grundy—a fact attested to by several members of the audience and one juror—and that he had been in opium dreams since about nine p.m. and knew nothing more. There had been no other customer in the den when he smoked himself into oblivion and he did not seem fully aware yet that there had been a corpse in the room when he was carried out of it. Neither Barre's examination nor Dr. Falcon's cross-examination could get anything more out of the genuinely bleary fellow, so he was given over into the custody of Sergeant Edwards, who carried him away to a cozy cell to sleep it off. The judge beckoned to the usher and gave him the folded note, gesturing toward someone in the audience. The usher nodded and delivered the billet to the ambassador's wife.

The foreman of the jury, yawning, moved that if all the evidence was in, they might be allowed to deliberate and get it over with. The judge, however, obviously eager to wait and see what effect his message would have on the pretty Japanese lady, shook his head and pounded his gavel once or twice. "Oh, the testimony can't be all in yet," he said cheerfully. "Come, come, gentlemen, surely one of you must have another witness to call?"

Barre rose at once and said, "Indeed, m'lud, counsel for the crown would have been confidently content to rest its case, but at the behest of the court, we call Dr. Charles Falcon to the stand."

"With pleasure!" Chuck rose and strode to the witness stand. But as he was about to take the oath, the judge leaned over and remarked,

"I say, my lad, if you're acting in the capacity of witness, the court really must insist that you remove your wig."

Dr. Falcon removed his wig and was sworn in. The judge returned his attention to the Japanese lady, who had folded his note into a fan and was alternately fanning herself and tapping the paper coyly to her lips. Her large husband seemed, like the jury, to be dozing.

"Now then," said Barre, "you were with Captain Edward Corcoran, R. N., at the time he arrived in the upper room of number forty-seven, Etched Moon Street, that notorious den of iniquity?"

"Objection," said Dr. Falcon.

"Sustained," observed the judge, without, however, glancing down nor giving the court any further instruction.

"Well, were you?" persisted Barre.

Dr. Falcon decided not to press the objection. After all, nr. 47 really was a den of iniquity. "I was."

"And you agree that Captain Corcoran's testimony is substantially correct?"

"As far as it went. It was also circumstantial—"

"Objection!" cried Barre.

"Sustained," said the judge, this time tearing his gaze away from the ambassador's wife long enough to glance toward the witness stand. "Ah, I see! Doctor, you really must remember when you are acting as witness and when as counsel."

"But you were, I believe," continued Barre, "the first party actually to discover the corpse—aside from the heinous murderer, of course?"

Dr. Falcon controlled himself, biding his time. "I was."

"And would you mind very much describing to the court the relative positions of the occupants of the death chamber as they were when you found them?"

"Mrs. Cripps was nearest the door, the corpse a few feet beyond her, the defendant some paces beyond that, in about the middle of the room, Mr. Solomon Grundy—"

"Oh, I hardly think we need bother abut Mr. Grundy," said Barre, waving his hand. "And the defendant held a cudgel, or bludgeon, in his right hand, I think?"

"Yes."

"A *bloody* bludgeon, I think?"

Chuck looked at Sir Ruthven, who seemed to be following the proceedings with something like moral satisfaction. "It was."

"And was there blood on the defendant's hand, also?"

"There was," said Chuck, "and he was—"

"Thank you," said Barre, "that will be all. You may step down now."

Instead of stepping down, Dr. Falcon slapped his wig back on his head and said loudly, "Objection! My witness, m'lud!"

"What? Oh! Eh! Certainly, certainly," said the judge. "Cross-examination. Yes, of course. But you must make it perfectly clear to the court when you are speaking as counsel and when as witness."

Dr. Falcon followed this instruction by alternately wearing his wig and removing it. The court was too sleepy or too preoccupied to insist on his also alternately descending from and returning to the stand.

Dr. Falcon (with wig): Which of the occupants of the room was physically nearest to the victim?

(Without wig): Mrs. Cripps.

Barre: Objection!

Judge: Sustained.

Dr. Falcon (with wig): In your opinion—

Barre: Objection!

Judge: Sustained.

Dr. Falcon (with wig): The court understands, Dr. Falcon, that you hold a high degree in the field of mental health, psychiatry, and psychology. In your *professional* opinion, was the defendant in a competent state of mind to understand his actions?

(Without wig): No, in my *professional* opinion, he was not.

Barre: Objection!

Judge: Sustained.

This time, Sir Ruthven looked as if he shared Barre's objection.

Dr. Falcon (with wig halfway back to head): What's your objection now?

Barre: Defendant's action on trial, not his competence at time of committing same. Unfortunate seaman equally dead either way.

The Judge blew a kiss to the Japanese lady. Dr. Falcon shifted tactics a little.

Dr. Falcon (with wig): Did you actually see the attack which resulted in the victim's death?

(Without wig): No.

(With wig): The crime could have been committed some moments before you arrived?

Barre: Objection!

Judge: Sustained.

Having noticed that the judge's response seemed automatic and unconscious, a reflex action to the word "Objection," Dr. Falcon ignored it.

Dr. Falcon (without wig): Yes, it could have been.

He paused, expecting Barre to object again, but the barrister seemed absorbed for the moment in watching the exchange of winks between the judge and the ambassador's wife. Counsel for the defense continued.

Dr. Falcon (with wig): Then the crime could have been committed by a third party or parties unknown, who had time to press the bludgeon into the defendant's hand and escape, either down the stairs by which you shortly afterwards ascended, or by some other way?

Barre: Objection!

Judge: Overruled.

Apparently his honor had decided that varying his response would create a favorable impression of his grasp on matters.

Barre: Nonsense! This hypothetical third party of yours would have had time to make his way down two flights of stairs, out the front door, and down the street in one direction or other and so out of sight without either you, the good captain, or the good Mrs. Cripps noticing him?

Dr. Falcon felt he would be well within his bounds to object to Barre's cross-questioning out of turn; but it did not hurt his purpose to answer the question. "I think it entirely possible that the third party could have made it down the stairs, hidden somewhere on the first floor while Captain Corcoran and I entered the house and mounted to the upper room, then escaped through either the front or back door while we were upstairs. In fact, some unseen person did open the door to us, apparently hid behind it while we ran upstairs in response to Mrs. Cripps' screaming, and was gone from the house by the time we came back down. As for what Mrs. Cripps saw or did not see, I can't answer, but—" (throwing on his wig) "I move the court proceed no further in this business until the good woman can be summoned to give her evidence."

"Objection!" said Barre.

"Sustained," said the judge, at whom the Japanese lady was tenderly shaking her head. "What? Oh, ah, I really believe we can settle this affair to a turn without troubling poor Mrs.—what's the name?—Buttercripps. Now if that's all, doctor, your witness may stand down."

Dr. Falcon glanced around. The jurors dozed in their box without displaying much sign that they had been swayed either way. The judge might well call for acquittal or committal on the basis of whether or not the ambassador's wife chose to return his flirtation. A few of the more alert members of the audience seemed impressed with the latest testimony, but not sufficiently so to change their bets on the outcome. In fact, Chuck had been pleading his case, not with a view to winning it in the court proper, but with a view to winning it in Lozinski's own mind. Stepping down from the witness stand, he was about to play his last, desperate hole card, when Barre played it first.

"Have we time for another witness, m'lud?" Barre asked of the bench, and, receiving an abstracted nod, went on, "The crown calls as witness Sir Ruthven Murgatroyd."

There was no sensation. Chuck guessed that most of those present had forgotten the defendant's name. The judge remarked, "Eh? Who?" and the usher looked everywhere but at the lawyers' tables as he called the name. Meanwhile, Sir Ruthven had risen and started forward.

Dr. Falcon intercepted him for a muttered word of advice. "You don't have to give incriminating evidence against yourself." The proceedings were so much a hodgepodge of bits and pieces gleaned from Old Earth movies and screenshows that he felt tempted to add, "You can always plead the fifth."

"If you please, doctor," replied the baronet, shaking off Chuck's hand. "I do not appreciate being presented as mentally incompetent." Then his tone changed to wistful enthusiasm. "But that was an inspired thought of yours, about the unknown third party. I wish it had occurred to me in time!"

He mounted the witness stand and stood waiting for the usher to bring the bible and swear him in. The usher had by now reduced the well-known formula to a rapid monotone mumble punctuated by a loud "Do you…" at the beginning, a couple of forceful "truth's" in the middle, and a clear "…so help you God?" at the end.

One hand on the book and the other raised, Sir Ruthven responded, "I don't," clearly enough, but quickly and rather low. If any members of the court besides Dr. Falcon noticed the irregularity, they gave no sign of it, and the baronet, trembling very slightly, sat down with a sigh as of relief.

Secretly, Dr. Falcon sighed too.

"Now, then, Sir Ruthven," Barre began briskly, "how do you plead to the charge?"

"Ah!" said the judge. "*That* Sir Ruthven." And, enlightened as to the identity of the witness, he returned his attention to the lady in the audience.

"Guilty," said the baronet.

"You did kill the late, unfortunate, greatly-lamented Mr. Dead-eye, cutting down that staunch British seaman, one of the bulwarks of our nation, in the very prime of his manhood and usefulness, eh? Answer yes or no."

"Yes."

"Thank you, Sir Ruthven, that will be all!" Barre stepped back and spread his hands with a flourish.

Dr. Falcon rose to claim the right of cross-examination, but Sir Ruthven had already jumped to his feet, crying, "No, it will not be all!"

"Eh?" said the judge with a blink. "Witness not to talk except to answer questions, I think? Usher?"

"I wish to speak in my capacity as defendant, my lord," said Sir Ruthven. "I believe every defendant has the right to speak in his own behalf?"

"Ah! Oh, yes, yes, quite right, now you mention it. You may proceed, sir, but do try to refrain from saying anything that might confuse the court." Confusable as the court was, that seemed a tall order.

Dr. Falcon sat again, having decided it was best, now that Sir Ruthven was ready to say something at last, to let him go on in his own way, even at the risk of losing the cross-examination, which might have doubtful value anyway, after the baronet's ruse with the oath.

"My lord," began Sir Ruthven, somewhat nervously now that the room was giving him its silence, "gentlemen of the jury, honored members of the court, when the…the late Mr. Deadeye met me at Number Forty-Seven, Etched Moon Street, it was for the purpose of enlisting me as a witness to the nature of the activities carried on in the upper room of that—establishment. Those activities have been made sufficiently clear during these proceedings, but I have yet to hear one word about putting a stop to them!

"I...I insisted that in order to testify to the nature of these activities, I first be allowed to sample them. I spent some time, perhaps even hours—days, it almost seemed—inhaling those noxious fumes...I..." The baronet put his hand to his head and swayed a little. The gaslights flickered, and Dr. Falcon got to his feet.

But Sir Ruthven propped himself against the short wooden railing and continued, "I believe I stand here a living testimony to the evil of that opiate... Gentleman, that place and all others like it must be...must be closed, and to prevent the knowledge from dying in this room, I am ready—in fact, I demand—to swear out an affidavit before...before such sentence as this court sees fit to pass on me is..."

The lights seemed to dim suddenly of themselves, and Sir Ruthven fell forward across the railing.

Dr. Falcon sprang forward. But, halfway to his client, he vanished from the courtroom.

CHAPTER 14

SECOND INTERLUDE AND SENTENCING

"*Why?*" Chandra demanded, looking at her virtual helmet in Misaki's hands. "Why did you yank me out? What happened this time?"

Misaki bowed her head in apology. "Some kind of glitch—virtual bug—viral gremlin… I'm sorry, Dr. Falcon, the cleansweep must not have been quite clean enough, or the filtering not quite pure enough."

"Okay. Try another cleansweep and filter-back." Chandra sighed.

"Still wanta keep on trying, Doc?" asked Deuteronomy Osborne. "Damage done, now. We've got one uh the sphincters who did it right here, and the other three can't slip past security much longer, not now folks're getting things goin' again in other pylons. Ship's big. Not that big."

"We've got intraship communications restored with uptown, downtown, both neighborhoods, and the monastery pylon," Sister Harriet expanded. "And the core. It looks like the core is on its way back to normal. We haven't got contact with the convent pylon yet, but it's only a matter of time. And the insul-tubes are still locked down, no traveling yet from pylon to pylon."

"They want my advice," said Osborne, "leave 'em locked down till we have the sphincters, all four uv 'em."

Chandra said, "You seem to take it for granted they're all guilty. All equally guilty."

"All tryin' t' hide out, ain't they? All but this one—" Osborne gestured at Lozinski, lying still in his virtual suit, living through… what?

Chandra shook her head. "I'm not convinced of that at all. Right now, I'm especially convinced that Bob Lozinski is either innocent, or wanted to make a full confession—give us a warning—of anything he maybe only suspected, himself."

The security man shrugged. "Too bad he didn't make that confession, give us that warning in time. *If* that's the way it was. Now...whoever's guilty, chances are they're gonna freeze 'em."

"*Freeze* them?" whispered Sister Harriet. "Oh, no...surely...I know Papa Gadore let them put the death penalty on reserve, but... life is too precious in *Papa's Pride! All* life."

"So's compost," Osborne returned matter-of-factly. "So's oxygen. So's food an' water. Wanta go on spendin' food, water, and air on sphincters who put the whole damn ship at risk with their double-damned computer bug?"

Misaki said, "We're already spending food, water, and oxygen on two manslaughterers in the core prison."

"Ask me, that's wastin' precious core space, too. Oughta have the security lock-up in th' tropical forest pylon, where it's good and hot. Or at the bottom uh one uh the water pylons."

"We don't even know yet that these four were the ones who did it," Sister Harriet protested. "I really can't believe it of any of my Antique Terra people."

"In hidin', ain't they? The three of 'em."

"You thought Pete Schultz was coming to meet you at Ishmael's Downtown," Misaki pointed out. "Along with Steve Davis and maybe Bob Lozinski. And now, with communications still just in process of being restored, and the insul-tubes shut down, as far as we know, all over the ship, they might not be hiding out deliberately. Any number of people could be temporarily displaced, hard to catch sight of."

"And *whoever* did it—" Sister Harriet repeated—"and I still can't believe it was anybody in Antique Terra—we did *Blankout* just two seasons ago—Efren Plover's play about the devastation—comparatively mild devastation—a computer virus causes on Old Earth...*whoever* did this, I'm sure he, she, or they must have thought of it as just a practical joke. To lose your life—to be frozen to death—for a practical joke!"

"Yeah?" said Osborne. "A 'practical joke' they figured was worth murderin' Steve Davis to cover it up ahead uh time. Assumin' it was these four involved," he added sardonically. "The ones right there when an' where Davis got himself killed."

"And from the way Bob's virtual fantasy was going," Chandra insisted, without further details. "I feel surer and surer that he does *not* deserve to be frozen. Misaki, get me back 'in there' just as soon as you safely can."

* * * *

Someone was chafing Sir Ruthven's wrists, patting a cool, damp cloth over his forehead. He opened his eyes. He was lying on the floor with a single figure, comforting in its largeness, bending above him. Beyond this figure, the courtroom was dark and seemed to be in confusion; but, as he continued to gaze upward, the gaslights slowly came back up and, although the clamor went on, a few voices came into it of people trying to restore order. The judge's gavel, which seemed to have been pounding raggedly and sporadically for some time, fell into a regular rhythm.

The man bending over him was the reverend vicar of Plover-leigh.

"Ah, my dear young friend!" said Dr. Daly. "Are you feeling a little more like yourself now, I hope?"

"Yes—a little." Aided by the vicar, Sir Ruthven sat up. Several jurymen and members of the audience had fallen into either slumber or swoons, but the lord high ambassador of Japan had awakened, and he and his lady sat facing each other, engaged in what appeared to be a contest of snapping and waving their fans. In one corner, a seedy-looking man, perhaps a thespian, was juggling a seemingly infinite supply of sausage-rolls, while a number of men and women in classical Greek attire were catching and eating those he dropped. Sergeant Edwards was dancing a hornpipe with Solomon Grundy. True, the solemn usher, the foreman of the jury, Mr. Barre, a very respectable-looking middle-aged governess, and his honor the judge were all calling for order, but on the whole, Sir Ruthven inclined to the theory that he was hallucinating to some extent, possibly a lingering aftereffect of the opium. Dr. Daly, for instance, ought to have been asleep in his bed at the George Inn. Logically, then, it was Dr. Falcon bending over him, and his overwrought imagination was transposing the vicar's benevolent, comfortable features on his stranger and more unearthly friend.

"Dr.... Daly?" he asked. He had meant to say "Falcon," but it came out "Daly."

"Right here, my good young friend. A glass of water, perhaps?"

"Thank you. It would be greatly appreciated. But where is Dr. Falcon?"

Producing a water decanter and glass which he must have brought from one of the tables, the cleric began to pour. "Dr. Falcon? The strange gentleman you were telling me of earlier this evening? He's been here, has he?"

"He was acting as my counsel. You may ask anyone here, whenever they calm down again." Fear that the vicar might doubt his sanity added a slight edge to Sir Ruthven's voice, though he tried to avoid the effect.

"I don't doubt you in the least." Sighing, Dr. Daly handed him the glass of water. "I fear, however, that if he acted as your counsel, he must have made a sorry mess of it. Indeed, that may account for his sudden departure."

"No. Dr. Falcon muddled nothing. I think he was probably the most conscientious person here."

"You remind me of the duty of charity, my friend." The vicar heaved another sigh. "Finding you in such…such a predicament, if I may so express it, and your counsel gone, I assumed the fellow had bolted. But we are not put here to judge our fellow creatures. How do you account for his disappearance?"

"I…don't know. This is not the first time—he may appear again at any moment. But how do you come to be here, Dr. Daly?"

"A restless night. Sleep would not find me. At last, rather than continue to tangle the bedclothes, I dressed and went out for a walk. In the street I heard rumors of a young gentleman arrested at a house in Etched Moon Street. Remembering the note you had received of that sailor chap, I came on here." Noticing that the courtroom around them had nearly quieted again, Dr. Daly lowered his voice. "Believe me, my friend, it was a bitter shock to find my worst fear confirmed, and if there's any way I can help—"

"I say," inquired the judge, leaning down over the top of his rostrum, "are you feeling better now, defendant?"

"Yes…better now."

"Up to standing to hear the verdict?"

With the vicar's help, Sir Ruthven stood. He glanced around, looking again for the dock and wondering whether, in the absence of one, he ought to return to the witness stand.

"Oh, don't move about," the judge remarked with offhand kindness. "You're well enough there. Verdict!" He rapped his gavel several times and then unfolded a small piece of violet paper—a curious scrap for a legal document—and began perusing it eagerly, with smiling glances toward the audience.

Standing in an angle between the judge's bench and the rail of the witness stand, Sir Ruthven could see most of the audience, especially the Japanese ambassador and his lady. The ambassador's bulk was comforting somehow; the lady's smile, which seemed to flicker back and forth between judge and defendant, was not. He could not see more than a corner of the jury box, so the foreman's voice, when at last it came, reached his ears as if from a disembodied entity, an invisible judge of Hades. "My lord, we find the prisoner guilty as charged."

Though he had been prepared—had, in fact, actually dug his own grave—the baronet suddenly realized how greatly he had been hoping for acquittal. He closed his eyes for a moment, and must have swayed slightly, because he felt the vicar's hand on his arm to steady him. "It's all right," he whispered, opening his eyes and groping for Dr. Daly's fingers.

The learned judge tapped his gavel lightly, as if in annoyance. "Bother," he muttered. "'Not guilty' is so much simpler—release, end of whole business. Now, what is the usual sentence in such cases?…Mr. Barre—"

Happening to look in their direction, Sir Ruthven saw the ambassador's wife give her husband a sharp nudge.

"M'lud," said the ambassador, rising to his feet, "we claim custody of the prisoner on behalf of his majesty the mikado of Japan."

"You do?" said the judge blankly.

"On what grounds, may I ask?" said Mr. Barre.

The ambassador turned to his wife. After they had whispered to each other for a few seconds, he straightened, opened his fan with a flourish, and said, "On grounds that he is under suspicion of flirting with my wife."

"Eh?" The judge leaned over to peer at the defendant. "Have you been flirting with the lady, young man?"

Sir Ruthven, who did not know whether to regard this astounding development with terror or hope, could only shake his head.

"I beg to point out," said Mr. Barre, "that the party in question has just been convicted of the murder of an English subject on English soil, which is a rather more serious crime than flirting."

"It is not in Japan," replied the ambassador. "Nor with a Japanese woman on any soil. As the woman in question is my wife, and thus imbued by association with a measure of the inconceivable dignity, both inherent and acquired, residing in myself, the offense is proportionably heightened. Not to turn the culprit over at once into my custody will undoubtedly result in war between Japan and Britain by this day week. Still, I neither insist nor threaten; I merely point out the fact to you. Our warriors in their serried ranks assembled, I am told on reliable authority, present a particularly formidable array in battle."

"Stop a bit!" said the judge. "His majesty the mikado has published an exhaustive treatise, I believe, in three or four folio volumes, on the ideal relationship of the punishment to the crime? Our problem is solved very nicely!" Beaming, he rapped his gavel thrice, seemingly for the pure joy of it. "Let the prisoner be bound over to his excellency the ambassador. I'm sure our estimable neighbors of Japan can handle the sentencing much better than we could, and now we can all go to supper and bed."

CHAPTER 15

THE HIGH ROAD TO LONDON

After consideration, Chandra Falcon had Harriet Sanford splice together a medley of *Pinafore* tunes for Portsmouth, *Trial by Jury* music for the court house, and a few bars of "A Policeman's lot is not a happy one" for Sergeant Edwards. "Bailey Barre," said the sister, "comes from the next-to-the-last Gilbert and Sullivan opera, but there he's *Sir* Bailey, so Bob must have taken him from a much earlier point in his career than *Utopia, Limited* covers. Besides, he was hardly congenial enough for us to desire his continued presence in the virtual fantasy, was he?" Nor did she use any tunes from *The Mikado,* for though the Japanese ambassador and his wife—whom Harriet agreed must be Pooh-Bah and Pitti-Sing— had been present at the proceedings, Chuck had only seen him dozing and his wife apparently recast in the role taken by the first bridesmaid in *Trial by Jury.*

Dr. Falcon landed outside the Portsmouth courthouse just as the hour of ten a.m. was sounding. But on what day? The morning after that kangaroo-court "hearing"? Or had any number of days passed 'in here'? Probably, the best he could hope was to pick up the trail. If he could find and question Sergeant Edwards, or even the learned judge...

Making his way around a bridal party that was gathered on the courthouse steps as if awaiting its cue, he entered the courthouse. The spectators' section was crowded today, and the audience alert, even though, as he learned from a portly, reverend-looking gentleman sitting next to the aisle in the last row, there was nothing more spectacular on the docket than a breach of promise case and a civil suit brought by a military officer seeking a restraining order on his wife to make her stop treating him as if he were a pet dicky bird. "We heard a rather interesting case Wednesday, though," Chuck's informant went on. "Young gentleman of utterly blameless life who had made up his mind to commit one criminal deed merely by way of experiment, to see what it was like. Unhappy fellow forged a party's will for five hundred thousand pounds or thereabouts—lived quite handsomely for a month before he was found out. His defense was that the temptation to acquire a sum of that size was too overpowering to resist, therefore, the guilt attached to the action must be negligible; whereas, had he stolen a mere penny from someone's till, *that,* being unmotivated, would have been a crime of the worst description. The bench, I fear, did not see it that way, and the youth drew a sentence of life; still, it was a pretty moral point, and I'm more than half inclined to suspect that, purely in terms of individual conscience, the young man may have been quite correct in his reasoning."

"Do you come here often?" Chuck inquired.

"I have been, every day this past week. Never before in my life. It's been an education, but I confess I'd as lief it end soon."

The court was in a state of muddled preparation for the breach of promise case—nothing important had actually begun as yet, but the time was obviously unpropitious to approach the judge, who was peering around the audience as if searching for the prettiest female face. Chuck thought of leaving the chamber to try to locate Sergeant Edwards, but for the moment he decided to question the informant at hand, who seemed familiar somehow. "Has there been any case connected with drugs—opium, hashish—this week?"

"None, unfortunately. I say!" The clerical gentleman looked at Chuck more closely. "You wouldn't be—pardon my seeming rudeness, but this may be rather important—you wouldn't be—"

"Order in the court!" sang the usher, striking his wand loudly on the floor. The defendant, a happy-go-lucky looking young rogue, had appeared, and the jurors and front rows of the audience were hissing and shaking their fists at him.

The clerical gentleman lowered his voice. "You wouldn't be one Dr. Charles Falcon?"

Chuck almost gripped the man's arm in a reflex action. "The same. Let's get someplace where we can talk!"

* * * *

Once on the street, Chuck's courtroom acquaintance introduced himself as Barrington Daly, vicar of Ploverleigh, "to which pleasant village I should have returned before now, but for the promise I made to that unfortunate young gentleman, our mutual friend Sir Ruthven. I fear it does not seem very kindly done of you, Dr. Falcon, to have left him so abruptly at such a time."

"It wasn't," Chuck agreed, "but it wasn't my own choice, either. I was…pulled away while off my guard. You're talking about that farce of a midnight trial about—would it be a week ago?"

"A week ago tonight. I only arrived for the end of the thing myself—after you were already gone, as it seems, and I had some misgivings, perhaps justified, as to whether I would recognize you on sight, in spite of Sir Ruthven's excellent description."

"And this promise you made him?"

Daly blinked. "Oh, did I not mention it? My promise was to wait here for a reasonable length of time, in hopes of meeting you on his behalf. I elected to haunt the last place you were known to have been in this city, and a very fortunate thing you did not wait much longer before making your reappearance, doctor—but tush, I sermonize." Reaching into an inner coat pocket, the clergyman brought forth a folded piece of pale violet paper. "I am to give you this, if you wish to receive it."

Chuck accepted it, glancing at the blob of unstamped crimson wax that sealed it.

"I added the seal later," Daly explained. "His lordship the judge was willing to supply ink and paper, but had neither wafers nor wax at hand. I assure you, I have not read the contents."

Wasting no further time in speculation, Chuck broke the seal and unfolded the sheet. The note showed signs of having been penned in haste.

"My Esteemed Fr [these two letters lined out] *Dr. Falcon, This is to assure you that, tho' I do not entirely understand your actions, yet I understand you may well have reasons beyond the comprehension of the rest of us. If you should find it convenient and desirable to resume the acquaintanceship, please be assured I will be at your service in whatever place we may happen to meet again—assuming that possible—If not, very little blame could attach to one who chooses to*

sever relations with a recognized and convicted felon—indeed, quite the reverse—but know that I shall ever remain grateful for the privilege of having known your conversation. I remain, &c., your servant, R.M."

Finishing the note, Chuck glanced at the vicar again, wondering why he looked so familiar. "Where is he now?"

"Dear me, sir! Were there not even any illustrated papers in that limbo to which you seem to have vanished for a week?"

"None from Portsmouth."

Daly tsked, less in censure than wonderment. "Then you truly know nothing of what's happened since your mysterious disappearance from our midst? Doctor, I could almost begin to credit something of what our mutual young friend told me of you. 'For some have entertained angels unawares'? You were aware, at least, that the jury brought in a verdict of guilty?"

"No, I didn't even know that. I was afraid of it. Well, what happened next? Any chance for an appeal?"

"A very difficult question, that. Well, briefly, just as the court was about to pass sentence, his excellency the new ambassador of Japan, who happened to be present—dear knows why—claimed custody of Sir Ruthven's person, on grounds that our friend had been flirting with his excellency's wife, which, as it seems, is a rather more serious offense than murder in their country. Under threat of causing immediate and devastating war with Japan for non-compliance, the court bound him over into the ambassador's keeping. They departed next day for London in the ambassador's personal carriage."

"Railway carriage?"

"Landau. His excellency mistrusts more modern conveyances and will travel only behind horses or via sedan chair."

"But you do have the railroad here?"

"My very good sir," Daly replied, "do you take England for a benighted nation? Our railway system is the best in the civilized world!"

Chuck could not resist asking, "America, too?"

"Well, yes, if you take the *pro* stand in the debate on whether to include America in the civilized world."

So at least America was somewhere in Lozinski's virtual world. How, exactly, it fit on the map, might be interesting to investigate later. "How long would it take to reach London by train and by landau?"

"Roughly four days by the latter, an overnight trip by the former. One has the advantage, of course, of choosing one's own time of departure when traveling by personal carriage. I think the next train for the City does not leave Portsmouth until after ten p.m. this evening, assuming it is not delayed in Penzance or Plymouth. I must mention that as yet there's been no notice in the papers of the ambassador and his party arriving in London. Of course, neither have I been able to obtain a London paper more recent than day before yesterday's. City papers arrived on schedule yesterday evening, but remain bundled due to a stationers' strike."

Chuck made rapid mental calculations. Barring delays on the road, the Japanese ambassador could have had Sir Ruthven in London for two days by now. By waiting in Portsmouth for the train, Chuck would need at least another day to reach London. By making a rapid trip 'outside,' putting on music from one of the operettas with a London setting—at least two came immediately to his mind—and returning at once, he might get there sooner. Even a few hours might be crucial. That Sir Ruthven was still alive and in good health was evidenced by this world being in functional existence under a sunny blue sky; but in *The Mikado* the Japanese penalty for flirting was decapitation, and if the lord high ambassador, who had one or two lines like "Chop it off, chop it off" in the opera, were to press his accusation to the uttermost, it could be fatal. Unless Lozinski existed in more than one mental persona... but, judging from what Chuck had witnessed happening both times Sir Ruthven was losing consciousness.... Besides, Chuck did not relish the idea of kicking his heels around Portsmouth for the next twelve hours or so in order to endure an overnight train trip.

"I'll get to London by my own means," he told the vicar. "Will you meet me there?"

Daly coughed. "I would have been on my way to London a week ago had I been able to act in this as a free agent. May I ask whether your own means are faster and smoother than the railway, sir?"

Chuck looked again at the cleric, who was clearly making valiant efforts to remain polite in the face of what must appear to him extreme high-handedness. (How independently aware *were* these virtual-reality creations?) "Dr. Daly," he said, "I'd take you along with me if I could. Unfortunately, it's impossible—you'd be pulled apart into atoms before we got halfway."

Daly gazed back at him. "If you'd favor me with any further explanation of this phenomenon, sir, I'd feel honored."

Chandra's fingers already groping for her virtual helmet (invisible inside the virtual world), Chuck hesitated. Maybe it was the continued conviction that he already knew Daly from somewhere else that decided him. "I'm not quite sure how much Sir Ruthven may have told you about me, reverend, but the truth is, I come from another world, a world in a sense 'outside' your own. I'm going to return to that world and come back into yours in London." He traced a triangle in the air. "Something like getting from point A at this side of the base to point B at the other side by jumping up to the apex and back."

"Perhaps I see, perhaps I do not," said the vicar. "Dr. Falcon, are you God?"

Chuck shook his head. "Hardly, friend. Nor an angel, either. Simply a human being from another plane of existence. You're read Abbott's *Flatland?*"

It was the vicar's turn to shake his head.

"Well," Chuck went on, "in my own world, my race finds God considerably more elusive than you find me."

"And has your world the same Deity as ours?"

For a moment, Chuck was stymied. (What might a member of the Order of the Cosmic Christ say to this question?) "I'm not sure. I suppose in some ways yes, in other ways no. I guess you might say that your God, in the strict sense of your creator, is very close to home—you might even find him wandering around incarnate and unaware of it himself."

Daly glanced toward Chuck's hands, hovering near his ears. "Well, Dr. Falcon, we'd best resume this fascinating but unorthodox conversation at a later date. Where shall I look for you in London?"

Good point. Even Lozinski's virtual London must be pretty big, especially for people who in actual life had no adult memories of

Old Earth, only exaggerated ideas retained from childhood or fed by classes and movies. "How well do you know the city? Do you have any favorite hotel there?"

"I've been to London thrice only," the vicar replied, "two of those times in passing through, when I changed trains at Victoria Station. And the establishment in which I spent a happy week in my youth has since been torn down, to make room, I believe, for a gallery of illustration. Am I to understand that you don't know London, either?"

"Only by studying about it. We'll have to find out where they are, the ambassador and Sir Ruthven—the Japanese embassy, maybe, or—" A hotel came to Chuck's mind that ought to have made it into Lozinski's virtual world. "If nowhere else, try to meet me at the Savoy."

The vicar nodded and took out his memorandum book to make a note. Chandra found her helmet by feel and lifted it off.

CHAPTER 16

THE QUEEN OF THE FAIRIES

But it turned out there were only three G. and S. operettas with London settings. One of them—*Trial by Jury*—had already been adapted to Portsmouth, and another, *The Yeomen of the Guard,* took place several centuries earlier than most of the operettas in the series. Not that the anachronism made as much difference in *Papa's Pride* as it might have made back on Old Earth, but the fact that *Yeomen* had been in rehearsal at the time Steve Davis was killed could ring associations and overtones Chandra would just as soon avoid for now.

The computer virus attack made that backstage tragedy seemed longer ago to *Papa's Pride* than Chandra could imagine Tudor times seeming to Victorian times back on Old Earth. But if that death had any connection with the virus, they still had to find out what it was. Even more important, to the three women if not to Deuteronomy Osborne, was establishing whether and how far Bob Lozinski might share guilt for the virus or the murder or both.

"If I understand you," said Sister Harriet, "some of the virtual characters—maybe not all, but some of them—represent people Bob knows 'out here.' Some people possibly appearing as more than one character. I've tried to make up a list, my guesses." She handed it to Chandra. It was hand printed on a reusable film slate. Not only because computer applications were more precious just now even than usual, but also because the move back to conserving power, paper, and graphite had already been prepared for at Liftaway.

Chandra read Sister Harriet's list:

Sir Ruthven—Bob
Mad Margaret—also Bob? Judi?
Bunthorne—Steve? and/or also Bob?

Dick Deadeye—Steve
Ruth—Barbara?
Buttercup—Barbara?
Pirate King—Pete?
Capt. Corcoran—Pete?
Dr. Daly—Pete?
Pooh-Bah—Pete?
Pitti-Sing—Judi?
Learned Judge—Deuces?

"Yes," said Chandra, "this isn't a bad working list. A lot of your guesses would also be mine, even though I never knew the Antique Terra people as well as you do. But I should maybe remind you that gender lines can cross between reality and virtual scenarios."

"You're proving that yourself, Dr. Falcon. Chandra."

"And we've got a lot of question marks here."

"Of course. It doesn't seem likely, does it, that Pete could be *all* the ones I've got under consideration for him. The only characters I'd guess we can probably feel confident about are Bob as Sir Ruthven and poor Steve as Dick Deadeye."

Chandra thought, And a bludgeon in the virtual version of Steve's death. Definitely a murder, 'in there.' Whatever the truth of it, 'out here.'

Sister Harriet went on, "For the rest, I went by roles they've either played or want to play. Barbara says she was predestined to the heavy contralto roles by being born a Cripps."

Deuces Osborne was standing in the other side of the room, beyond Bob's hospital bed, watching Misaki at the keyboard. Not wanting the security man to overhear her, Chandra tapped "Learned Judge—Deuces?" with the tip of her right forefinger.

"I know G. and S. better than I know psychology," Sister Harriet murmured, "but don't people in coma sometimes understand a lot more than we might think about what's going on around them? Now, I'd have called Sir Roderic Murgatroyd a likelier role for..." She nodded toward Deuces. "But couldn't that be why Bob is running away from Ruddigore Castle? Whether he's guilty or not, just knowing...he—" Another nod. "—suspects him? Then jumping him into a comic but incompetent judge...defused him, made him less threatening."

"Only I was the one who started our trip away from Ruddigore Castle," Chandra pointed out. Though she wondered, now, if she'd really had as much control over that move as she'd thought, or if Bob's scenario had been pushing Chuck the way Sir Ruthven wanted to go. "And when it came to the crunch, by what Daly told me, that judge—threatening in and of himself or not—would have sentenced Sir Ruthven."

"And Pooh-Bah—Pete?—stepped in at that point. With Pitti-Sing, who could so easily be Judi." Sister Harriet sighed. "I wish you had a third virtual suit for this equipment. So I could 'go in' with you."

"You're already 'in there,'" Chandra told her. "Forget this one." Tapping "Dr. Daly—Pete?" she went on, "I'm about ninety-five percent sure I've figured out why Daly seemed familiar when I met him. Sister Harriet, Dr. Barrington Daly is *you.*"

* * * *

With two of the London-setting operettas out of consideration, they ended with the second act of *Iolanthe* to provide music for guiding Dr. Falcon 'in' this time. He landed just behind the sentry box in a moonlit and heavily populated palace yard. Unnoticed himself, he watched the scene over the shoulder of the sentry, a man almost as broad-shouldered and tall as Chuck Falcon himself—the high military shako made him even taller—and considerably thicker about the waist than you saw anybody 'outside' in *Papa's Pride* today, after the best part of a decade of being completely self-sufficient about food, as well as everything else.

The House of Lords, dressed for a session, were filing haughtily back into a building that had to be Westminster Hall. They must have just enjoyed a brief recess from a midnight debate. Hovering all around the edges of the yard, gazing after the peers, were two or three dozen delicate, feminine creatures. Their bodies—not their chiffon draperies—were semi-transparent, they were about three-quarters the size of ordinary young women, and their wings, translucent and fine-veined as those of mayflies, and extending from their knees to a level with their eyebrows, were as expressive and as obviously an integral part of their anatomies as a dog's ears to the dog. Chuck reflected that the mind had more flexibility in costuming a chorus of fays than had any production company limited by the need to use human beings.

As the last peer disappeared into the hall, there came a thunder-clap and a brilliant flash streaked into the air above the yard. The flash gathered itself into a shimmering cloud, shot through with rays of gold, silver, and blue; the cloud descended until it almost touched the ground, where it resolved into another fairy woman, as youthful and translucent as the others, but almost human-size and of a robust girth in bosom and hips that gave her more appearance of solidity. Her apparel, too, looked more substantial, her torso being clad in glittering, close-fitting chain mail of gold and silver links, below which her gown flowed twice as full as the skirts of the other nymphs. She was crowned with a bright silver light, car-ried a gold-headed spear, and her wings extended from a hand's-length above her head down to her ankles. This was a production that would have turned even an animation-film studio aquamarine with envy.

"Oh, shame!" cried the queen of the fairies, looking about on her women as she stood a foot or so above the paving-stones. "Shame upon you! Is this your fidelity to the laws you are bound to obey? Know ye not that it is death to marry a mortal?"

"Yes," replied one of her bolder subjects, "but it's not death to *wish* to marry a mortal."

"If it were," added another, "you'd have to execute us all!"

"Oh, this is weakness!" cried her fairy majesty. "Subdue it!"

"We know it's weakness, but the weakness is so strong!" wailed a third nymph.

"We're not all as tough as you are," said she who, Chuck thought, had spoken the first.

"Tough!" The queen fluttered down until her skirts brushed the pavement. "Do you suppose that I am insensible to the effect of manly beauty? Look at that man!" She turned to the sentry, who had all this time been standing motionless. Her mouth fell open in surprise. "Oh—*look* at him indeed! Who—Who *are* you, sir?"

The sentry gave the first sign that he had been following the action—he snapped to attention. "Private Willis, B company, first grenadier guards, mum."

"No, no!" said the queen. "That *other* fine fellow behind you!"

Willis looked over his shoulder, grinned at Chuck, and executed a military step to one side.

The queen took a deep breath, as if trying to get back into her lines after a stage mishap. "Now, here is a man whose physical attributes are simply godlike."

"I seem to be intruding here," Chuck put in. "If you'll excuse me, I'd better be getting on about my own business."

"Don't go!" cried the queen, pointing with her spear. Private Willis flashed out one hand and caught Chuck by the arm, the rest of his body remaining as stiff as before.

Her majesty advanced on Chuck, gliding smoothly above the pavement. "This man has a most extraordinary effect upon me. If I yielded to a natural impulse…"

She yielded to the impulse—she fell down at Chuck's feet and commenced hugging his ankles.

Chuck tried to disengage himself, but though he pulled free of Willis' arm with a single tug, the fairy queen clung fast. He thought quickly back over *Iolanthe* as he had crammed it into his head from the librettos. "Your majesty, don't you have a song to sing here? Something about putting out the fire with the hose of common sense?"

"Oh, Shaw!" The queen moved her embrace upward to Chuck's knees and held tighter. "She wrestles with her fire in vain, who lives by loving thee!"

Another fairy appeared, issuing from the sentry box. This one was dressed in simple gauze, like the chorus, but was covered with seaweed and water lilies; a couple of frogs hopped out of her waist-length, pale blond hair. Iolanthe herself—but making her entrance as per the first act rather than the second.

"Oh, fie, your majesty!" cried Iolanthe. "And you, who banished me to the bottom of the Thames for a far more respectable (though also more serious) affair than this with a mortal!"

"This—*this* is no mere mortal!" returned the queen. "This is indeed a god—another immortal!" She gazed up into Chuck's eyes with such intensity that he wondered if she had in fact recognized him as an outsider from a higher level of reality.

"This is madness, your majesty!" cried Iolanthe. "Subdue it! Wed him and you perish!"

"Nay—oh, my divinity!" the queen replied, apparently talking partly to Iolanthe, partly to Chuck, and partly to herself. "Death it may be to *marry* a mortal, but hast thou never heard, O foolish fay, that love may take other forms than matrimony?"

"Your majesty," said Chuck, trying to get free without kicking her, "I really don't have the time right now."

Iolanthe seized the spear out of the queen's hand and pointed it at her. A spray of water came from the golden point, drenching her majesty.

Wet and bedraggled, still the queen held tight, gazing up at Chuck and chanting,

> *"If heart of stone for heart of fire*
> *Be all thou hast to give,*
> *If dead to me my heart's desire,*
> *Why should I wish to live?*

Save us!" she added in a whisper, staring straight into Chuck's eyes.

Iolanthe screamed. Chuck looked at her. Her hair was no longer blond—it had become red. Her clothes were no longer merely wet and covered with seaweed—they were coarse linsey-woolsey and hanging in rags. She no longer stood above the ground, but on it.

"Our part is played out until Tuesday week," she remarked, staring at Chuck with wide, dark eyes. Then she turned and ran between the rows of silent, perplexed fairies, singing as she ran,

> *"The cat and the dog and the little puppee*
> *Sat down in a window-seat, staring at me.*
> *The lightning flashed, and the window-pane shone,*
> *And when it was cleared, I was all, all alone."*

She reached the wall, climbed it, and perched there for a moment to tell Chuck solemnly, "The pictures have all been moved to the tower, every one, and stored away in wild honey to keep the glow." Then she jumped off on the other side. There was a splash.

"She'll be carried out to sea!" exclaimed one of the fairies, peering over.

"No—she's safe! See!" Added another. But no one specified how she had attained safety.

Meanwhile, Private Willis had blinked. "I don't mind inconwenience, mum," he said, "but I don't think I can allow irregularity. Might I ask if things are going quite as planned?"

A light, high laugh floated down from above their heads. Chuck glanced up and saw a young person in silver tights sitting cross-legged on a cloud.

"Yes, a terrible muddle you've got matters into now, haven't you?" the newcomer shouted down. "And so now I suppose it all falls to me to set things straight again, eh?"

"And who are you?" said Chuck.

"Why, I'm the celestial drudge! I do everybody else's work, watch everybody else take the credit for it, and set everything straight again when everybody else has botched it!"

"Since you do everybody else's work in the first place," said Chuck, "doesn't that make you the one who must have botched it?"

The celestial drudge frowned and stood up on the cloud. "Fairies—to your places! Droop! Sigh! Look soulful and lovesick! Fairy queen—to your feet, ma'am! Olympus commands it! The gods, madam, take precedence over a mere fairy monarch! Private Willis! 'Ten-shun! A little more respect, sir! We'll take it from the line, 'Oh shame—shame upon you!' And as for *you*, sir—" (turning to Chuck) "—we'll have no intruders on *this* set! I give you fair warning, sir, either you or your head must be off, and that in about half no time! Now!"

Chuck's fighting instincts were roused. He had a hard time stifling them. He guessed that, with a jump, he could have reached the drudge's ankles and yanked him/her down. But everybody else had obeyed the godlet instantly, and, freed at last from the queen's clinging arms, Chuck knew the chance to get away to some other part of London was too good to miss. Ducking just as the celestial drudge hurled a thunderbolt at his head, he turned and strode away.

CHAPTER 17

DR. DALY'S NEWS

A ragged figure came stumbling toward Chuck in one of the moonlit streets surrounding Westminster. "The Regent Street Station?" it howled. "For mercy's sake, do you know the way to the Regent Street Police Station?"

The man was, or once had been, a London bobby; but his uniform now hung faded and torn upon a frame no longer plump enough to fill it, and his beard grew grizzled and unkempt round his cavernous mouth.

"I'm sorry," said Chuck, "I'm a stranger here myself. But if you can get me to the Savoy Hotel—"

"Lost! Lost! Lost!" wailed the one-time officer of the law.

"Possibly not, my man," chimed in a third party, who had just come up at Chuck's shoulder. "If you were to double back on your way down this street, take a sharp left at the fourth street but one, follow Heathcliff Mews to Little Dombey Way, then turn right at Abercrombie Terrace, proceed uphill toward Victoria Rise, downhill at Pudding Lane to the new houses in Pondicherry Crescent, then another left at Threadneedle Street, a right at Simmary Axe, a left at Macbeth Alley, a right at Lower Sudbury House, and a circle round Regent's Park, you might be surprised where you would find yourself."

The wretched bobby, who had listened to this with mouth open and panting as if to help him memorize it all, keened a thank-you and turned to retrace his steps.

"Oh, and you might just take this crown and buy yourself a few mugs and a sausage roll somewhere," his informant went on, tossing a coin. The departing figure paused to catch it, added a second, semi-coherent thanks, and lurched on out of sight.

"I was going to buy him a hot dinner," Chuck remarked, studying the individual beside him, who was tall and spare, with a hawklike nose, a pipe in his mouth, and a deerstalker cap on his head.

The individual chuckled. "Peter the Wag? He'd never have got you safe to the Savoy, nor to anywhere else in London, for that matter. Lost his own way some twenty-odd years ago."

"And the rest of you go on misdirecting him in revenge for his having misdirected everyone else before he got lost himself?" Chuck remembered the hapless Peter Forth now, from the *Bab Ballads.*

"Bless you, whether one gives him sound directions or unsound makes very little difference! As a matter of fact, the experiment has been tried of pointing out to him the true way back to his police station, but if ever he finds Regent Street again, I fear it will be by pure accident. As for the Savoy, sir, I can take you in that direction myself, though I cannot advantage myself of the dinner you were about to offer your guide. My business will require that I leave you a few houses away from the hotel."

"And you are?" said Chuck.

"Incognito, at the moment." The man in the deerstalker hat chuckled again. "But my last employment, I think I may safely tell you since it is terminated now, was as private detective to one of the crowned heads of Europe—no less a personage than his grace the grand duke Rudolph of Pfennig Halbpfennig. The last two words serve a dual purpose, naming both his grace's dukedom and the salary I drew from him."

The Grand Duke was the last and one of the least-known of the Gilbert and Sullivan operas, but a detective was mentioned somewhere in it. Had Chuck gone on suspecting the one present before him to be Sherlock Holmes, he would have tried to enlist his aid—probably better to have Holmes on your side than to risk finding him pitted against you. But a Gilbert-and-Sullivan detective was unlikely to prove so formidable, so, when their ways parted, Chuck bade him good-night and watched him enter one of the buildings, without paying more than cursory attention to which building it was.

* * * *

The private detective stood in the dark foyer and listened to the other man's footsteps fade away down the street. Then he chuckled, emerged from that building, and slipped into the one next door. "Probably a disinterested stranger," he remarked to himself with another chuckle. "Still, never any harm in a little extra precaution."

He threaded his way through the ground-floor curiosity shop, found the stairs, and mounted to a second-floor apartment where a pallid and thin young man sat covering sheets of foolscap with lines of verse by the light of a single candle, and pausing occasionally to sniff at a bunch of withered violets in a tumbler before him on the table.

"Well?" said the poet, glaring up at his visitor. "I trust you've better success to report this time than the last. I tell you, sir, it is unendurable for a man of my talents and fame to languish here in enforced obscurity—not to mention the lack of that luxury to which I have been accustomed."

"Patience, Mr. B., patience." The detective rubbed his hands over the candle flame. "We can start for Ploverleigh within the week. My lovely little Olga has managed to convey the information we need out to me—it cost the dear some ingenuity, since her Hungarian highness has banned the *mail* from your castle grounds—" here the detective laughed outright—"and I believe we have but to convince the delightful scholars of your utter chasteness to provide you with a larger and more faithful following of beauties than those you recently lost. We might, indeed, persuade them to adopt you into their midst as an honorary woman!"

Since the poet was occupying the only chair, the detective sat down on the floor to enjoy a few convulsions of mirth. The poet continued to scowl and pen his verse.

"And there is always this," the detective went on, wiping his eyes. "If nothing else, we may hope that the play you made up to vent your feelings makes you enough capital out of the situation to pay my fee."

* * * *

The Savoy Hotel of Bob Lozinski's London represented the heights of Victorian opulence as it could be gleaned from classic movies. In his first glance around the lobby, Chuck recognized the twins of the great branching staircase and the plush circular couch featured in so many screenshows that they deserved a line in the credits.

Despite the lateness of the hour and the fact that the streets had been almost deserted, the hotel lobby and ground-floor rooms were—not crowded—but sufficiently well filled to justify their existence. About every third or fourth seat was empty, but the rest were occupied with elegantly animated folk in evening dress, to whom liveried waiters carried trays of refreshments on a scale to gladden any cashier. Chuck guessed this was the theatre crowd.

A short, balding doorman approached him, looked up and down at his khaki hiking clothes and leather knapsack, and said, "If I might suggest, sir, that you would find the Red Lion, a short walk from here on Wellington Street, more to your taste..."

"Thanks," said Chuck, "but don't worry. I'm not here to book a room. I'm here to meet someone."

He started for the desk, but the doorman blocked his way. "Does the party expect you, sir?"

"He does."

"I trust you know the number of his room?"

"We weren't in London when we arranged to meet here. He didn't have a room reservation yet." In fact, Chuck wondered if the vicar of Ploverleigh could afford to stay here.

"That is unfortunate, sir. We do not divulge the room numbers of our guests. May I suggest you leave a message and return some-time to-morrow for the reply?"

Chuck stifled the impulse to flex the muscles of the inner male, pick the doorman up like a doll, and move him out of the way. "Thanks, I'll do that. If you'll let me get to the desk."

The hotel minion took another look up and stepped prudently out of Chuck's way. He was not too overawed, however, to hold out his palm. Well, Chuck might have to hang around the Savoy for a while, and it wouldn't be the worst idea to get on the good side of the staff, so he dropped a virtual half-crown into the waiting hand—as easy for the computer to provide money as a seemingly hard and bound copy of the Gilbert and Sullivan librettos.

Ignoring the glances of such bluebloods as deigned to observe him, Chuck left a message at the desk, where he was informed that as yet no Dr. Barrington Daly seemed to have registered, and then began a search through the public ground-floor rooms. In the second one he entered, a sitting-room off the lobby, he found the vicar.

Whether through his clerical status or his own charisma, Dr. Daly had obviously won acceptance into even these rarified social circles. He sat sipping from a teacup and chatting at ease with a small knot of swells near the fire. Catching sight of Chuck at almost the same instant Chuck saw him, he rose, set down his cup, and beckoned. Chuck joined the group.

"Your graces, my lady, my lord," said the vicar, "allow me to present my friend Dr. Charles Falcon. Dr. Falcon—their graces the duke and duchess of Dunstable—he is late of the thirty-fifth dragoon guards—Lady Sophy Brandram, Lord Dramaleigh."

"Delighted," said the duke of Dunstable, extending his hand at once. "Any friend of Dr. Daly's, sir…"

Introductions over, Daly's tone grew more serious. "If you will excuse us for a few moments?"

"Of course," said the duchess of Dunstable, a plain, portly woman who looked at Chuck as if she entertained a keen appreciation of the eccentric. "I'm sure your friend is more eager to learn the news you have to impart than to listen to Lord Dramaleigh's views—excellent though they are—upon the state of the modern theatre."

Lady Sophy, whose reaction to Chuck's out-of-place attire had been the opposite of the duchess's, conquered her visible distaste and said, "But of course you will join us afterwards for a dish of chocolate, Dr. Falcon? Or perhaps you would prefer coffee?"

Chuck put in his order for coffee, bowed to the ladies, and turned away with the vicar to an unoccupied divan nearby. Lady Sophy was saying to Lord Dramaleigh, "But if you dislike Mr. Bunthorne's new play so, my lord, why did you license it to be played?"

"Necessity, dear lady, necessity." Dramaleigh sighed. "If you could see the vile selection that comes to me—which I do not advise your seeing, since most of them are unfit for the printer, much less for the stage—and yet I must, perforce, license a few of them, if the theatres are to be kept supplied. And the notion of ladies in love with their mirrors and sundials is at least such as can be seen without bringing the blush of shame to the cheek of modesty."

Chuck and the vicar brought their heads closer together. "Our friend," the vicar began, "is being held in the Tower."

"The Tower of London?"

Daly nodded. "As a sort of potential international prisoner—until it can be settled which crime should take precedence. He himself freely confesses to the murder, but denies the flirtation."

Chuck reminded himself of the peculiar rules of logic applying to this world. "And flirting is a more serious crime than murder?"

"According to the criminal code of Japan. But he would have to be extradited to Japan, or at least to that nation's embassy here, and tried according to Japanese legal processes. He could hardly be tried for flirting in a British court of law, despite the opinions Lord Dramaleigh and the dear Lady Sophy may tell you to the contrary. Whereas he has already been tried, found guilty, and all but sentenced by a British court in the case of the murdered seaman. The problem bristles with diplomatic thorns, but the crown refuses to give him up until there is more evidence against him in the case of flirting than the sole word of the ambassador's lovely wife. I may add that several gentlemen, including the Tower gaoler (if one can call him a gentleman) have been observed in the act of what the vulgar would no doubt term flirtation with that sweet young woman—I may even say, unless this aging heart is very much mistaken, that she has attempted to turn her charms full upon me—but no one else except Sir Ruthven has been accused."

"So they need his confession before extraditing him?" said Chuck. "And then?"

The vicar sighed. "The legal processes of that quaint and curious nation are said to be somewhat arbitrary. And their mikado's penalty for flirting is decapitation. Our hapless young friend not unnaturally maintains that he would prefer to be hanged with British rope on British soil. But since the learned judge did not actually pass that sentence in Portsmouth before binding him over..." Daly shrugged. "As I said, the case is a veritable legal and diplomatic hedgehog."

"Is he being held *incommunicado?*"

"That, at least, he is not; he is allowed visitors every day from nine to five. The Tower closes at five." Daly's brief smile faded almost at once. "But my gravest news I have yet to impart. An international arbiter from a presently neutral country has been summoned. He arrived today—his distinction Don Alhambra del Bolero…you know the name?"

Chuck did. "The grand inquisitor of Spain?"

The vicar nodded soberly. "He entered the Tower at once this afternoon on his arrival, and is said to have taken his lodgings as a house guest of Sir Richard Cholmondeley's—the lieutenant of the Tower—so as to be as close as possible to the problem."

Chuck whistled softly. He thought that Don Alhambra was sometimes played as a bumbling incompetent, sometimes as a genial soul whose attachment to the Inquisition was all but ignored, and sometimes as a cheerfully—or dourly—menacing sadist. Which interpretation was Bob Lozinski, in his present state of mind, most likely to attach to the character? Might Don Alhambra be an embodiment, filtered through layers of coma, of Deuteronomy Osborne?

"There has been no word of any curtailment in visiting privileges," Daly went on. Then, lowering his voice still more, "And I think—I say I *think*—that his grace the duke yonder has a great fancy for the idea of rescue. For myself, I hardly dare think of the possible international repercussions of such a thing in a case like this, but if you, with your…wider perspective on our world… should opt for it, I am ready to do what I can. In any event," he finished, "there is very little we can do until the Tower opens again in the morning."

"I'd like to sound out the duke a little," Chuck said slowly. "And did I hear them talking about the poet Reginald Bunthorne?"

"Mr. Bunthorne? He's believed to have come here to London after his castle was seized by the Hungarian princess…what possible connection can he have with our young friend in the Tower?"

"Maybe none, maybe a lot," Chuck replied, unwilling to go into the situation more fully. "It's rather complicated. Well, let's sound out the duke, and then we'd better try to get a good night's sleep."

"Let me recommend the Red Lion," said Dr. Daly. "A very clean establishment. I'm stopping there myself."

CHAPTER 18

THE PRISONER

Lozinski's Tower of London was a theatricalized piece of the late Middle Ages set down in the middle of a basically Victorian city, with the residents of neither area showing any awareness whatever that their garb and speech patterns were in any way incongruous.

A friendly beefeater, after insisting that Chuck leave his knapsack in the gatehouse, directed him, as he had expected from Daly's information, to the southwest bastion of St. Thomas' Tower. He made his way there and entered, to find the ground floor occupied by a single circular chamber, where two men sat engaged in animated discussion at a table littered with papers, diagrams, and small pieces of paraphernalia.

The two were of much the same body build—they might have made good linebackers—and both were dressed in black, the younger one in plain, close-fitting tunic and trunk hose, the older in cassock and wide-brimmed clerical hat with crimson lining and trim. Wilfred Shadbolt and Don Alhambra del Bolero. They had not yet noticed Chuck.

"My unenlightened young friend," Don Alhambra was saying, "if you cannot trust a grand inquisitor to be up to date in these matters, whom *can* you trust? Only observe—" (holding up between his thumb and forefinger a thin sliver almost invisible from where Chuck stood in the doorway) "—neat, simple, compact—an entire morning's supply can be carried in a packet in one's pocket without producing a noticeable bulge—and yet capable, withal, of causing the most prolonged and exquisite results, with scarcely more than the minimum skill in application. Even you, my bucolic *confrere*, might be trained in their use in a few hours. Shall I demonstrate?"

"No. Newfangled," said Shadbolt with a scowl. "Give me a well-oiled screw. In the hundredth part of a single revolution lieth all the difference between stony reticence and a torrent of impulsive unbosoming that the pen can scarcely follow." His fingers were fidgeting with a small thumbscrew, and as he talked he caught his own thumb in it and ended his speech with a yelp.

"Better to newfangle than to mangle," remarked Don Alhambra. "Though perhaps one should not look to find the loftier refinements of human intellect in this benighted island."

Shadbolt glanced up, sucking the tip of his thumb, and saw Chuck. "No sightseers today," he said. "Not in this building. Come back next week. Or better, next month. Or best, in a year or three."

"I'm not sightseeing," said Dr. Falcon. "I'm here to visit one of your prisoners. Sir Ruthven Murgatroyd."

"Murgatroyd? Why?"

"Personal friend."

"Oh," said the gaoler. "That's all right, then. Verily, I took thee for another one of these fools and jades that do come daily to gawk and stare." He brought out a ring of keys, disengaged one, and threw it to Chuck. "Here. Mount to the cell at top of yon stairs, and mind thou lockest him well in again whenever thou dost take thy departure."

* * * *

Once out of sight of the pretty pair, Chuck lengthened his stride, taking the steps three at a time. He was in a state of wary confusion. Shadbolt's features, beneath a scowl that might have been laid on like precious make-up, had been youthful and open. And, if his expression was not overly intelligent, neither could Chuck recall that the Wilfred Shadbolt of the operetta had ever treated his gaoler's duties in quite so casual a fashion as to toss a visitor the key to the cell. Logically, this Shadbolt was Bob Lozinski's friend and housemate Pete Schultz, cast in the same part as in the production they'd been rehearsing when Steve Davis was killed. So Shadbolt could be sympathetic toward his charge. On the other hand, weren't Shadbolt and Don Alhambra traditionally played by the same performer? And hadn't they seemed to be arguing the relative merits of thumbscrews and under-fingernail splinters?

Was Bob Lozinski casting Pete Schultz in a villainous role or roles through knowledge Schultz was guilty of murder or—worse—the shipnet virus? Or was Lozinski bent on self-punishment? Chuck thought back to the scene of Deadeye's murder, but could not remember any counterpart characters of Shadbolt and Don Alhambra in the Portsmouth opium den. Unless sex lines had crossed and made Schultz into Little Buttercup in that sequence… or unless the derelict Solomon Grundy had not been so unconscious and supernumerary as he had seemed.

As far as Chuck could remember, though there were enough jokes about and references to torture and unpleasant death scattered throughout Gilbert's works that some critics called him sadistic, Sir Ruthven Murgatroyd was the only character in the operettas who actually came in for such treatment on stage—with the possible exception of John Wellington Wells, who was supposed to sink down through a flaming trap-door at the end of *The Sorcerer*…and who was another Grossmith character, like Sir Ruthven. Chandra had learned almost as much about all this as the small, hard core Gilbert and Sullivan enthusiasts in *Papa's Pride*.

Mounting the stairs as far as he could go, he found himself on the open ramparts, looking across the moat and Tower Wharf to the Thames. Shadbolt had neglected to tell him that the stairs led up beyond the topmost cell. St. Thomas' Tower straddled Traitors' Gate, where a short channel cut through the wharf to join the river with the moat. Everything seemed to be working very neatly—perhaps too neatly—in favor of Plan "A." Filing the layout in his mind, Chuck retraced his steps down one flight to the last door he had passed on his way up, unbolted and unlocked it—the key made a heavy, rattling sound—and went in.

Sir Ruthven stood by the fireplace, warily watching the door. On seeing Chuck, he relaxed and stepped forward, right hand extended. "Dr. Falcon! Sir, I am honored—deeply honored. Honored beyond my deserts."

Chuck shook his hand and glanced around his room. The fire was burning brightly, with a generous supply of extra wood stacked up on one side of it and a washstand on the other side; the remains of a roast fowl, a bowl of apples and oranges, a couple of bottles of wine and a silver coffeepot stood on a sideboard; a pillow squnched haphazardly on the bed, as if it had been used for a punching-bag; and the table nearest the fire was littered with papers, some of them lying torn and crumpled on the floor; but otherwise the chamber was clean and neat, as well as comfortably furnished.

"I'm only sorry to have flashed out on you like that back in Portsmouth," said Chuck. "We could have won that case. But why the hell did you plead guilty?"

Sir Ruthven blushed. "As matters turned out, it was fortunate I did. Poor Deadeye's death is the only thing that stands between myself and the snickersee of some Japanese lord high executioner. Had I been acquitted of the murder, I would most probably be even now in a dank and loathsome Oriental dungeon, rather than a snug English cell."

"Nor would you be facing the arbitration of the grand inquisitor of Spain," Chuck pointed out.

He had touched a nerve there. Sir Ruthven's facial muscles tightened and he turned to give the pillow a hard punch. "Threatened! Yes—what right have they to allow any foreigner—grandee or not, official or not, to *threaten* a true-born Englishman?"

"Maybe you should be thankful it hasn't come to anything more than threats."

"No...not yet," Sir Ruthven mused. "But he brought me all the illustrated papers this morning."

"And my guess is that it won't come to more than threats and illustrated papers—unless *you* want it to."

Sir Ruthven blinked. "You aren't still harking back to that weary old philosophical conundrum? Really, don't you think the jest is worn a trifle thin by this time? Here," he went on, crossing to the sideboard, "may I offer you some claret? Or perhaps you would prefer sherry or burgundy?"

"Coffee, if you have it."

"Coffee will take a few minutes to prepare—no matter. I find I am in the mood for it myself."

As Sir Ruthven filled a kettle with water, hung it over the fire, and fetched out coffee beans and a hand grinder, Chuck bent over the table, hoping to discover without asking whether the "illustrated papers" Don Alhambra had brought up were simply the current periodicals or something more sinister. He found a few sheets of the *London Times,* open to an artist's conception of life in Castle

Bunthorne under the occupation of the Hungarian princess, but the rest of the papers were either blank or penned in manuscript. "And what's all this?" he said.

"My forgeries." Sir Ruthven looked up with a kind of pride in his smile. "Incarceration limits a man's opportunities for criminal activity, but with a few scraps of paper and an inkwell I believe I have found a very neat way round the difficulty. Indeed, I may even have lit upon my true *metier*."

If Dr. Falcon could achieve his own, private plan "D"—a breakthrough to Bob Lozinski's consciousness—plan "A," "B," nor "C" might none of them be needed. And he thought he might just have found, among the completed forgeries, the tool to bring it off. "And this one?" he asked, holding the document up at arm's length.

"Ah! Yesterday's effort—one of my happiest inspirations. You hold the forgery of a party's Will for five hundred thousand pounds. Would you perhaps care to add your signature as witness?"

"But *which* party's Will?" Dr. Falcon pointed to the name preceding the words "being of sound mind and healthy body."

"My dear sir, do you suppose I would stoop to forging the Will of a *real* party? I merely chose a name at random."

"At random? Take another look at the name."

Frowning slightly, and still turning the coffee-grinder, Sir Ruthven crossed to the table and peered at the name on the Will. "Robert Lozinski. Well? It seems an unlikely name enough, but if it *should* prove to belong to some actual possessor of five hundred thousand or so, that may perhaps be so much unexpected profit..."

"You don't recognize the name?"

Sir Ruthven turned the grinder more slowly. "No... Wait! Yes— I believe I first heard that name from your lips, didn't I? Yes, that explains where I got it... Why, I believe it was the name you tried to tell me I myself possessed in some other dimension!"

"And it's *your own Will* you're supposed to forge." Since starting this project, Dr. Falcon had naturally used as much available time as possible for a concentrated study of Sir Ruthven's operetta.

"My own Will?... Yes, that had been my original thought, but how did you...read my mind?" Sir Ruthven put down the grinder and stared at his friend.

"And how old are you?"

"Old enough, I suppose, to know my own mind. But what has that to do with it?"

"You ran away from home and hid under an assumed name for twenty years before accepting your proper title. You had to be old enough to make that decision to run away—it isn't usual for babies of one and two years old to make decisions like that, or at least manage to carry them out." (Never mind the one or two who actually did it in the *Bab Ballads*.) "At a bottom guess, you have to be at least twenty-six or twenty-seven years old."

"As a matter of fact, I am thirty-five, having run away at the advanced age of fifteen. With the detailed study you have obviously made of my life, from what source or sources I can only conjecture, I am surprised you did not know that much as well."

"Have you looked at yourself lately in a good mirror?"

"Only as long as absolutely necessary for decent grooming."

Dr. Falcon picked up the small hand mirror from the washstand and thrust it at Sir Ruthven. "Then look now!"

"I was once rather nice-looking. I have no desire to behold the ravages of a life of crime writ large upon my features."

"Look!" Dr. Falcon repeated, forcing the mirror into his hand. "Take a good, hard look."

Sir Ruthven accepted the mirror and gazed at himself. At first his features registered morbid curiosity, then some satisfaction at seeing crime had not yet made any visible inroads upon his countenance, then a growing astonishment. In a moment he sat down and held the mirror closer, turning to get the best advantage of daylight from the barred window.

"Does that," said Dr. Falcon, "look like a thirty-five-year-old face?"

"Not even thirty-five years of innocence…it scarcely looks like a face out of its teens."

"Sir Ruthven Murgatroyd is thirty-five, by your own testimony," Dr. Falcon told him. "Bob Lozinski is twenty-three."

"But I *was* as old as my years!" Sir Ruthven stood and hurled the mirror into a corner of the room. "I had a definite crease in my forehead—wrinkles at the corners of both eyes—I may not have wished them, but they were undeniable! I had six plainly visible silver hairs—and I haven't plucked them for a fortnight! And all this *before* taking up my title and its obligations!"

"And what," Dr. Falcon went on ruthlessly, "is your relationship to Mad Margaret?"

"Meg? Why, I—I feel a brotherly regard for her—what gentleman would not?"

"Brotherly! And when did you start feeling this brotherly regard? Come to that, what is she still doing running around Great Britain in rags? She was supposed to have married your brother and settled down to a life of respectability when you took the title."

Sir Ruthven sat again, looking up at Dr. Falcon in bewilderment. "Yes…but I suppose… But how in heaven's name do you know all this?"

"It's all written in a book."

"What?"

"Sir Ruthven Murgatroyd," said Dr. Falcon, "is a character made up by an author named W. S. Gilbert."

"Are you implying, sir, that I am a figment of someone's imagination—a mere cipher on the printed page?"

"Not *you*. Sir Ruthven Murgatroyd is. *You* are a young colonist named Robert Lozinski, bound through the galaxy in the great starship *Papa's Pride,* and the question we've got to solve is why your own memories are so painful that you made a subconscious decision to bury them and adopt the identity and memories of a fictional character with a curse on his head and a potentially painful future."

Maybe Dr. Falcon had overplayed his hand. The baronet rose with a certain determined dignity. "If a man could not depend upon his own memory, sir—upon his own identity—then there would be no discernible purpose in the universe, no reason for existence. To be the last baronet of Ruddigore may not be enviable—it is hardly a fate I would wish upon my worst enemy—but I find it preferable, with all its drawbacks, to being some total stranger of clearly unbalanced mental faculties. I can only suppose, since you have seemed inclined towards friendship in the past, that this is your notion of an intellectual game to lighten the hours of my captivity; but I must tell you, I almost think I would rather face the threats of the grand inquisitor of Spain."

Chuck sighed and shrugged. "All right. Forget it." (*For now,* he added to himself.) "Let's talk about something else. Are you determined on seeing how well you can withstand torture, or would you just as lief escape instead?"

CHAPTER 19

THE RESCUE

Cupping his chin in his right hand and his right elbow in his left palm, the baronet thought this over. "I see three objections to escape. First, I fear such an action might exacerbate the international situation—hardly a patriotic gesture on my part. Second, it would be almost sure to cause Shadbolt some embarrassment. Third, what would Dr. Daly think of such an irresponsible escapade?"

Chuck noticed that difficulty, danger, and impracticality were not among Sir Ruthven's objections. "First," he replied, "I can't say for sure abut the international ramifications, but I'd guess there's a fifty-fifty chance you'd do more good than harm by escaping."

"Oh? If you would explain your logic, I should be infinitely obliged."

"As long as your person is in custody, the two countries have a tangible bone to fight over. If you disappear, the squabble falls flat—or, at worst, becomes a matter of abstracts."

"I take your point. Like two dogs fighting for a bone, or two children for a toy. Remove the source of contention, and while the parties may cry for a while, they will also cease delivering their blows. Hardly a flattering comparison…"

"You were the one who made it," said Chuck, secretly gratified that Sir Ruthven had assimilated his argument so readily. If Bob Lozinski believed that an escape would defuse the international crisis, Japan and Britain were that much more likely to come to a friendly agreement in this particular virtual fantasy.

"So I did—though I believe you first suggested it by your metaphorical allusion to me as a bone of contention. But have you considered that the disappointed wails of national governments may in themselves be rather more serious than those of dogs or small children? Besides, they would most likely pool their resources in the effort to recapture me."

"Then you'd have united them at least temporarily. And if you're really interested in the most patriotic course of action, why not get your government out of its bind by confessing to this flirtation?"

Sir Ruthven shuddered. "If it were any other offense, perhaps I should, if only to oblige the lord high ambassador. But her ladyship his wife—my dear sir, I have no wish to speak ill of any woman, and the beauty and charms of the gracious Lady Pitti-Sing are patent to the world...but I believe she is capable of anything... I would rather face his distinction of Spain! No, sooner than confess, I should prefer to escape and try whether that might not have the salutary effect you suggest upon international relations. But what of poor Shadbolt, who might be made scapegoat in my place?"

"Your gaoler? 'Poor Shadbolt' handed me the key to your cell with a readiness that suggests either he wouldn't mind seeing you escape, or else he's too stupid to keep his post here long in any case. And if he doesn't secretly want you to escape, then before you expend any more pity on him, maybe I should tell you that I left him discussing methods of torture with Don Alhambra. Shadbolt was holding out for the thumbscrew."

Sir Ruthven considered this. "As an assistant tormentor and a connoisseur of torture-chamber anecdotes, he would naturally have a professional interest in such things, but I cannot think it is mixed with any personal animosity towards me. Why, if he did not actually take my part this morning against the don, he at least served as a welcome buffer. I owe much of my comfort in this place to Shadbolt, you know. And he's rather good company, when he isn't repeating stories out of poor old Hugh Ambrose. If he really did slip you the key on purpose to facilitate your plans, it would seem ungrateful not to take advantage of it... But what would dear Dr. Daly think?"

"Dr. Daly is waiting right now, in the duke of Dunstable's yacht tied up at Tower Wharf, for a signal from me. The three of us worked out several alternate plans last night."

"Since you did so without consulting me, I fancy the more exact word would be 'rescue,' not 'escape.' And the reverend doctor of divinity is in this with you? But unofficial enlargement from a state prison in which one is lawfully confined…it can only be regarded as a…as a crime!"

"And I imagine you still have a crime to commit today?" Chuck pointed out.

The baronet smiled. "Well, well, forgery *has* grown a bit monotonous, even if first Don Alhambra's visit and now yours had not put me quite out of the sedentary mood this morning…. Very well, why not? I can always allow myself to be recaptured. What's the plan, Dr. Falcon? Am I to slip up to the rooftop battlements and wait until nightfall, whilst you relock the door and return Shadbolt the key?"

"Too risky. We can't depend on their not investigating before nightfall, especially if they're planning something for this afternoon. And once they found you gone, the battlements would be the first place they'd search."

"You might tell them I am indisposed—a toothache or a slight cold, perhaps."

"You think they'd hesitate to put a slightly indisposed man to the torture?"

"It would seem to go against all sporting instincts to do so. Besides, I doubt they can be planning anything of the sort until after five, when the Tower closes to the general public…unless they mean to sell tickets, of course," the baronet went on thoughtfully. "For entertainment and instruction of a morally edifying nature, it would beat even Madame Tussaud's Waxworks all hollow. You didn't see any sign that they might be selling tickets, did you?"

"I wouldn't put it past them. But whether they are or not, once I went down and returned the key, I'd have a devil of a time getting back up to you." Chuck thought of his knapsack, down in the gaoler's room; but virtual supplies could easily be reconstituted, and he did not quite trust Sir Ruthven to handle the rooftop end of the escape by himself. "We'd better take our chances right away."

"A daylight rescue? And you call *my* earlier proposal risky?" The baronet shrugged. "Well, an unsuccessful attempt should fulfill my criminal obligation as well as a successful one, and I daresay you can simply vanish into the air again, and Dr. Daly and the good duke pretend to be innocent bystanders if worse comes to worst. Very well—Lead on, MacDuff! Or would you like your coffee first?"

Regretfully refusing the coffee in favor of immediate action, Chuck rolled up pillows and blankets to make a dummy figure in the bed and then ushered Sir Ruthven out of the cell, relocked the door behind them, and tucked the key snugly into his pocket, both to slow down the investigations of gaoler and inquisitor and to guard against the baronet changing his mind and taking it upon himself to go back.

They reached the ramparts. "Well, what now?" Sir Ruthven inquired, leaning on the battlements to gaze down at the wharf and river.

"Now I signal." Chuck pulled a small mirror from his pocket and flashed it three or four times. (This was for Plan "A." Plans "B" and "C" would have entailed his first returning, alone, from the Tower.)

"Mirrors again," said the baronet. "And next? I should perhaps have warned you, I rather question my capability to plunge into the moat from this height and then swim until picked up from the river."

"With luck, you won't need to. The duke will try to bring his craft in nearly to Traitors' Gate and throw us a line."

The baronet whistled. "I repeat the sentiments I hinted a few minutes ago concerning heroics by daylight."

"I may have a trick up my sleeve to solve that problem. Are you game for an experiment?"

"I've agreed to go along with you in this rather original rescue scheme, have I not?"

"All right. I've seen the world go dark and foggy on two occasions when you were fainting—"

"If you're back to suggesting a cause and effect relationship, Dr. Falcon, I fear you're trying to carry milk in a cracked pitcher. The world certainly does not—to the best of my knowledge—fog over each time I drop off to sleep."

"No, not when it's a *natural* sleep. Those times I saw it happening, you were not going unconscious in the regular order of things. Now, I think I might be able to simulate that condition—"

"Not, I hope, by rendering me unnaturally unconscious with a sharp blow to the crown?"

"No, with an anesthetic." Chuck patted the virtual vial in his pocket and wondered whether he would need to explain anesthesia further.

But, as befit the spirit of Lozinski's whole fantasy world, Sir Ruthven seemed to be up on his anachronisms. "That sounds suspiciously like the trick Carton put upon St. Evremonde. You don't propose to spirit some innocent look-alike back down to my cell to take my place, do you? I really could not allow that."

"I'm having enough trouble getting you out, without trying to get a look-alike in. Even if I happened to have one up my sleeve."

"Very well, then," Sir Ruthven said with a sigh, "I doubt it will come to anything, except possibly to persuade you of your error. And to be rendered unconscious was not precisely the reason I consented to take this exercise, but I'll abide by your leadership. What do you want me to do?"

"Better lie down and make yourself as comfortable as you can. Don't worry, this won't hurt a bit."

"Had I asked if it would?"

Sir Ruthven succumbed almost instantly to the ether. As Chuck had hoped, the fog rolled in at once—or, rather, seemed to drop down on the Tower and presumably spread out from there. If fogs could be said to have personalities, this one, unlike the one that had fallen on the pirate ship off Penzance, seemed to be quiet, restful, dense but not menacing. Dr. Falcon's chief regret was that Sir Ruthven was asleep before he could see the results of the experiment with his own eyes.

Chuck stood and peered over the battlements. The duke had been coached not to bring his boat in unless and until he had some kind of cover. Now the moat was invisible in the thick grayness, and Chuck wondered if his grace of Dunstable would be able to stir from the wharf until the fog lifted a little as Sir Ruthven started to regain consciousness.

Chuck's memory helped him locate some lanterns he had noticed on the ramparts. He lit three of them and mounted one on each of the small watchtowers above the water gate. The danger of attracting unfriendly attention was outweighed by the need his grace would have for some guide to steer by.

Unable to see any lights below, Chuck wondered how far the lanterns penetrated the fog. Happily, he heard no sounds of consternation or even annoyance. Thronged as the Tower and Tower Wharf had been, the crowds of sightseers and citizens about their errands must have accepted the sudden pea-soup quietly and melted into the nearest taverns and teashops to wait it out. Chuck hoped that Shadbolt and Don Alhambra were also taking the business calmly. With luck, they might be too immersed in their debate to have noticed conditions outside. In any case, they should have no reason to connect the weather with a rescue attempt. They might, however, decide he was overstaying his visit...

The thin black lines of masts and yards loomed through the fog at last. But—they were too high to be those of the ducal yacht.

"Ahoy! The wall!"

A bulge on the masthead appeared to be a sailor on lookout. The fog seemed to be lifting very slightly in the immediate circle of ramparts and yardarms. Now Chuck could glimpse bits of rigging, suggestions of sails, a dark flag that might be...the skull and crossbones?

"Ruth?" he returned the lookout's hail. "Ruth, is that you?"

"Dr. Falcon? Aye, aye, sir! Stand clear, if you please!"

The *Divine Emollient,* vessel of the pirates of Penzance, was sailing up to St. Thomas' Tower!

Where had she come from? Chuck couldn't remember seeing her on the Thames or at Tower Wharf before the fog. He stood clear, making sure the baronet also was safe behind a battlement. An iron grappling-hook flew through a crenel, bit rock and was drawn tight.

"Haul in, there!" called the piratical maid-of-all-work.

Chuck found the end of a rope ladder attached to the cord of the grappling-hook. He pulled it taut and made it fast. The pirates seemed bent on taking the duke of Dunstable's place in the rescue. Why not? The baronets of Ruddigore, in this world, were honorary members of their band. "Can you throw us another line?"

"Another line?"

"Sir Ruthven's unconscious. I'd like to have a safety rope before I try to carry him across."

"One moment, doctor." Ruth shouted down to her shipmates on the deck, but at that moment Chuck heard noises on the level beneath him in the tower—Shadbolt and Don Alhambra pounding on the cell door and arguing between themselves.

"Quiet! Stand by!" Chuck directed, just loudly enough for Ruth's ears.

The pirate maid promptly bawled down to the decks, "Avast there, messmates! Stow all sound!" Chuck braced himself for a rousing chorus of "Carefully on tiptoe stealing." Fortunately, none came.

Scarcely was the rope ladder independently attached to the masonry before Chuck heard Don Alhambra and Shadbolt stop pounding on the door and start mounting the stairs. The inquisitor seemed to be tongue-lashing the gaoler about demanding that all visitors present letters of reference.

Chuck tied the free end of the cord around Sir Ruthven's chest and hoisted him up on his shoulders. But the rope ladder was occupied by Ruth, on her way to the battlements.

"Get back!" Chuck urged her. Shadbolt and Alhambra had emerged on the ramparts. By peering around the edge of the crenel Chuck could make out their forms some yards away, although thanks to the fog and the protecting masonry they seemed not to have spotted him yet.

"I think, doctor," Ruth replied, climbing into the niche, "with all respect, I'm better used to the ropes and rigging than you are."

"I hear them!" cried Don Alhambra. "But where? Confuscate your London fogs! In Venice, at least, there's nothing to worry about except unusually wet seasons."

"Down there, y'r piety?" came the gaoler's voice. "Methinks I heard a splashing in the moat."

"A splashing indeed!" Don Alhambra must have espied the shadowy shape of the pirate ship. "Here's Jonah's very whale or its second cousin swimming up to knock at your watergate! Oh, my young friend, if I had the management of your security for one day..."

"Lend my your cutlass," Chuck muttered. "I'll hold them off until you're over."

Ruth gave Chuck her weapon and shouldered the unconscious baronet. Balancing him expertly on her back, she started her return across the rope ladder. Close thing, that, Chuck thought, for here they come!

The two black-clad figures lumbered through the fog, Don Alhambra carrying a small lantern and Shadbolt an arquebus.

"There!" shouted the inquisitor, and the gaoler lifted his weapon and fired—wildly, missing Chuck by several meters.

"Clod!" grumbled Alhambra. "Why not wait for a better aim?"

"I e'en thought the knave about to jump from the wall."

That sounded almost like a hint, but Chuck did not act on it. Glancing round, he saw that Ruth was only about halfway across with her burden. Tucking the cutlass into his belt, he charged the pursuers.

They stepped apart. He made a quick decision and went for Alhambra as the more hostile of the two. For all his build, the inquisitor was unathletic. Chuck threw him in one movement.

But Shadbolt now seemed less cooperative. Closing with surprising speed, he already had his arms round Chuck in a bear hug from behind.

As Charles, Dr. Falcon was taller, his muscles harder, and his weight better distributed; but having Don Alhambra shouting and twisting under him interfered with his stance. And Shadbolt was maybe thirty kilos heavier—possible in virtual scenarios, not 'out there' in *Papa's Pride* after almost a decade of rationing ship-grown groceries. For a few seconds it was jujutsu against sumo wrestling, with Don Alhambra as an unwilling mat.

Space was limited between Don Alhambra and the wall, and by the time they got clear of the inquisitor they were grappling in one of the crenels, Chuck wedged beneath the gaoler. Chuck glanced around. The dark double shape of Ruth carrying Sir Ruthven was just reaching the masthead.

Chuck finally broke free of Shadbolt with a knee thrust and jumped up on the masonry, intending to make a dive for the water.

But while he strained his eyes to judge where he should aim to avoid the deck of the pirate ship, a scorching pain attacked him from the rear. He started to turn in the narrow space, and a black-sleeved arm gave him a shove. Already off balance because of the burning, he fell.

His trousers felt as if they had caught fire, and he was going to miss the water—he was hurtling down toward the deck of the *Divine Emollient.*

* * * *

"Ods bodkins!" cried Wilfred Shadbolt, peering down from the battlements. "Yon knave hath vanished into the air!"

"Snatched back by his infernal master, I shouldn't wonder," Don Alhambra pronounced, still contentedly nursing the candle from his lantern. "It serves him well for stamping on my gout. Excellent lanterns, these—ever-ready flame under peculiarly trying conditions. If the patentee can be persuaded to market them in Venice or Spain, he shall have my ready endorsement. Well, I suppose your security is such that this vessel will sail away down the river and gain the open sea before pursuit can even be organized?"

The gaoler sighed. "We must bring these news to his excellency the lord high ambassador. Properly speaking, 'twas his prisoner."

CHAPTER 20

DESTINATION CASTLE BUNTHORNE

Sir Ruthven opened his eyes with a sense of double *deja vu.* The vicar of Ploverleigh was bending above him, and they were in the guest cabin of the *Divine Emollient.*

"Dr. Daly?" he said. "I take it the rescue has succeeded, but Dr. Falcon had led me to believe the duke of Dunstable's yacht would be the craft involved."

"Their graces are following in the *Silver Churn,*" Dr. Daly replied. "I believe the duchess had the naming of their yacht, though the exact significance escapes me. Something to do with an old, old love, long thought hopeless, suddenly and unexpectedly requited." He heaved a sentimental sigh. "But on encountering these...er, excellent fellows, we deemed it best to allow them to take part in the effort. They proved to be old friends of yours, and most enthusiastic to join us."

Sir Ruthven guessed that the vicar was rambling on in order to soothe him. "The pirates of Penzance," he agreed. "Yes, I recognize this cabin. And Dr. Falcon?"

The vicar hesitated. Could the mysterious Dr. Falcon have been vulnerable to human dangers, after all? Sir Ruthven hoisted himself to a sitting position. "I'm quite hale, Dr. Daly. My condition when I was brought aboard was the temporary result of some drug Dr. Falcon had administered to me. He *is* all right?"

"So we must assume." With some difficulty, due to the movement of the ship, the vicar poured a glass of water for the baronet and another for himself. "I believe I'd best tell it briefly from the beginning. Mrs. Ruth scaled masts and rigging to throw a grappling-hook to the battlements and bring you safely across. But Dr. Falcon lingered behind, so as not to overburden the ropes, as well as to hold off the pursuing gaolers. I fear that somehow they must have got the better of him, for scarcely had Mrs. Ruth gained the masthead with you than we saw him fall from the top of the tower." Dr. Daly held up one hand as if to reassure his listener. "We awaited the worst—he seemed bound to strike the deck—but in midfall the man simply vanished into air."

Sir Ruthven leaned back with a sigh. "His best way of saving himself. He's returned again to…to wherever he comes from."

"Some higher sphere beyond our own," the vicar said softly. "He had told me as much, but I confess I had not entirely believed it until actually witnessing this." He drained off the last of his water and eyed the empty glass. "I believe some stronger beverage is called for. The kettle should be on the boil by now. I'll just brew us a jorum of tea."

"And so the Pirates have finally attacked a stronger party than themselves and triumphed," Sir Ruthven mused as Dr. Daly cautiously poured hot water into the bottom of the teapot during a moment when the ship seemed less liable to lurch. "For I suppose the Tower of London must count as a stronger force than the *Divine Emollient*. I should like to have seen them sailing up to Traitors' Gate to issue their challenge. By the by, I don't suppose a sudden fog could have settled down over London in good time for my rescue?"

"As a matter of fact, one did." Dr. Daly swirled the teapot, letting the water warm it. "Rather remarkably thick. We all but rammed the ship into the tower—at least, so it seemed to my untrained eye. Not unlike that phenomenal fog some time ago over Portsmouth and so much of the West. But how, having been unconscious at the time, did you know of it?"

"Dr. Falcon thought there might be a fog. That, I believe, was part of his experiment." Sir Ruthven shook his head to clear it of the peculiar miasmas that seemed to be building up in his brain. "Unusual weather, but not inconvenient for our purposes. Where are we bound?"

"By good luck or kindly Providence, to my own village of Ploverleigh." The vicar smiled. "We are not the only passengers, my friend. The pirates had originally and opportunely come up the Thames this week by special arrangement to take aboard a Middle European prince, his highness Hilarion, and two noble young companions of his. It seems that, quite by coincidence, they wish to journey to Castle Bunthorne at this time, and her majesty's government has refused to authorize their passports to that part of our country, for fear of rousing another international situation. So they have little choice but to have themselves unofficially smuggled through. Since Ploverleigh lies between the coast and Castle Bunthorne, we'll all be put ashore near home, and I misdoubt anyone will come looking for you in my tidy little country vicarage."

"Very much obliged…but why should I not help smuggle this royal party all the way to Castle Bunthorne? Yes," the baronet went on, pleased with the prospect of engaging so cheaply and harmlessly in a bit of desperate lawlessness, "this intrigues me. Why do they desire to go to Castle Bunthorne? And how can it concern our great nation whether they arrive there or not?"

Dr. Daly winked and sighed. "The matter of the Hungarian princess. The question of whether or not her seizure of Castle Bunthorne constitutes an invasion is already ticklish enough, but for it to be complicated by an attack upon her therein, even though called a siege of love, by another foreign body—the problem, I think, is whether we can permit two foreign powers to fight their war upon our own sovereign territory."

* * * *

Meanwhile, his grace the duke of Dunstable was having an unenviable time steering the *Silver Churn* down the Thames in the fog, avoiding other craft whilst keeping the *Divine Emollient* in sight. When his wife remarked, "Oh, South Kensington!" his first reaction was that they must be passing that neighborhood.

"Really, my love?" said the duke. "I had thought we were heading east, to the open sea. It's this beastly fog, I suppose. I wonder where they hope to hide a pirate ship upriver."

"No, dearest, you misunderstand me," said the duchess. "I was not playing the tour guide. I was uttering an exclamation of consternation, surprise, and confusion. We've stowaways aboard."

"Too crushing a word," a man's voice corrected her. "Call me, rather, an outcast of the hollow world, seeking temporary haven with one from whom he once commanded some admiration."

"Bunthorne!" said the duke, without taking his gaze from the river. "I say, old fellow, is that you?"

"It is, heart-weary shade that I am of my former self."

The duke became aware of yet another party behind him, this one chuckling. "I think you remarked, my dear," he inquired, "that we had stowaways, in the plural? Or perhaps I ought to say outcasts of the hollow world, in the plural? Of 'outcasts,' that is, not of 'world.'"

The chuckle became a laugh. "Pardon me," said the second stowaway, speaking around his laughter. "I hadn't considered myself an outcast, though I might enjoy as much claim as my present employer to that distinction. Allow me to introduce myself. I have the honor just now of being Mr. Bunthorne's private detective, but you may call me a stowaway, if it pleases you."

"We are in the midst of rather a desperate rescue," the duchess told him. "*Do* you think you can laugh with a bit more restraint?"

"In the name of that old passion you tore up with such sudden ease by its very heart's-roots," the poet went on, "in the name of All That Might Have Been, Jane, I believe the least you owe me is a little ride aboard your yacht."

"Well, old fellow, you really had but to ask, you know," said the duke. "I ought to point out, however, that just at the moment we are engaged in that bit of a desperate rescue my wife mentioned, and it might turn out rather sticky for us all if we're caught with our fingers in the jam, so you may not want to be involved."

"It hardly signifies," said the duchess, "since I really cannot see how we could put them ashore without the pirate ship sailing out of our sight."

"As to that," said Bunthorne's detective, "I have a pistol, you know. I had meant to use it to force you to take us along, but I can just as well use it to force you to put us ashore at the nearest dock if my esteemed employer so chooses."

"Bullied!" cried the duke, his eyes shining. "I say, by Jove, bullied at last! My dear, it's a dream come true. *She* absolutely refuses to bully me, you know," he went on, half-turning for a moment to get a glimpse of the stowaways.

Bunthorne heaved a great sigh and looked at the duchess.

"I had supposed," she was saying to the detective, "that persons of your description were concerned, at least in theory, with upholding the law. How, then, do you justify forcing folk to do your bidding at gunpoint?"

"Dear lady, you seem to be misinformed. We detectives uphold the law?" The private detective went into another gale of laughter, in the force of which he almost but not quite let the pistol drop from his hand. "Why, the detection of lawbreakers is our very bread and butter! We are forced by the demands of our calling to *encourage* criminal activities in order to have objects for our pursuit. And if we become our own malefactors, we don't have far to pursue, do we? But," he went on, wiping his eyes, "you need not alarm yourselves unduly. I never load my gun, for fear it might go off."

"Oh, I do wish you hadn't told us," said the duke. "In fact, we could have put you ashore easily enough, if you had meant to force us. Knowing our ultimate destination, I think we could catch the lead craft up again."

"My dear duke," the detective assured him, "I shall force you as cheerfully with an unloaded gun as with a loaded. Indeed, more cheerfully, being less apprehensive."

"Yes, and a pretty help that'll be to us if you don't force him to take us to Ploverleigh," said the poet.

"Ploverleigh?" cried the duke. "What a coincidence—our own destination exactly. You're going home to Castle Bunthorne, I take it? Oh, yes, we can bring you to Ploverleigh right enough, without even going out of our way."

"If you're wiling to become a fugitive from the law with us," added the duchess.

"As well that as attempt to purchase train tickets with tulip petals," Bunthorne remarked.

"You see, after my last experience with an employer," the detective explained, "I am insisting on a rather generous fee, and so far Mr. Bunthorne's new play has earned him only enough to pay me, with nothing left over for our traveling expenses."

"How very awkward," said the duchess. "But what do you mean to do when you reach home, Reginald? Etherealize the occupying army?"

"And why not?" the poet replied. "They are said to be educated young women. They may prove capable of appreciating my poetry as it deserves."

"Good old Bunthorne!" said the duke.

* * * *

"Escaped, you say?" The lord high ambassador shook his fan at Shadbolt and Don Alhambra, who had made their way to the Japanese embassy as soon as the fog began to lift.

"Rescued, y'r excellency." Shadbolt shifted from one foot to the other and fumbled with his key ring. "Rescued by plain force, and the rogue would e'en now lie dead in the river were it not for the ship. Faith, 'twas little less than a siege."

"Rescued by a fiend out of hell," Alhambra added calmly, consulting a small black memorandum book and prodding Dr. Falcon's knapsack—which they had brought along for evidence—as if it were an incubator of imps. "What would you have had a simple English Protestant gaoler do, my benighted Oriental friend, against a fiend out of hell?"

The ambassador closed his fan with a snap. "You would do well to refrain from applying the term 'benighted' to one who can trace his ancestral roots, and consequently his racial memory, back to a protoplasmal primordial atomic globule."

"The sun rises in the east, you know," said the ambassador's wife, opening the knapsack and digging into its contents with her dainty hands. "Therefore you Occidentals must remain benighted longer than us Orientals."

"I detect no odor of sulfur or brimstone," said the ambassador, wrinkling his nose at the knapsack. "Dirty socks, at worst, but those are not generally considered the property of a cloven-hoofed fiend. You observe, I am well versed in the finer points of your Western theology."

The three large men frowned at one another whilst the small woman turned over the mysterious rescuer's abandoned possessions—spare items of clothing (both clean and soiled), blanket, tinned food, canteen, matches, a camp cookery kit, basic articles of masculine toiletry. "I shouldn't think a daemon would need such stuff as this," she remarked. "Ah, but what have we here?" She untangled a book from the blanket, opened it, and began turning its pages. Her fine eyebrows went up very high, but she said nothing.

"And the rest of them sailed unmolested downriver and away on this piratical vessel?" the ambassador was saying.

"Followed, I believe, by a much smaller craft," said Don Alhambra. "Though sharper eyes than mine might have been deceived in that fog."

"Hum." The ambassador chopped open his fan. "Well, I myself have a pair of the sharpest eyes in Europe in my present employ. Or at least so their owner advertised them when I hired him. We shall hope, for the sake of continuing good will and peaceful trade between our nations, that he is able to track the miscreants to their destination."

Believing their destination to be the infernal regions, the grand inquisitor seemed to have little hope of anyone's ability to track them. "If and when affairs should come to a crisis, of course," he said, "I feel no hesitation in assuring your excellency that the government of Spain, and very likely that of Venice as well, will stand with Japan against England."

"Of course," said the ambassador's wife, looking up from the book with an inscrutable Oriental smile. "What are Venetian leather and Spanish altar lace if not surmounted with something Japanese?"

It was she who had suggested that her husband hire a private detective to help the British government keep guard of their prisoner, but she did not mention that now.

* * * *

"Thanks for yanking my helmet off," Chandra told Misaki. "What clued you?"

"You yelped," Misaki explained. "And then you yelled. And you were not even groping for the helmet yourself."

Chandra wondered just how far it really was possible to get 'sucked in' to a virtual scenario. It had never happened to her in one of her own invention or one pulled from the public databanks; but people did sometimes have to be extracted almost catatonic from a recreation booth, and taken to the hospital for medication and recovery. It had happened a dozen times in the year after Lift-away, then only once or twice a year for several years, and now up to twice a month since "pylon fever" got prevalent enough to be named. But getting sucked into a shared simulation—a scenario constructed essentially out of the other person's comatose mental processes? This was the first time anything like this had ever been tried in *Papa's Pride,* not counting Chandra's test-run with Omar before the illness that put him into cold storage. They might have known what to do for such cases back on Old Earth…maybe there were real dangers here; maybe that was why Old Earth had never uploaded this data to *Papa's Pride* until after the descendants back home had stopped caring very much about a colony starship they'd never see again, one whose own weakening communications had stopped making much sense to the mother planet.

Meanwhile, Sister Harriet and the others were asking her to fill them in about what had happened so far. Chandra filled them in, adding, with a direct look at Osborne,

"Worrying about what his escape might do to the international situation 'in there'—does that sound like anyone irresponsible enough to put a virus into the ship's computer?"

"Could be remorse," said Deuteronomy Osborn. "Why the bloody hell didn't you use that cutlass thing instead of going for 'em with your bare hands? Kind of a Samson unbound 'in there,' aren't you?"

"We still don't know exactly who and what I could have risked destroying."

"Then why ask for the sword in the first place?"

Chandra sighed. "Suppose Ruth is Barbara Cripps, and suppose Cripps is involved in planting the virus and/or killing Steve Davis? Suppose Lozinski knows it, and sees her as wanting to get him out of the way, too? I took a risk just letting her carry him—but that rope ladder probably wouldn't have supported all three of us at once, and we didn't have time to argue. And it could've been a worse risk for me to start across and leave her at my rear. By taking her cutlass, I figured to cut the risk to a minimum, especially with Sir Ruthven already attached to a lifeline so that she couldn't just drop him."

Sister Harriet said, "As nearly as we can make out, Pete and Barbara seem to have run Judi Oshita to earth in a corner of one of the uptown pylon museums. That makes it appear that Judi alone was responsible for the virus…" Harriet sighed. "Poor Judi."

"Poor ship!" Osborne grunted. "And we'd just better make damn sure the others ain't tryin' to scapegoat Oshita to cover their own behinds. Wouldn't put it past 'em to've drawn straws."

"Doesn't that in itself," Sister Harriet asked him, "show there's still a lot of good in them? A lot that's worth saving, whoever has done what."

"Cousin Deuces," Chandra Falcon said deliberately, with another look at the security man, "you're 'in there,' too. You're appearing as Don Alhambra, the grand inquisitor of Spain."

CHAPTER 21

EXPRESSIVE GLANCES AT CASTLE BUNTHORNE
(AS GLIMPSED FROM A DISTANCE)

Dr. Daly and Sir Ruthven sat at supper in the snug vicarage of Ploverleigh. "Well, my friend," said the vicar, "do you really have no regrets? To share the company of an aging cleric when you might have been enjoying that of a hundred beautiful young maidens?"

"Like the country mouse in the fable," Sir Ruthven replied in the same spirit, "I prefer a crust in safety to a banquet in danger. Figuratively speaking, of course." He helped himself to a generous serving of apple tart. "If you would pass the cream?"

Dr. Daly passed it. "And yet I'm not sure the simile holds true. Who knows but that you might not have been safer inside the castle, after all? In terms of the national and international situations."

Sir Ruthven contemplated being one of four handsome men amongst a hundred or so bold and beautiful young women, and suppressed a shudder. "Safer in terms of the political situation, perhaps, but at what a price for a painfully bashful Adonis like myself!"

They had proceeded inland to Castle Bunthorne early that morning, rolling softly in hired gigs and curricles through the pearly dew along with Prince Hilarion, his two noble companions, and a small escort composed of the pirate king, his lieutenant Samuel, young Frederic, Mrs. Ruth, and the duke and duchess of Dunstable, as well as Mr. Bunthorne the poet and his private detective, who were in the party but not quite of it, having reasons of their own for the expedition.

Arriving at Castle Bunthorne just as the dew was beginning to glitter in the rays of the rising sun, the prince and his two friends had disappeared inside the edifice according to a set of directions

Mr. Bunthorne had provided them. He had not provided them entirely willingly, for he maintained that as the castle's rightful owner he ought to make one of their force. But Florian had argued that their safety would lie in a smaller rather than a larger number, Cyril had quipped that Bunthorne reminded him too much of the Princess Ida's royal father for his company to be desirable, and Hilarion had asked whether the poet would be game to disguise himself as a girl graduate, which was their plan if they could find suitable garments before being themselves discovered in the castle grounds.

Dr. Daly, seeming a little disturbed by the fact that so many persons originally unconnected with Sir Ruthven's rescue now knew all about it, had suggested (when Bunthorne was out of hearing) that the baronet might go into the castle with the prince and his comrades; but, though they had shown themselves readier to accept Murgatroyd than the poet, they had also pointed out that there might be a certain degree of danger for any males discovered within their fair enemy's domain. On the whole, now that he considered himself to have helped perpetrate a legal irregularity by escorting them this far, Sir Ruthven preferred to lapse into inaction for the rest of the day.

Hopeful of receiving a further fee from his highness should his plan succeed and he wish transportation back across the Channel, the pirates pitched a tent in the meadow below the castle, where once twenty lovesick maidens had sung to their mandolins. The duke and duchess, Bunthorne and his detective had settled down in this pavilion along with their pirate hosts to await the outcome. Sir Ruthven, however, having ridden alongside Mr. Bunthorne most of the way from coast to castle and discovered that a mutual interest in poesy did not necessarily provide a basis for pleasure in another man's society, had opted to return to Ploverleigh with the vicar.

"And yet," Dr. Daly mused now, over his apple tart, "I daresay you could have worn a feminine disguise as well as any of our three gallants. Though if Achilles himself managed to lie hid in damsel's attire for a time, I suppose Prince Hilarion has a reasonable chance of carrying it off. And young ladies, I believe, behave far differently towards those they believe to be of their own sex than they do towards attractive members of ours."

Sir Ruthven rubbed his chin, which had not been shaved since morning, and tried to imagine such a situation. "I conceive that the disguise successful would hardly be less uncomfortable than the disguise penetrated. I wonder how they'll manage their shaves."

"On the other hand, each day that you spent in disguise amongst the young ladies might have been made to count as the fulfillment of your odious obligation." Finishing his sweet, Dr. Daly brought out the cheese. "I may in time find it a trifle tedious to be cheated every day at backgammon," he went on with a wink, "even though I was myself the one to propose the expedient."

"Oh, it need not be backgammon every day. We can begin tomorrow with draughts, the next day dominoes, then reversi, followed by backgammon and so on up to chess. There's five days of variety, without even considering the various card games available to the enterprising."

"You would hardly need to cheat me at draughts or reversi. I profess to be no master of those games. But I fancy that I could give you a close run at fox and geese."

"That sport," said the baronet, "you would have to teach me, and it's not easy to cheat when one is the learner."

A knock at the door made both men start. Then the vicar smiled. "Clergymen, like medical men, must expect summons at awkward hours. My own flock is very considerate as a rule—allow me to keep shop, so to speak, from ten to four, with the usual half-holiday on Saturdays. They're so exceptionally steady a parish that they require little special counseling in any case…save in matters of the heart, and there, alas! I am but ill qualified to guide them. But I've been away for some weeks now, so an extraordinary summons was only to be expected."

Meanwhile, Dr. Daly's housekeeper-cook was answering the door. She presently came back to the dining room, still wiping one soapy hand on her apron. She totally ignored Sir Ruthven. She had been instructed that his presence was to be made known to none of the villagers. And, while from seven in the morning to six at night she counted herself one of the vicar's household, when she went home in the evenings to her own cottage she became a simple villager. Tonight, although she was staying a little past her usual time, she obviously considered herself to have gone off duty in the official way half an hour ago and thus lost all knowledge of the fugitive's existence. Dear only knew how, in her capacity of ignorant villager, she accounted for the extra dishes she was washing up. "Here, sor," she said, holding out a letter on a silver salver to Dr. Daly with her dry hand. "I told 'im there was never such a person of this name in Ploverleigh, but he said to bring it to you regardless."

"Thank you kindly, Mrs. Partlet." The clergyman took the letter and examined the superscription. "Very curious. Very curious indeed. Well, I suppose we must set it aside in case the individual in question should ever turn up here. In the interim, I fear you'll have to tell the bearer there can be no immediate reply, and send him away again with our sincere regrets if he has wasted his effort."

The housekeeper nodded and departed. Dr. Daly put the missive on the table near Sir Ruthven's plate. The baronet read the superscription twice in the evening light that still traced through the windows, then lifted the letter to the candlelight and read it through again, even though it would hardly have seemed to be worth such scrutiny, consisting as it did of a single name. His own. But the handwriting belonged to that species which appears clear and peculiarly elegant until one actually tries to read it, and though the surname was clear enough, when one knew what letters to look for, he found it harder and harder to determine whether the abbreviation of his Christian name was "Ruth." or "Robt."

"I rather think it must be meant for you, nevertheless," said the vicar. "But if you accidentally lifted it just a little higher, it might catch fire and burn unread." Lighting his pipe, he went on, "I have heard of an officer, in the military bureaucracy as I think, who for thirty years or thereabouts kept his department working at the top of efficiency and order by the simple expedient of storing all potentially bothersome correspondence under the carpet."

"Thank you," said Sir Ruthven, "but there seems to be an enclosure. And I fear that curiosity might prove as dangerous a commodity unsatisfied as satisfied." Still, he hesitated a moment longer before wiping his butter knife on his napkin and employing it as a letter opener.

The cover letter was from the pen of his grace the duke of Dunstable:

"Old son—

We're sending this by the hand of Bunthorne's Private Detective, who claims to be a very bang-up for discretion. Whether you choose to act on the enclosed or not is entirely up to you, but in any case, you'd best be warned that the Lord High Ambassador and his Lady are with us, having come up this morning by railway to Puddleby—her instigation and insistence, he abhors the modern 'monstrosity' of this type of conveyance—and from thence the rest of the way East by carriage to the castle. I suppose it must have been from them that Her Highness learned of your existence—the word is that she and her bluestockings tried taking in some of the illustrated papers at the beginning—and that was stretching a point because it's the *mails* that bring them up from the City—but they gave it up after a few days when Her Highness found that after cutting out all the references to our sex, she had lace-paper doilies instead of news. But she allowed the Lady Pitti-Sing inside the walls to negotiate this afternoon. The latter stayed inside for two hours, and brought out the enclosed terms."

The enclosure had been sealed with a small gob of blue wax bearing the impress of what appeared to be an Oriental design. When Sir Ruthven lifted the seal and unfolded the message, yet another enclosure fluttered out—a small, wafered note on the same blue stationery as the duke's letter. The principal enclosure was in heavy, black, official-looking calligraphy on pale buff paper. The baronet read it first:

> **"Their lives are forfeit who invade our walls**
> **And dare defile our cloisters with their manhood.**
> **Yet if three other men should pledge their faith**
> **And prove the boasted courage of their sex**
> **By offering their persons in exchange**
> **As hostage to redeem the Prince**
> **And his two erring fellows, well and good:**
> **Hilarion, Cyril, Florian shall go free.**
> **For this our strain-ed mercy we'll accept**
> **Lord Pooh-Bah of the nation of Japan,**
> **Bunthorne, call'd poet (we abhor his rhymes),**

**And Ruthven, baronet of Ruddigore.
No others need apply.
(sign'd) Ida, R."**

The second enclosure, again in the duke's hand, read:

"Frightfully sorry, old fellow. I offered to make one of the hostages myself, but Her Highness is adamant."

Sir Ruthven silently passed the communications to Dr. Daly, who read them through and then sat for a few moments in silence, energetically but absently puffing his pipe. At length he said, "It isn't too late to burn all this…"

"But why us three?" said the baronet.

The vicar shrugged. "Deep are the thoughts of each human heart. She may, of course, know of Bunthorne's part in showing the prince and his friends a way into the castle. But why call specifically for you in preference to any of us others who merely accompanied the party? And why include his excellency the ambassador at all?"

"At the Lady Pitti-Sing's suggestion? For some reason of that… rather sinister if completely captivating lady's own?… Well," Sir Ruthven went on, "the princess implies that they will be killed if we do not offer ourselves up hostage, but she does not seem, on the face of it, to specifically threaten *our* lives if we do."

"Unfortunate that his grace neglects to mention how amenable Bunthorne and the ambassador are to the plan."

Sir Ruthven grinned. "I imagine the mystic poet will jump at the chance to get back within his own castle walls and captivate the damsels with his verse—he might not even be aware of Princess Ida's own opinion of it. But the lord high ambassador… I wonder if the bargain is to be all or none, or if her highness would be willing to break the set? In the latter case, I'd as lief go for Florian."

"Then you intend to go?"

The baronet watched his own finger tracing geometrical designs on the tabletop between his dessert bowl and the milk jug. "At least to talk it over with the others, study the situation at closer hand."

"Good man!" approved the vicar. "Shall we start this evening, or wait until morning?"

In the end, they started that evening. As Sir Ruthven observed, sleep would probably have been impossible for him that night in any event.

CHAPTER 22

PRINCESS IDA

The pirates' black silk tent, much torn and mended, was taking on a glow like jackdaws' feathers against the deep twilight when Sir Ruthven and Dr. Daly arrived in the meadow below Castle Bunthorne. They lifted the tent flaps and entered, along with a number of moths which flew straight to the oil lamp and tried to beat their way through its glass chimney to the flame.

"If those insects admire the light so very much," said Bunthorne from his corner of the tent, "why the deuce don't they fly about by day and tuck up in their beds for the night like sensible folk?"

"Perhaps the fiery eye of day would be too grand a goal," replied the vicar. "And, not unlike most of their biped brethren, the little creatures prefer aspiring to a lesser but more readily attainable light."

"Bosh," said the poet.

The lord high ambassador waved his fan slowly back and forth, whether to stir away from his face the tobacco smoke that filled the tent or to gather it closer to his own nostrils, seemed unclear. "It is obvious," said he, "that the young persons within the castle show some measure of commendable perception in requesting a man of such high degree as myself. What is less clear is why they should not recognize me as a far more than equal trade in my own august person for all three of their captives."

"In weight, perhaps," said Bunthorne. "But if it comes down to worth, I'll wager we could bargain me for more heads than you."

Sir Ruthven cut in with hopes of keeping the peace. "No doubt it's the ladies' sense of symmetry that demands an exact and equal *number* in exchange."

"And as for *weight*," quipped the private detective, who sat near the lamp whittling comical monkeys and elephants out of peach stones, "two small and one jumbo should about equal three of somewhat broader chests than average."

"That remark," said Bunthorne, "comes out of your fee." He took out his memorandum book to note the fact. "To the tune of about two and six, I believe."

"Too high," returned the detective. "Say a bob and I'll call it a fair price and worth every penny."

"Is the exchange to be all or nothing?" the baronet asked of the others in the tent—the pirates, the duke and duchess, the ambassador's wife.

"It could hardly be one for one or two for two, by our detective's reckoning," said the pirate king. "Though Bunthorne alone might purchase the prince's torso, or Bunthorne plus one of his excellency's legs go for the whole of that Cyril fellow…"

"As all three of you gentlemen seem ready to show your noble generosity," said the ambassador's wife, "the question don't arise."

Sir Ruthven seated himself at the camp table and accepted a cup of pirate sherry from young Frederic. "As to that," the baronet confessed, "I've as great an admiration for self-sacrifice as the next man, but I fear that my own inclination to the present gesture is more or less open to be influenced by whether or not her highness proposes to treat her hostages as she would have treated her prisoners."

"Her law," replied the ambassador's lady, "encompasses the death sentence for any male who intrudes upon her realm *unbidden.* In all fairness, that would not apply to any who had entered, so to speak, by invitation."

Sir Ruthven recognized the circumlocution, being adept in that art himself. "A telling point, your ladyship, but—with all respect—it is not a direct answer."

"Sir," rumbled the ambassador, "having flirted with my wife, do you now dare compound the offense by doubting her veracity?"

"Not her veracity," said the duchess. "The extent of her information. Lady Pitti-Sing is the one person from the world outside, even from among her own sex, with whom the princess has treated face to face. Would it surprise any of us if her highness had not admitted even her ladyship into all her secret counsels?"

"Exactly!" said the ambassador's wife with a shrug. "I can't say for sure what the princess may do with you. I can say only what I would do in her place, and I shouldn't wish to waste even such specimens of manhood as you three." Winking, she tapped her husband on the shoulder with her fan. "Would I urge my own Pooh-Bahlet to do it if I thought he might be going into danger?"

"Well, my dear," the piratical maid-of-all-work observed, "but *you* wouldn't have threatened to execute the prince and his comrades, neither."

"One might *threaten* anything," Lady Pitti-Sing replied. "The threats must be divided by a bit of commonsense in order to calculate what the threatener may actually be likely to *do*."

"That's if her highness has any of the said commodity," said the pirate king, "which I'm not convinced she does. What does she gain from this proposed trade of prisoners?" He shook his head. "No way to run a business."

The ambassador began to swell dangerously. "She gains *me*, fellow."

"I conceive it's a form of bond, or bail," the duke interjected in an obvious effort to smooth troubled waters. "To insure her highness can call back her original three, when and if she wishes."

"And if that's the case, of course she'll keep the hostages safe," said Frederic, although he looked doubtful.

"So you three have nothing to worry about." The private detective tried to stand one of his peach-pit animals up on the table. "Just soft beds and a hundred pretty girls to bring you breakfast in same."

"My own beds," said Bunthorne. "And breakfast cooked from my own stores. No more than my due."

Sir Ruthven was not so sure that as hostages they would have nothing to worry about, but the ambassador's reference some speeches ago to the alleged flirtation had raised a doubt as to whether the whole situation might not have been manufactured for the purpose of flushing him out to face some international trial; and though a few moments' reflection showed him the unlikelihood of Lord Pooh-Bah's enlisting the pirates or the duke and duchess in such a scheme, the fact remained that now the ambassador and his lady had him in their sight again, the baronet's alternative to Castle Bunthorne might be a return to the Tower or even immediate shipment to some quaint Japanese dungeon. "Well," said he, "the only way to learn the mind of the princess is to accept the situations she offers us. And though I don't pretend to any excessive heroism or self-sacrifice, I do feel a certain curiosity."

"It's arranged, then?" Lady Pitti-Sing stood and smoothed her kimono. "I shall go and notify them at the castle."

The private detective folded his pocket knife. "Good men. Well, Mr. Bunthorne, sir, if you can borrow the ready from one of our friends here, I'd as soon take my pay before you go."

* * * *

The exchange was made late that same evening, by torchlight. The drawbridge creaked its majestic way down on hinges purposely touched with an inadequate amount of oil, for the effect. The torchbearers, four damsels in chain mail tunics, issued forth to take their places, two on each side about midway across the drawbridge. Next came a tall woman in half-armor, bearing a battleaxe and looking quite capable of wielding it to effect. And, after this graying amazon, came the prince and his companions, each one escorted by a helmeted and breast-plated guard who held the end of the rope that bound her prisoner.

After some squabbling between Pooh-Bah and Bunthorne about which of them should take precedence, the volunteers had agreed to walk strictly abreast, Sir Ruthven in the middle, with Pitti-Sing to go a few steps ahead and the duchess of Dunstable a few steps behind, by way of honor guard. Pitti-Sing met the officer with the battleaxe and gave a Japanese curtsey. The officer replied with a nod of her head and stepped to one side, between the two torchbearers on the left, motioning the ambassador's wife to stand opposite her between the torchbearers on the right.

"Is that female the princess?" Bunthorne muttered with a sniff in Sir Ruthven's ear.

Whether or not in response to Bunthorne's overheard remark, the tall woman turned a little towards the volunteers and announced:

> *"I am the Lady Blanche,*
> *Second in this place to none but Ida's self."*

"Charmed, madam, I'm sure," replied the poet. "I trust you've been keeping my house in order for me?" Sir Ruthven could just hear him add under his breath, "Makes poor old Jane look like a gift from the gods."

Meanwhile, the guards had been unbinding Prince Hilarion and his companions. Cyril's guard took longer than the others, because even though he stood on the prince's right, directly opposite Bunthorne and almost under Lady Blanche's very nose, he seemed determined to flirt with the maiden as she untied him.

"*And have you done at last?*" said Lady Blanche. Seeing that they had, she gave the Latin command: "*Ligate omnes!*"

The guards turned and approached the hostages, holding out the ropes that had just come off the former prisoners' wrists.

Lord Pooh-Bah folded his arms across his wide torso and frowned down at the guard. "Hojojutsu," said he, "is beneath my protoplasmal dignity. Not to mention my ambassadorial immunity."

"Even further beneath mine," said Bunthorne, planting his hands firmly on his hips, "if you mean binding. What? Is this any way to welcome a man back into his own castle?"

The middle guard looked pleadingly at Sir Ruthven, biting her lip a little. He hesitated, torn between the idea that he might get her into trouble if he refused to let her carry out her orders and the idea that he really ought to join the other two men in a united front. Their guards were casting perplexed glances at Lady Blanche.

The formidable second in command ruled:

> "*Ah, very well. As special favor, you*
> *May leave the portly one unbound. Small doubt*
> *But that he is more air than substance in*
> *The final count. But this our other knave—*"

She pointed to the poet.

> "*—Must wear the ropes.*"

"I rejoice, madam," said Bunthorne, "that in me you recognize more substance than air."

Pooh-Bah heaved his chest and chin a few inches higher. "Occidental barbarians," he observed, "with ancestral trees reaching no further back in antiquity than to the apes."

Beginning to feel ignored by everyone except the young woman who waited to bind him in particular, Sir Ruthven held out his hands to her. But as she gratefully lifted the rope, Cyril stepped forward and took it from her, saying,

> *"Allow me, sweetest child. The work's too coarse*
> *By far for those small, dainty fingerlets."*

Turning, Cyril winked at the baronet and began looping the cord loosely about his wrists.

"I prefer," said Bunthorne, "that yonder fair damozel perform that operation upon me." And he put out his hands for the guard waiting in front of him. Watching with the educated eye of an experienced ligatee, Sir Ruthven thought the poet might have made a mistake: whereas Bunthorne's young woman seemed to perform her task conscientiously, Cyril was creating a bulk of loops and coils that looked impressive but would fall apart at the wearer's first tug. Bunthorne, of course, was being bound beneath the direct scrutiny of the formidable Lady Blanche, who had seemed far from deaf to his insults, so she might not have permitted Cyril's rope tricks on the poet's wrists. The baronet was surprised she permitted them on his. The lord high ambassador, meanwhile, seemed in some inscrutable Oriental fashion to have sent his mind far from the petty scene about him.

Prince Hilarion said:

> *"If Her Highness grants you audience,*
> *I pray you, friends, to bear her this from me—*
> *Her hapless prisoner:*
> *Whom she has chained must wear his chain,*
> *She cannot set him free.*
> *Though my corse walk at liberty abroad,*
> *My heart and soul are now and evermore*
> *Enchained to her fair light."*

Florian added,

> *"And should you find the chance for speech with one*
> *Most pretty maiden called Melissa, say*
> *To her that if my death could bring her aid,*
> *Ne'er would I break my promise not to leave*

Without her."

Cyril finished,

> *"And there's a saucy fair dame scholar there*
> *Inside those walls, one Lady Psyche called.*
> *No blushing sweet shy thing with downcast eyes,*
> *But you might let her know she'll do to haunt*
> *My dreams until some virgin of the latter sort*
> *Should come along."*

"It sounds as if the angling's not so bad inside, after all," remarked Bunthorne, with a side glance at Lady Blanche that suggested his first impression of the scholars had been far from favorable.

Lady Blanche sniffed and waved her axe. The prince and his companions crossed between their replacements and joined the duchess. Lady Pitti-Sing stood on tiptoe to give her husband a peck on the cheek and then joined the departing group. Two of the guards gathered up the ends of their hostages' ropes; the third young woman stood a moment in perplexity, staring up at Pooh-Bah, and finally tucked one end of her rope into the crook of his left elbow. He huffed, but permitted it to remain. Preceded by Lady Blanche and flanked by the torchbearers, the guards led the hostages the rest of the way across the drawbridge. It occurred to Sir Ruthven that there was probably some indignity, even ignominy, intended in the whole process; but he was too busy keeping Cyril's handiwork from falling apart prematurely to worry about the disgrace.

"Those three," said Bunthorne, with a backward twitch of his head at the departing footsteps of Prince Hilarion and his friends, "have no more poetic sentiment than a beetle."

"I thought their messages rather pretty," the baronet replied.

"Yes, *you* might." It was typical of the poetic discussions they had shared on the way to Castle Bunthorne. Sir Ruthven thought that Bunthorne had not always been this unpleasant…and yet when had he known him before, to make the comparison? For no apparent reason, Deadeye, the seaman who had made the ultimate sacrifice in Portsmouth in the cause of checking the opium trade, came to the baronet's mind.

They gained the courtyard. The original Castle Bunthorne dated from the Conquest, and the courtyard must once have been large; but numerous additions over the centuries to the living quarters and stables had reduced it to little more than a carriageway, lighted now by torches and lanterns.

"I'll say this for 'em, they're excellent little housewives," said Bunthorne. "My courtyard ain't been this tidy for years. Well, is *that* the princess, then?"

He indicated a gracefully buxom young dame in academic robes who came forward with a bouncing step to meet them, exclaiming,

> *"Good Lady Blanche! And are these same the three*
> *New men?"*

Lady Blanche replied,

> *"They are. And seems our currency is down,*
> *For to my thought we've lost by the exchange."*

To which Bunthorne snapped, "And you, madam, wouldn't fetch more than half a crown in any open market."

"This one's not bound," the newcomer observed, inspecting Pooh-Bah.

"Nor needs in my opinion so to be," said Lady Blanche, meanwhile looking thoughtfully from the battleaxe in her hands to the poet's head.

The new lady commented,

> *"Why, I would say they none of them need be,*
> *But for the orders of our Princess wise."*

Lady Blanche told her:

> *"And I, my Lady Psyche, elder am*
> *Than she, by several years. Let her for once*
> *Take counsel from experience, I say."*

"So you're Lady Psyche, eh?" said Bunthorne. "Well, one of yonder young fools, Cyril I think 'twas, had a parting message for you: If you were to learn the arts of blushing sweetly and casting down your eyes, you might haunt his dreams."

"That wasn't quite the way he put it," said Sir Ruthven, but could not bring himself to transmit a more authentic statement of Cyril's message with so many standing round to overhear.

Lady Psyche laughed.

> *"I fancy I can reconstruct what words*
> *He said. Well, Lady Blanche, our Princess may,*
> *Perhaps, know what she does, for all your plaints.*
> *These three are hardly like to turn girls' heads,*
> *As did the last."*

To which Lady Blanche replied:

> *"You speak from life, my dear:*
> *Yours was the first head turned."*

Lady Psyche laughed again, then explained,

> *"My brother and two childhood chums, no more.*
> *I tease Lord Cyril more, much more by far*
> *Than he plagues me. But Ida watches from*
> *Her tower room. So let us not lose time*
> *Beneath her very nose."*

Lady Psyche took the end of Pooh-Bah's rope from his guard, and, after a moment's consideration, the end of Sir Ruthven's as well. Lady Blanche appropriated Bunthorne's, and they led the way into the main residential building, the three young lady guards trailing in the rear. At the foot of the stairs Lady Psyche looked round and laughed a third time, remarking,

> *"Darwinian man at best is monkey shaved,*
> *And dry old maidenhood, they say, will end*
> *By leading apes in Hell."*

"But since you're leading us upstairs, madam," Sir Ruthven pointed out, surprising himself, "one might say without too much fear of dispute, that we men are about to rise considerably in the world thanks to woman's lead."

"*Follow, then: I lead,*" Lady Psyche teased with yet another laugh and a tug at the ropes.

"Don't do that!" cried the baronet, without explaining why. Cyril's loops had withstood the shock, but he feared they would not take many more such. Though it might not have mattered as far as Lady Psyche was concerned. Pooh-Bah's rope had slipped from his elbow, and he simply followed the dangling end up at a stately pace.

Five flights later, after several pauses for the ambassador to fan himself majestically, they gained the tower room and found the princess.

She sat in the light of several candelabra and the chimney fire, with the window at her right hand, a table at her left, and an open space of floor between her and her newly arrived audience. She wore a mortarboard hat and a dark academic robe, open in front to reveal a loose white gown of Norman simplicity. A telescope was in the window; astrolabes, gyroscopes, papers and other studious paraphernalia covered the tabletop; and the princess held a book closed on one finger. The book was in a nondescript binding but somehow it looked to the baronet as if he ought to have remembered its title and author.

"You've made some improvements, anyway," said Bunthorne with a glance around. "But what, madam, have you done with all the lumber I had stored up here?"

Her highness ignored the question. She indicated Pooh-Bah with a nod.

> *"Why comes that man of bulk*
> *Unbound into our presence?"*

Lady Blanche replied:

> *"A small concession, ma'am, that I saw fit*
> *Upon mine own authority to grant."*

She made it sound like a very large concession, and herself very important for granting it.

The Princess and her second-in-command exchanged frowns. Lady Psyche cut in:

> *"Consider, ma'am, that this*
> *Tremendous Swell has some importance in*
> *His native land. Should harm or insult fall*

On him, Japan might war with England here,
And dames as well as men fall in that fray."

The Princess nodded, looked Pooh-Bah up and down, smiled, and pronounced:

"Then take him to our choicest suite of rooms,
And let the finest meats be spread for him,
And treat him with the utmost deference.
The Lady Psyche will attend his wants."

The lord high ambassador snapped his fan open and gave it an intricate flutter than might have been his dignified equivalent of the bow some less consequential being would grant his hostess by way of acknowledgment. Then he swept from the room with Lady Psyche, who was quivering delightedly and holding one hand to her mouth.

The Princess went on to the guards:

"And any man of his great consequence
Will want all three of you to guard his wake."

She waved her hand, and the three filed out after Pooh-Bah and Lady Psyche.

"Shall I remain, your Grace?" said Lady Blanche.

"Madam, as you will, but close the door," the princess answered carelessly, as if no kind of bodyguard could be required against the two men left. Remaining in the room, Lady Blanche closed the door and stood with her back to it.

"Your highness," said Sir Ruthven, fearing an awkward silence or worse, "his highness Prince Hilarion sends a—a message to you. He bids us say—how did he put it?—that you may chain, but you cannot unchain…that though his body now walks at large, his heart remains in your thrall forevermore."

The Princess replied:

"He means until I own myself his bride.
And then he will enthrall me flesh and soul.
I menace him with swift and mortal death.
He threatens me with lifelong chains of mind."

"You're quite right to refuse the fellow as unworthy of you, ma'am," said Bunthorne. "For a prince, he is an atrocious poet. Though I must say that even Prince Hilarion's poesy, bad as it was to begin with, suffers in our baronet's translation."

"*Perhaps.*" The Princess rose, laid her book down on the table, picked up a jeweled dagger, and strode forward ready to plunge it into Bunthorne's chest.

"NO!" cried Sir Ruthven, freeing his wrists with one hard tug and hitting the dagger from her hand. It clattered into a corner of the room, one jewel rolling loose from the hilt. The baronet stepped backwards as the princess turned to stare at him.

"*Away with yonder poetasting fool!*" said her highness, waving at Bunthorne, and going on:

> "*Give him no lesser cheer than Pooh-Bah has,*
> *But get him from my sight!*"

Lady Blanche laid her hand on the poet's shoulder and steered him, speechless for once, from the room, reclosing the door behind them.

Sir Ruthven fell back until a bookshelf set against the far wall stopped his retreat. How had he known Princess Ida's intention in time to shake off Cyril's ropes and stop her attempt? Had it seemed a recurrence of that scene in the Portsmouth opium den? Engulfing these thoughts came the sense that he himself was the most important hostage, the one whom the princess had chiefly wanted all along. But superimposing on this was the humbling notion that both of them were the mere weapons of larger—and unseen—antagonists.

Never turning her gaze from him, the princess sat. Laying one hand on her book, she said:

> "*I mean to know and understand, young man,*
> *What war is being waged in earth and heaven.*"

CHAPTER 23

PISTOL-PACKING PITTI-SING

As her prisoner stood silent, Princess Ida went on:

"The ancients tell of folk possessed by devils.
What, have I rung a chord?"

He had shivered. "It reminded me of…not devils, precisely, though…well, never mind."

With a glance at her dagger, where it lay on the floor, she said:

"Not mind? What but some devil forced my hand?
It was not I who meant to stab that fool."

"If your Highness will forgive the observation," Sir Ruthven began hesitantly, "your attitude towards our sex in general may, perhaps, explain…"

"You blame me for my sentence on the prince
And his two friends. You hold it out of measure?
Those three, in fullest knowledge of my law,
Did slyly come with close-concealed intent
To ruin all my work: like wolves disguised
In woolly skins to snare my women here
And trap me out of this my chosen life
Into a hateful role of playing shadow
To my self-styled lord. I passed on them
The sentence first devised by Man, and long
Accepted by your world as meet and just
For any captured spy in time of war.
You hold me so unfair as to extend
That doom to you who come here in their place,
In open honesty, without pretence, and by

My invitation, one might say?
At least consider this: if you were dead,
I could not change you for the prince again.
My hold were lost on those of deepest guilt.
What motive had I, then, to stab the poet?"

"It is his castle."

"We doubt not he has heirs, and heirs perhaps
More violent to recoup their loss."

"But why us three in particular, your highness?"

"I seek the answer to that point myself."

She tapped her book.

"Were you to read what lies beneath my hand...
But no, the answer seems not here—at most,
One half the key, some scattered clues."

Leaning forward, she said slowly and deliberately,

"Why did you start at mention of the devils?"

He had hoped she would not return to that. Nevertheless, if they were both seeking the answers to the same or related riddles... "I've been told," he confessed, "with rather alarming frequency and vehemence, by one who claims to hail from beyond our sphere, that I am...possessed, I suppose...though not, as I understand it, by a devil."

"By what, then? Or by whom?"

He stared at the floor so as to avoid meeting her gaze. "As I understand it, by the...the creator of our world."

"You?"

She opened the book and riffled through its pages, ending at the front.

"This spirit is called 'Gilbert,' by some chance?"

"No…no, I'm sure that's not the name."

She pondered a moment, holding the book in both hands, before asking:

"And who is it that told you this?"

Thinking of her potential for violence, he decided that cooperation was one thing as touched himself, another as it touched a fellow male. "Forgive me, your highness. If it were one of your own sex, I should not hesitate to give you the name, but as it is…"

"You fear I'd wreak my fury on your friend?
And if I offer him all amnesty?"

"Your highness might," he acknowledged with all the respect at his command. "But this devil you hint may be possessing you seems rather less predictable than your august self."

She rose and tugged a bell pull. Lady Psyche, having apparently completed her task of settling the lord high ambassador into his rooms, answered the summons at once. The princess instructed her:

"Good Lady Psyche, pray assemble some
Of our best scholars. Bring them, in an hour,
To my laboratory, there to hear
A lecture and instructive exercise,
The subject being Man, his vaunted strength
Of loyalty and fortitude. We have found
A specimen with which to demonstrate."

* * * *

Assuming that the pirates had followed the original rescue scheme with Dr. Daly and their graces of Dunstable, Dr. Falcon decided to aim for Ploverleigh. To avoid as far as possible getting Sir Ruthven and Dr. Falcon mixed up in the effects of John Wellington Wells' love philtre on the gentry and villagers of Ploverleigh, Sister Harriet suggested and selected music from the beginning of *The Sorcerer's* first act, well before the title character was even mentioned by anyone onstage.

Chuck expected this to bring him in on a scene of two gently born young lovers sealing their troth to choral accompaniment.

Instead, when he landed on the lawn before Sir Marmaduke Point-dextre's country house, he found it in a state of early morning desertion.

Making his way from Sir Marmaduke's estate to the village itself, he found Dr. Daly's vicarage, identifiable by a neat brass nameplate, and learned the reason why the music had not produced its corresponding scene. Dr. Daly's housekeeper, who was just arriving at the vicarage from the opposite direction, and who introduced herself as Mrs. Partlet, informed Chuck that her employer was from home. Since Daly had a part to play in the opening sequence of *The Sorcerer,* the scene could not materialize without him, whatever the music.

To Chuck's query as to where the vicar had gone, the good woman glanced at her old-fashioned watch and said, "Well, I didn't rightly ought to tell you, sor, being as how he left last night after I was officially off-duty. But if ye care to bide and drink a dish of tea, I'll just have a little look around inside and see has he left us a note or some'at."

She settled Chuck in the parlor, returning to him ten minutes later with a tea tray and a note. "Aye, here 'tis, I thought the dear man would ha' left us one, though all as he writes is how he's called away unexpected, and ought t' be home again in a day or two. But I think, sor, I think as how I seen him driving out last night, after I was off-duty, you know, down the road westwards. There's been some goings-on up to the castle—Castle Bunthorne," she added helpfully. "Mayhap he's gone there."

"Many thanks, Mrs. Partlet," Chuck told her with a sober nod. "You've been a great help." He did not mention that, while walking around the room waiting for her, he had already found a packet addressed to Sir Ruthven, leaning against the mantel clock. Mrs. Partlet clearly considered herself bound to a certain degree of secrecy as to her employer's doings, but Chuck Falcon had had no such scruples about reading the communications from Princess Ida and the duke of Dunstable. It was quite possible, taking into account what deep awareness Lozinski had of events in the objective world around him and the various levels of his control over his inner scenario, that he had transferred the messages to the parlor mantelpiece from wherever they had previously lain, in order for his strange friend to find them now.

Walking the four miles to Castle Bunthorne—a pleasant little jog, in the clear, country-cool British morning, for a man of Chuck Falcon's virtual physique—probably got him there as conveniently as if he had hung around trying to hire a horse or bicycle. The first individuals he met on coming in sight of the castle were Pitti-Sing, whom he remembered from the gala reception for the lord high ambassador and the later episode in the Portsmouth courthouse, and the private detective he had encountered briefly in London. They were strolling across the meadow, chatting amiably, but when Pitti-Sing glanced up and saw Chuck, she nudged the detective's elbow and cried, "There! Arrest him!"

The detective blinked. "What for, ma'am?"

"That's the man who engineered Sir Ruthven's rescue, I'm sure of it!"

"Yes, but that don't injure my present (more or less) employer, and I'm not in the pay of either your government or her majesty's. Now, if your ladyship means to employ me to arrest this felon, my going rate for that kind of job—"

"Oh, never mind, I'll do it myself!" She snatched a small revolver from the detective's coat pocket and aimed it at Chuck.

"It's still three and six for gun rental, ma'am," said the detective.

Deciding to play along to a certain extent, Chuck raised his hands in deference to the gun. But Pitti-Sing ignored this sign of surrender and fired. Chuck dodged. The bullet plowed into the earth some yards behind him.

The detective blinked again. "Damme, I didn't know it was loaded. I'm afraid the rental's seven and six for a loaded gun, your ladyship, plus three bob for the cost of ammunition."

"Your prices are outrageous," she replied. "You ought to arrest yourself for a swindler. As for you, sir," she went on to Chuck, still pointing the revolver, "are you or are you not the culprit who left your moth-eaten knapsack behind at the Tower of London when you engineered that infamous rescue?"

"And if I am, madam, does that give you any right to—"

"Now, there's a delicate point," remarked the detective. "If she was a British subject, of course, it wouldn't. But as she's a citizen of Japan, also here with full diplomatic immunity and privileges and all that, do we apply British Common Law, or Japanese, or—I say, old boy, what nationality are you?"

"International citizen," Chuck said, as the closest thing that applied 'in here.' He went on, more or less bluffing, "And I think it's recognized international usage not to shoot a man in the act of giving himself up, though what I'm supposed to have done to give myself up for, I wish you'd explain to me."

By now people were hurrying to the scene from the distant tent and other parts of the meadow. Chuck recognized the Penzance pirates, Dr. Daly, the duke and duchess of Dunstable. Since they were all apparently running at large, either they had not been arrested and should be reluctant to betray him, or else Pitti-Sing was only using the rescue as a trumped-up charge, and had some other reason...

His abandoned knapsack. It had contained his virtual copy of Gilbert's *Savoy Operas.* If Pitti-Sing had gotten hold of that volume... Chuck tried to read her face. Behind the determination, beneath the self-control, he thought he glimpsed terror. The Red King's Dream came to his mind. If creatures of a virtual fantasy could become aware of the nature of their own existence...if she had read Gilbert's libretti, recognized Dr. Falcon as the man who had carried the book, she might well have pegged him as a visitor from another sphere. That might explain her firing on him—to destroy a demon or test a god.

But no, if she had figured out anything like the true picture, or mistaken him for her dreamer-creator, she would hardly take the chance of destroying herself and her world along with him. More likely she feared him as the bringer of a mysterious, possibly menacing oracle from the realms of the unknown.

Or maybe her attack had little to do with the book. Maybe it was not Gilbert's little maid from school who had squeezed the trigger, but...

"Doctor!" cried Daly, the first to reach the tense little group. "Dr. Falcon! Good heavens, your ladyship, what...?"

Pitti-Sing turned. For a moment it looked as if she might fire on the clergyman, and Chuck prepared to spring. But she smiled and lowered the gun. "So you know this man, Dr. Daly?" she said. "I suppose you can vouch for him?"

And on Daly's assuring her that he did and could, she tossed the gun back to the private detective.

CHAPTER 24

THE INFILTRATION

Across the camp table, Prince Hilarion was telling Chuck what the others present already knew:

"The Princess Ida is my own dear wife.
I'll not consent to any plan soe'er
That puts her into danger of her life."

"Nobody's going to be in any danger." Chuck wondered how many times he'd have to repeat the statement before he could wear down the impression some of these people seemed to hold of him as a dangerous desperado, thanks to Pitti-Sing's little show with the revolver.

Florian, perhaps the steadiest of the three who spoke in blank verse, said:

"Good doctor, with all right and due respect,
So strong and muscular a man as you
Could tear those maids apart if they attacked."

Cyril added:

"Nor could you featly pass in maiden's dress."

Wondering if he could switch into a virtual version of his real identity as Chandra while still 'in here,' how quickly he could do it, and whether or not it would be advisable, Chuck assured them, "I don't attack any weaker parties than myself. Ask our friends the pirates."

"Quite true," said the pirate king. "But while it's clear that any individual one of those damsels would be weaker—"

"E'en to the Lady Blanche herself," Cyril cut in with a grin.

"—so would any given one of us men," the pirate king went on. "Why, I'd even fight you myself, sir, with no compunction, man to man, if it ever came to that. But the question is, would the maidens still count as a weaker party if they rushed you en masse? If you conceived they wouldn't, and felt justified in fighting for your life, you might take down a number of the pretty dears with you."

"And Ida doubtless in the forefront fray," said Hilarion.

Chuck sighed. "I'm not going to give any of them so much as a torn fingernail, and if they rush me, I can disappear again. Don't make me demonstrate. Take Dr. Daly's word for it, and the pirates'—they've seen me do it." Why, he thought, couldn't the prince and his companions have been on deck to see it for themselves the last time?

Hilarion said:

> *"If this phenomenon you tell us of*
> *Be very truth, then why, I pray you tell,*
> *Can you not simply vanish from our midst*
> *And reappear within yon castle walls?"*

"I wish I could. Unfortunately, it isn't that simple. Without going into technical details," Chuck expanded, thinking that a long technical explanation might serve his highness right, "let's just say there are limits even to my powers."

The prince protested:

> *"But, this much granted by your own account,*
> *What triumph can you hope to win therein,*
> *Where we with our advantages have failed?"*

Advantages? thought Chuck. Aloud, he said, "You forget, my aim is entirely different. You went in there after Princess Ida's heart. I'm only going in to check on the hostages."

Cyril inquired,

> *"And if you bring 'em safely out again,*
> *Shall we three then in honor be compelled*
> *To yield our necks for Ida's block and axe?"*

"It's a nice point," said the vicar, "but on the whole I think not. Fortunes of war, you know. I'm a man of peace myself, by profession as it were, but I seem to remember reading something of such cases. Unless they've given their words not to attempt escape, which they hadn't when they went in, and I see no reason why they should have done since."

"Yes," Pitti-Sing said demurely, "but we've no idea what the princess may have done to them in there. We've had no communication with the castle since last night, you know."

"My dear," said Lady Jane, "I thought you were the authority on what her highness was likely to do or not to do."

Pitti-Sing smiled and spread her fan. "If the so-powerful Dr. Falcon can confess he's not omnipotent, I don't feel ashamed to confess I'm not omniscient. I think—I say I *think*—she won't have hurt them. At least, not seriously. But we really can't be sure, now can we?"

"No—no, we can't." Dr. Daly drummed his fingertips on the table. "Poor fellow...poor fellow*s*. Well, we would seem to risk nothing. I assure all of you that Dr. Falcon can escape from danger himself at any time, at the merest moment's notice, so there's no risk of her highness acquiring a fourth hostage. And if anyone can get those three gentlemen safely out again, it will be he."

"Is that your professional or your personal opinion, Reverend?" asked the private detective.

"Yes," said Dr. Daly.

"Ain't you aware by now it was Dr. Falcon who planned Sir Ruthven's escape from the Tower?" said the duke of Dunstable. "Yes, and did most of the work, too. The most dangerous part, that is."

Florian put in,

> *"I think, your Highness, that it might be best*
> *To let him try."*

Hilarion sighed and looked at his other courtier:

> *"And Cyril, you? Your thought?"*

Cyril replied,

> *"Why, sire, since he does not mean, I think,*
> *That we should run our heads into the noose,*
> *I vote it will not hurt to let him try.*

Your royal veto would, of course, o'errule."

Hilarion looked around at everyone present and sighed more deeply before declaring:

"My royal veto I will not employ,
Since my opinion seems outnumbered here.
Well, sir, you've won. When darkness falls we'll show
You to that passage in the wall shown us
By Mr. Bunthorne, two days since, 'tis now."

* * * *

Chuck made the attempt at dinnertime. At least, from their half a day as Ida's prisoners, Hilarion and his friends knew that they had been given dinner at eight, and assumed the princess and her women took it at the same hour. Emerging from Bunthorne's secret passage into a bushy corner of the castle's walled garden, Chuck proved the correctness of the assumption. Not only was the garden deserted, but a clatter of dishes could be heard through the high, arched windows of an adjacent building.

Chuck climbed a few feet up on the old, wrist-thick ivy branches for a look through one of the windows. Not even Hilarion knew the exact enrollment of Ida's academy, but the dining hall was sufficiently crowded to suggest that the school ate all together. The dark young beauty sitting in the central place at the head table, with a regal air and a gold tassel to her mortarboard, had to be Ida herself.

Had Chuck been in charge of a beleaguered castle, he would have fed his command in shifts; but considering the nature of the forces encamped outside the castle, Ida's way no doubt made as much sense as any. He climbed down the ivy, turned, and discovered that the garden was not deserted after all. On the other side of the sundial, Mad Margaret was unfolding herself from a bed of alyssum in which she had apparently been asleep.

She yawned, stretched, and looked at him. "The tortoise and the hare, they ran a race," she said. "And do you know what happened to them both? They turned into a clock. The long hand is the hare. He chases the shelly short one round and round, but never quite catches him up. Why do you come so soon?"

"Shh." Chuck put one finger to his lips. He approached as near as he dared, hunkered down on the gravel path facing her, and, figuring that he might as well talk sense as gibberish to her, countered with a question of his own. "I thought they hadn't let any visitors in from outside except the Lady Pitti-Sing?"

"What's all the world to them or me?" Margaret jumped up and did a few dance steps, waving her arms as if to include everything around. "Outside's in and inside's out," she sang, "all around and round about. For love and I had the wit to win, we drew a circle so very thin…" She knelt, stared Chuck in the eye, and added in a speaking voice, "They don't throw things at one here. That counts for a good deal. They give me food on a blue china plate, all willowy as the moon. Have you come to see *them?*"

Chuck took the gamble. "That's right. Where are they?"

"The fee is…the fee is…one last kiss from your cherry red lips?" She shook her head and rose. "Well, come on then, before they melt away."

He followed her out of the garden, through courtyard and corridors, up and down flights of stairs. At times he thought she was no longer aware of him, if, indeed, she ever had been. Here she paused to wave at a mirror, there to exchange the time of day with a bronze urn, or gaze through her cupped hands at an invisible point of interest. Chuck guessed the women must be finishing their meal in the dining hall by now. But he was accomplishing an exploration of Castle Bunthorne, and he had not yet encountered any of Ida's scholars along the way.

A few minutes after he had congratulated himself on this last point, as he was trailing Margaret down a long, badly lit, deep-carpeted hallway, a girl graduate carrying a tray laden with dirty dishes came out of a door between them. Chuck slipped back at once into the shadows of another doorway. The graduate apparently did not catch sight of him for glancing in the other direction. "Oh, Margaret!" she called. "Have you had your supper?"

Margaret called back, "Bread in the moonlight and dew all around, and circle, and circle, and circle…but they're all gone in, like so many mushrooms."

The graduate sighed, shrugged with a clanking of the empty crockery on her tray, and turned after the madwoman, who was disappearing in the shadows at the hallway's far end. At least

Chuck did not hear Margaret mention him. Maybe he had escaped her memory.

When both women were gone, he approached the door the graduate had issued from and put first his eye and then his ear to the keyhole. There were young women in the room, quite a few of them, but he could also make out Pooh-Bah's robes and Bunthorne's voice.

The door was unlocked. Chuck accepted the risk and went in.

The lord high ambassador was reclining on a chaise-longue, surrounded by girl graduates: two were fanning him, a third playing soft music to him on a mandolin, a fourth pouring him a cup of tea, and a fifth peeling him a grape. The mystic poet stood at a lectern on the other side of the room, declaiming his poetry to half a dozen more young women, who were dutifully closing their eyes, hugging one another, and looking as if they were trying to pretend to think of faint lilies, though Chuck noticed one stifling a yawn. The baronet was ensconced in an armchair in the far corner, reading a book.

Chuck threaded his way between the ambassador's entourage and the poet's. He got a few glances from the former, but as nobody voiced a comment or tried to stop him, he soon reached the baronet.

"Dr. Falcon!" Sir Ruthven exclaimed softly, looking up at his approach and offering to rise.

Chuck waved him to keep his seat, drew up another armchair, and sat facing him. "Well, you seem to have it comfortable enough."

The other shook his head. "On the contrary, Dr. Falcon, we are being exquisitely tortured."

"Oh? When?"

"Why, at present." Sir Ruthven gestured at the whole room.

Chuck took another long look around. "What? Here and now?"

"Here and now. It's a fiendishly ingenious method reportedly employed upon the Princess Ida's own father by a rival monarch, from whom her highness borrowed the idea. We're being allowed nothing whatever to grumble at."

"I should've known. You fellows seem to be bearing up pretty well."

"As a matter of fact, I don't believe his excellency and the poet are yet aware what's going on." The baronet smiled. "Lord

Pooh-Bah accepts it all as no more than the deference due to a man of his pedigree, and Bunthorne seems too busy enjoying the young ladies' adulation to notice it's as sham as he is himself."

"And how about you?"

Sir Ruthven shrugged. "Oh, I make shift. I ask for as little as possible, thus contriving to be left alone most of the time; and when I do find any trifling little matter for complaint, such as the impermissibility of walking out the front gate, I keep it to myself. Besides, it's infinitely preferable to…" He leaned forward and clutched Chuck's wrist. "Forgive me, doctor. I…I fear I've told her highness everything."

"Everything?"

"Your name, your description—I couldn't help it. Have you any idea what it is to be made a laboratory specimen for the instruction of half a dozen or more very beautiful young ladies of the most— no, I won't say 'forward'—but eager—curious—inquisitive na- ture? Oh, the giggles!" He shuddered. "I confess I saw no great harm in revealing your peculiar philosophy, down to the smallest detail…as I comprehend it, that is—not that I believe it. But your identity…"

"I forgive you," said Chuck.

"My only comfort was the reflection that your powers of com- ing and going at will should help to keep you safe. Nevertheless…"

"I forgive you," Chuck repeated. This time his pardon must have penetrated, for the baronet bent double and kissed his hand. Chuck disengaged himself and went on, "You've got the run of the castle?"

Sir Ruthven sat up straight and adjusted his neckcloth. "Yes, except for certain quarters reserved for the women exclusively… not that I grumble at *that!*"

"Good. How about the princess? Any idea where she'll be after dinner?"

"…Her tower, perhaps. Or possibly the library or conservatory or… I'm not really sure, you see, but I keep to our chambers here, despite the noise—" He nodded in Bunthorne's direction. "—so as to be sure of avoiding her."

Chuck stood. "Sorry to drag you away from your safe port, but you're going to guide me around to all these places until we find her."

"What? Oh, no, Dr. Falcon, you can't—Besides, I've only been here since last night, myself. Why not Bunthorne?"

"Bunthorne?" Chuck glanced at the mystic poet, who was leaning back with eyes closed and body in an improbable Anglo-Saxon attitude presumably meant to convey the agony of inspiration. "It may be his castle, but you know something of what's going on, even if you don't believe it yet. Think of the explanations I'd have to go through with him. Would you wish that fate on me—a man you've just betrayed?"

"You forgave me that," the baronet pointed out. "If I understood you correctly."

"Right. Nevertheless, you still owe me something, wouldn't you say?"

"But you could explore just as effectively and no doubt more safely alone, with your powers of—"

"That's where you're wrong, my friend," said Chuck. "Alone, I might have to wink back to my own sphere, and it isn't always simple to get back to just the right time and place in yours. If you're with me, there's a pretty good chance they'll let us pass unmolested, by terms of the torture they're applying to you. Come on, man, up!" he added, hauling on Sir Ruthven's arm.

"Oh, very well, although under protest." Sir Ruthven rose, shook himself, straightened his waistcoat, and grinned nervously. "At least there's this to be said for it: you're giving me something to grumble at."

CHAPTER 25

TO BEARD A MAIDEN IN HER LAIR

Chuck and Sir Ruthven met only two women on their way through the castle. It was hard to say which of the two made the baronet more nervous.

The first was Mad Margaret, wandering the passageways. "Meg," Sir Ruthven began, "don't be afraid…"

She eyed him up and down. "Have you washed your fingernails yet?"

He held his hands out pleadingly to her. She seized one of them and turned it back and forth, tracing the veins on the back as if she were reading his fortune and the lines on the palm as if she were reading a map. "The Nile's a very short river, but the Limpopo's a greasy one. Here's the Mount of Venus, where the lovers' laws came down. Ohhh…! Beware, beware!" She thrust his arm away and shrank back against the wall.

"Meg…"

"A watery life and a long death!" she cried. "Don't touch me! Don't touch me! They're closing in."

He took a step forward and she dodged through the nearest door. He looked at Chuck.

"All right," Dr. Falcon agreed, "We'll go after her—but just far enough to make sure she isn't getting into any immediate danger."

Sir Ruthven lunged through the door, Chuck following. They found themselves in the conservatory. Margaret sat on her knees on the tiled floor, humming softly and braiding several thin, dark green palm leaves without detaching them from their stem.

"Okay," Chuck murmured, twitching the baronet's sleeve. "Now let's get out before we startle her again—"

Maybe she heard him, because she looked up, although completely unstartled, eyed them, and said matter-of-factly, as if she hadn't run away from them a few seconds back, "Oh, it's you. A watery life and a long, long death. Beware." She winked and returned to her braidwork.

Chuck tugged his companion out of the conservatory. Sir Ruthven leaned against the passage wall, closed his eyes, took several deep breaths, and said, "How did…? I had no idea she was here, in Castle Bunthorne."

"Margaret? I guess I should've told you. I think Princess Ida's women have taken her in, sort of adopted her."

"Given her sanctuary from the world." Sir Ruthven nodded. "It's good of them. By far the best side I've seen of her highness. Well…" He shrugged and pushed away from the wall. The two men continued their search.

The second woman they met was Lady Blanche. Even before the baronet stammered her name, Chuck guessed her identity by her silvering hair, straight-backed height, and frowning face.

"And who is he that violates our walls?" she said, glowering at Doc.

"A…a friend of mine," the baronet explained.

"It rubs against our rule to have him here."

"If I am not allowed my friends in to visit me," said Sir Ruthven, "I shall have something to grumble at. And I will grumble, ma'am. Grumble I will."

Lady Blanche decided, smiling:

> *"Our leader's laws would seem to contradict*
> *The one, the other. Well, I'll wink at this,*
> *Though mind you keep him close, and do not give*
> *Our maidens matter to complain of him."*

"Madam," said Chuck, "it's the furthest thing from my mind." Her smile broadened.

> *"I'd counsel that you give our leader's self*
> *Wide berth. I warn, when last I saw her grace,*
> *She was at research in the library,*
> *There to remain some time. The library*
> *Is down that passageway. Words to the wise."*

She looked Chuck up and down.

*"Our Princess Ida is accounted, sir,
One of the greatest beauties of our day."*

Lady Blanche moved on down the passage at a stately pace, paying the men no further attention. Sir Ruthven let out his breath and wiped his forehead. "The princess' second in command," he told Chuck. "Florian says he believes if it were up to Lady Blanche, she'd as soon have seen the prince succeed, marry the princess, and take her away."

"Leaving our friend Blanche first in command. Yes, I remember," said Chuck. "That is, I guessed as much. Come on."

"Must I... Do you really think I'm still needed, Doctor? If you are determined to face the princess, wouldn't you as lief do so alone?"

One more drastic session might just be the thing to shake Bob Lozinski's own consciousness out of its self-imposed fog. "Yes," said Dr. Falcon, "you're still needed. Don't worry, I'm not going to blink out and leave you alone with her." He took Sir Ruthven's arm.

The other tried to shake free. "Oh, very well, but at least leave me some dignity of movement."

Chuck loosed his hold and they proceeded to the library door. It was ajar. Sir Ruthven pushed it open and Chuck stepped inside, controlling his doubts as to whether his companion would follow. His companion did, but stayed well back—within a step of the door, as Chuck observed out of the corner of his eye.

The room was large, high, and lined with floor-to-ceiling bookshelves everywhere except the outer wall, which was devoted to a bow window with window seat. The wall shelves were crammed to the point of buckling slightly here and there, and several freestanding waist-high bookcases accommodated the overflow. These did not match the wall shelves, being maple rather than oak, and they lacked the mellowness of age. One of them stood in front of the window seat, hiding all but its corners from view. On this case a book lay open.

At first glance the room appeared deserted. Then the princess rose up between the window seat and the bookcase, holding a volume she had presumably just selected.

The window was directly opposite the door. Ida stood, framed by the twilight showing through the glass panes, and gazed at her visitor.

"And this is Dr. Charles Falcon, then?" she said.

"I think I have the honor of meeting her highness, the Princess Ida." Chuck strode forward and extended his hand across the bookshelf, though he was hardly surprised when Ida, instead of shaking it, glanced down at it coldly and looked back up at his face.

She condescended to remark, however,

> *"It seems a pity, sir, that you are male.*
> *And so you come from realms beyond our own.*
> *What brings you to this little sphere of ours,*
> *To meddle in our ways, and fill our men—*
> *Or some of them—with thoughts above their due?"*

For the first time since they'd come in, her gaze flickered to Sir Ruthven.

"Exactly what I've been trying to tell him, myself, your highness," said the baronet.

Wondering what Ida would say if Dr. Falcon could change back into her true gender right here and now, Chuck glanced at the book that lay atop the waist-high shelf between him and Ida. It was his virtual copy of the *Savoy Operas,* opened to the last act of *Princess Ida.* "You got that," Chuck guessed, nodding down at it, "from Pitti-Sing?"

"And she, it seems, by ways unplanned, from you." Putting down the book she had just withdrawn from the case—a volume titled *Lost in a Good Book*—Ida began to flip Gilbert's pages, musing:

> *"I've read of Brobdingnag and Lilliput,*
> *The traveler's thoughts thereon. And Plato's works,*
> *And Twain's Mysterious Stranger. Flatland, too.*
> *And certain of Calvino's tales, and lore*
> *Of Tir Nan Og and Faery. I know*
> *The theories of worlds on worlds in worlds,*

Or nestled each in each like children's toys,
Or running somehow parallel, with doors
That open in uncertain times and ways.
I know that in such thought we may exist,
Each one of us, in worlds without end—
A million Idas, Blanches, Psyches too,
Hilarions and Bunthornes and the rest,
Innumerably echoed, every one
Unknown and unsuspected by its likes.
And all of us are here—*all, all of us—*
Save you alone. Now, Doctor, why?"

she finished, snapping the book shut and thumping it with her fist.

"Maybe because I wasn't born yet when W. S. Gilbert wrote that book."

"And Gilbert's the creator of our world?
Or is it Ruthven here, who thinks that's not
The secret name you told him was his own?"

"In a way, both of them. Gilbert wrote you first, Sir Ruthven—whose 'secret name' is Robert Lozinski—took you over from Gilbert." Chuck looked around, saw two armchairs by the fireplace, and waved at them. "Sit down, make yourselves comfortable, and I'll try to explain it all."

Ida settled regally into the larger of the armchairs, saying with a nod:

"We waive formality. You two may sit."

After some hesitation, Sir Ruthven drew up a straight chair for himself, leaving the second armchair for Chuck, even though Doc began his account standing.

At first he intended to remain on his feet, but this time he gave his listeners the whole story, beginning with Steve Davis' death, not omitting security man Deuteronomy Osborne and his suspicions of Lozinski, and even recapping, for Ida's benefit, his and the baronet's adventures to date in Gilbertian-Lozinskian England. It took longer than he had expected, and by the time he wrapped it up, he was sitting down after all.

Ida's comment was:

> *"And so it seems I am indeed possessed.*
> *And by the demon* you *have willed in me."*

She frowned at the baronet.

"Not *I,* your highness," he protested. "This intelligence who, by Dr. Falcon's account, is using me—just as you are being used yourself, and it's not entirely comfortable. I can quite sympathize with your highness…though still reserving the right not to credit any of this."

"So do you not?" Cocking one fine black eyebrow, Ida went on:

> *"Bring me that tablet from the table there."*

As Sir Ruthven jumped up to do her bidding, she went on to Chuck, though without lowering her voice:

> *"I think the baronet is not so good,*
> *Nor I so evil as this mind makes us."*

"Your highness flatters me," Sir Ruthven remarked, returning to hand her the tablet.

She tugged a handy bell pull, drew a pen from the case at her belt, and wrote while continuing to talk:

> *"I summon Lady Psyche, not my guard.*
> *Well, Dr. Falcon, I will lend my aid,*
> *And help you to unravel these events,*
> *But only if you'll somewhat do for me."*

"That depends," said Chuck, "on the 'somewhat' you have in mind."

She smiled.

> *"If I know anything of men, or if*
> *One half the tales told of gods are true,*
> *You'll have no grief nor pain of my request."*

Sir Ruthven started at the sound of the opening door.

Ida glanced up. *"Ah, Lady Psyche."* She wrote a few more words, tore the sheet from the tablet, folded it and handed it to the newcomer. *"Act on this at once."*

Lady Psyche curtseyed, winked at the men, and took her leave.

"All right," said Chuck. "Name your terms and maybe we can talk business."

Ida leaned back and regarded him over her tented fingers as she spoke.

> *"The doubt of murder hereupon reduced*
> *To business, cut and dried? Oh, no, my friend.*
> *Your malehood makes me more sure of you*
> *Than would your pledge—your sex so often breaks*
> *Its sworn and sealed treaties. We'll proceed*
> *To isolate the demon from my breast."*

CHAPTER 26

EXCHANGE OF FAVORS

Ida went on:

> *"Resuming, then, I take it you are sure*
> *Of some identities. As, Deadeye was*
> *The murdered Davis; Buttercup is Cripps;*
> *Sir Ruthven is Lozinski's self. And Schultz?*
> *Schultz was not present at the sailor's death.*
> *Unless as Captain Corcoran? Perhaps,*
> *And Schultz is also Pooh-Bah in our world?"*

"Maybe Shadbolt, too" said Dr. Falcon, "and I'm pretty sure
that Don Alhambra is our security man Deuteronomy Osborne.
But, having met Corcoran, I don't think he was Schultz."
Ida nodded:

> *"And Daly's Sister Harriet. Yet say*
> *Lozinski brought this Davis back to life*
> *From Deadeye into Bunthorne, casting me*
> *As his new murderer, but that this time*
> *Lozinski, as Sir Ruthven, foiled the blow."*

"Putting it simply," said Dr. Falcon, "I make that wish fulfillment. Suggesting that if one of the others killed Steve Davis deliberately, Bob Lozinski would have stopped it if he could have.

> *"Our task remains: to find who killed the sailor,*
> *And who it is in your wide world beyond*
> *That killer represents in our small sphere."*

For all her intelligence and imagination, Ida seemed incapable of understanding the computer virus as worse than the murder. Gazing with some distaste at Sir Ruthven, she went on:

"Is't possible that he and I are both
Of us possessed by your Lozinski's soul?
That through remorse Lozinski foiled himself
In this last re-enactment of the crime?"

Sir Ruthven coughed and looked at the floor. "I should think it very unlikely, your highness, that your majestic self and I could be animated by a single consciousness. As for poor Deadeye's murderer and, by extension, whoever planted this deadly seed in their communications system..."

As the baronet hesitated, Ida flashed at him:

"You lied when you confessed that murder foul—
We're sure of it! Now name the criminal!"

Dr. Falcon would have tried a different approach, but at this point he judged it best to give these people their heads for a while. None of his previous approaches to the question had been successful anyway.

Unfortunately, at first Ida's tactics looked no more promising than anyone else's. Whatever Sir Ruthven had been about to say concerning Deadeye's murder, he clammed up now, folding his arms, sitting back in his chair, and, after one glance at the princess, returning his gaze to the carpet.

But Ida pressed on undaunted:

"It must have been this Mrs. Buttercup.
For had it been a man, you'd not have felt
Yourself obliged to shield him, while a dame
Aroused your sense of specious chivalry.
Confess it now. Why, man, do you not see
It dangles death and life in larger worlds
Than our poor little sphere? Nay, it may be
This knowledge will help Falcon circumvent
The utter holocaust of all we know
By saving this man's brain in which we live
From catastrophic ruin of his world:

This viral end perhaps engulfing all!"

So, after all, she had grasped the seriousness of the computer virus. She finished:

"So will you speak, or shall I call again
My choicest scholars, eager to learn more
Of Man, with lab'ratory specimen?"

"You've no need to threaten and bully," said Sir Ruthven. "The truth is, I don't know who killed Deadeye—not for certain. When I...er...came round from my dream, Mrs. Cripps was bending over him, screaming. She had the bludgeon in her hand. I assumed she had done the deed and appropriated the weapon. I did not actually witness it—but I shall swear to what I have already stated on whatever book you like." He stared at the volume of librettos in Ida's lap.

The princess sighed and looked at Chuck as she theorized on:

"Then say there's more than one. And one is small...
That small attendant in the opium den!"

Sir Ruthven looked startled. "Yes...yes, it could have been... Mother-of-pearl! If I could have been sure of that, I should never have acted scapegoat in the affair."

"Unless the attendant was another woman," Chuck mused.

Ida said:

"Indeed, this guilty entity had seized
On me (though subsequently exorcised
By mine own will). Lozinski would not cast,
I think, though man himself, another man
As me. It stretches, too, to link me with
A Ruth, a Buttercup, a Lady Jane.
And yet I do not guess she's jumped direct
From opium slave to me without some third
And intervening host."

The princess raised the book to her chin, tapping the cover with her fingernails.

"Now, Lady Pitti-Sing it was who found

> *This book, this key—well, that was chance. But yet*
> *Her passing it to me was not. Nor was,*
> *We may presume, that sudden urge I felt*
> *To name those hostages I chose to name*
> *In spite of my own interest, which would*
> *Have best been served by keeping close the prince.*
> *If Pitti-Sing in some sense shares this force*
> *And brought it on to me... Who, then, is she*
> *In your wide world outside? Why, could she not—"*

"Judi!" cried Sir Ruthven, sitting forward. Then he glanced round at Chuck and the princess, strained them a grin, and shrank back in his chair. "I...don't know why I said that."

"Judi Oshita. Yes, that confirms it!" Chuck jumped to his feet.

Ida caught his hand and, holding it fast, rose more slowly.

> *"Your bargain, Dr. Falcon. You'll not go*
> *Until you've heard, at least, what I would have*
> *You do for me."*

He might as well. The people outside already knew that Pete Schultz and Barbara Cripps had cornered Judi Oshita. Lozinski's confirmation could hardly get her into secure custody any quicker. More important, Lozinski's balance did not seem to have been restored. It might be tricky enough to clear him from suspicion of worse involvement even with his coherent statement—without it, maybe impossible. Looking down into Ida's dark eyes, Dr. Falcon said, "All right, your highness. What can I do for you?"

Without looking away from Dr. Falcon, Ida said,

> *"Sir Ruthven, you will leave us now alone."*

"I'm not sure..." Chuck began, glancing at the baronet.

Sir Ruthven had also stood. "Oh, this time I'm only too ready to obey her highness' command. Don't worry, Dr. Falcon: I shall look out for myself. Though at the rate your theories have been going, it would be astonishing if I were the only vessel of Mr. Lozinski's intelligence in our world. It appears to me that any danger in that direction lies in your outer sphere, not our inner one." With this, he made his exit.

Chuck looked back at Ida. "Well?"

"I'd have you marry me."

"What?"
Ida shook her head and explained:

"Not for your 'godhead,' no.
But Gilbert dooms me to Hilarion,
And I'll not have the booby!"

"But aren't you already married to him? Not that I'm saying I'd make you live with him, if it were up to me. But legally speaking—"

"An empty form.
The marriage never consummate. Nor is
The very ceremony free from doubt.
For I, the bride, did never say those words,
Those fatal words, 'I do.' Indeed, I screamed
My non-consent aloud to all the world,
Until, had I been seventeen, e'en men
Of stony heart might grieve, and cry it shame
To force a maid against her will. But at
A year of age, I had not learned the words
With which grown folk converse, and so they did
But laugh and sate me with milk over-rich."

"But you wouldn't have much of a husband in me," Dr. Falcon argued. "You know I'm not going to stick around in your world much longer."

"And likely not return, Lozinski cured." She smiled and nodded.

"Why, Doctor, but an absent husband's best
To my own thought and taste! So go your way.
I ask but one short marriage night of you."

"And you aren't afraid you might find it…uh…a little distasteful…even with me?" (Oh, if you knew what I really am outside virtual reality!)
Ida shrugged.

"One night may be endured, if it frees me

From menace of a lifetime's chain. And you,
At least, show little of the ape so obvious
In other men. Perhaps because you hail
From higher planes. (Oh, Goddess! How the women
There must shine, if he is of the men!)"

"I suppose that means you wouldn't even consider choosing a proxy from the men of your own plane? Sir Ruthven, for instance, with his daily crime to commit—desertion should do it nicely..." (Not, strangely enough, that Dr. Falcon found Ida's proposal repugnant, now s/he'd had time to think about it a little more. From Omar and a couple of others, but chiefly Omar...dear Omar... Chandra knew what it was like from the woman's side. Why not try it, 'in here' in virtual reality, from the man's? She thought other people did it sometimes in the virtual privacy booths, looking to appreciate how the other sex had it. Still, marrying Ida might not be the worst therapy for Bob Lozinski.)

But the princess only laughed.

"Had I not known so much, I do confess
The scheme had crossed my mind, our baronet
To be the man. But would you have me wed,
At even second-hand, with one who cast
Me as a murderess? Not though he be
Our God incarnate, in a sense of speech!
And Bunthorne or Lord Pooh-Bah? By no means!
Now, let us have the benefit of form,
Though I think not that form will bind you, back
In your own sphere. I've sent for Dr. Daly."

"So that was the note you gave Lady Psyche?" At Ida's nod, Chuck went on, "Well, how about you? Don't you risk bigamy?" She snapped her fingers.

"The form is but the form. But if the Prince
Hilarion still wants me for his wife,
Once any other man has first enjoyed
My favors—why, perhaps, in such a case,
He'll prove his so-called love is truly love,
Not male pride. I'll chance it."

Thinking back over his impressions of Hilarion earlier that day, Chandra could hardly help sympathizing, in all objectivity, with Ida's preference for Charles Falcon over the prince. "All right, your highness," he said aloud, "if you can persuade Dr. Daly to read the ceremony over us, I'll be your husband for the night."

CHAPTER 27

WHEN THE NUPTIAL KNOT IS TIED

Dr. Daly, though sympathetic, could not be persuaded to perform the marriage ceremony for Princess Ida and Dr. Falcon. "Believe me, your highness," said the vicar, "having passed some time on shipboard and in camp with his royal highness, I feel for you most heartily. At the same time, alas, you *were* wedded to him in due and proper form, however questionable in its legality or binding power, so that in the absence of any official annulment of that earlier marriage, I fear I cannot in good conscience... Not, at least, without consulting my bishop, and even that interview might not produce the desired results, liberal though he's known to be.... But wait a bit! Richard—our friendly pirate king! As captain of the *Divine Emollient, he* might read the ceremony over you aboard his vessel. If you could see your way to make the excursion."

Sending the vicar back outside to arrange the details, Ida set about her own preparations at once.

"You're trusting Dr. Daly pretty far," Chuck couldn't help remarking. "He is a man, you know."

> *"Inhabited, as you assure me, sir,*
> *At present by the conscience of a woman—*
> *The generous, wise Sanford of your world."*

The princess left both Lady Blanche and Lady Psyche in temporary command of Castle Bunthorne, Blanche to keep up the defense and Psyche, Chuck suspected, to keep an eye on Blanche. Ida armed and armored Lady Blanche's daughter Melissa and half a dozen more of her likeliest students to ride in guard formation around the carriage—Bunthorne's carriage, drawn by Bunthorne's horses, in which she was taking along her three hostages.

She was taking them along for several reasons: she trusted their custody more under her own eye than under those of the Ladies Blanche and Psyche; she judged an attack on her party, even for rescue purposes, less likely if the hostages might be endangered; she would have them as witnesses to the ceremony; and she was so confident that her marriage with Dr. Falcon would end her troubles with Prince Hilarion that she even pledged her word to release the three once the union was accomplished. This last promise somewhat mollified Pooh-Bah and Bunthorne for the inconvenience of being bustled into a carriage the doors of which were then chained shut. Dr. Daly also rode inside with them as a voluntary fourth, for further security.

After some deliberation, Ida decided to drive the carriage herself. As for the bridegroom, she provided him with weapons but no armor—finding any large enough to fit his tall, athletic virtual frame would have been a problem—mounted him on a good horse and charged him with leading a better one close beside the carriage so that she could vault into the saddle in case of treachery. She seemed to trust Chuck's own dislike of Hilarion and eagerness for the marriage to insure that any betrayal would not come from Chuck himself.

At the last moment, as the drawbridge was lowering to let out the entourage, Mad Margaret appeared from a corner of the courtyard, dashed between the riders, and scrambled up to the seat beside the princess.

"There's laurel leaves for you," she said, dumping a handful of plant life, including a wreath of braided palm fronds, into Ida's lap. "And rosebuds for your hair. I must go down to the sea again…"

"Your highness!" Sir Ruthven cried, leaning out the carriage window. "Wouldn't she be safer to remain here?"

Ida looked at the madwoman and smiled.

> *"Safer? Aye, perhaps; but whoso harms*
> *This child further, answers with his life.*
> *And if she'd come with us, and if I wish*
> *Her for a bridesmaid, why, then, let her ride*
> *Along beside me."*

The baronet beckoned Chuck closer to the window. "But Margaret's warning? 'They're closing in—watery death' and so forth?" He kept his voice low and glanced up toward the driver's seat.

"If Margaret was sensing any evil inside the castle," said Chuck, "she could be better off outside. I think it's safe enough."

"Oh." Sir Ruthven nodded and slid back to the carriage cushions, just as Dr. Daly was making a diplomatic response to Bunthorne's testy inquiries why, having settled on this preposterous excursion—in *his* best carriage, moreover—they had not been on their way ten minutes ago.

* * * *

Ida's half-expected betrayal and attack never materialized, perhaps because of her precautions and perhaps because Lozinski's measure of control over his fantasy world was working in favor of the marriage. Hilarion rode after the party at a little distance, flanked by the faithful Cyril and Florian and serenading Ida with jingling triolets of shallow sentimentality. At the last, as Chuck and Ida got into the longboat to be rowed out to the ship, the prince bestowed on them a stare rather ludicrously compounded of jealousy and puppy love. But that was all the annoyance they had between Castle Bunthorne and the *Divine Emollient*.

The ceremony was held in due form on the quarterdeck, to the intense delight of the pirate crew, who had never seen a wedding aboard their own ship before, and who seized the opportunity to indulge their poetic sentiments to the full. The pirate king officiated, Melissa and Mad Margaret served as bridesmaids, and Sir Ruthven acted as best man. Ida refused to allow anyone to 'give her away'—*"Alone, I give, or rather lend, myself,"* she stated—but the other traditions were meticulously observed, and Bunthorne overcame his distaste, Pooh-Bah (for a generous insult) his snobbery, and Dr. Daly his scruples to join Pirate Ruth in signing as witnesses, giving Ida double the required number.

While the rest of the ship reveled with grog and cakes, the guest-cum-wealthy prisoners' cabin behind the pirate king's quarters was turned over to the newlyweds as a bridal suite. Ida was no more cold than coy, declaring:

"I did not buy your help to disappoint.

I'll taste this fully, so it be but once."

Chandra had never been in so much danger as now of being sucked into the virtual reality of Charles Falcon.

* * * *

Dusk was falling on this long, long summer's day when Sir Ruthven found Mad Margaret on the poop deck, leaning against the rail. She had caught the bride's bouquet (put together that morning with flowers from Bunthorne's gardens) and was eating one of the white roses petal by petal.

"Meg…" he began, and hesitated. Why *did* he care so desperately about her? "I wish…I wish you'd look upon me as…as a brother."

She shook her head. "The butterfly had a brother…and yet he meant well, for all of that. He wouldn't let them get her wet and muddy." She put another petal in her mouth and laid her hand down on the rail.

"I'm sorry, Meg." He put his hand out to cover hers.

"And have you come to throw me in at last?" she said, dropping half a dozen rose petals into the sea.

He gazed down at the white points floating into a constellation on the dark waters before being sucked under, one by one, in the lapping of the ship's wake. If he watched long enough, the water might form a surface and reflect back their two faces…but would it be *two?* Gripping the rail with both hands, he turned back to her. "Who has threatened to throw you in?"

"Here and there, hither and yon, the rocks, the coasts, the pools of water thick beside the tumbled towns, so clear, so cold… Oh, will the fir trees ever bloom again?"

She held up the bouquet, as if offering it to him like a box of chocolates. At that moment the world gave a lurch. The sun, that had all but set, jumped halfway up again above the western horizon. The ocean seemed to rise in a hot wave that scalded his chest and carried her overboard…

* * * *

"Falcon!" said Princess Ida, poking him in the ribs—

"Awaken, man, and to your sphere at once."

"Unh?" Chuck sat up, trying to separate the heavings of the ship from the rhythms of his dream, and the punctuation mark of Ida's punch from the recent jolt he sensed more by memory than awareness of it at the time.

> *"Return to your own world, nor waste your time*
> *In tender takings-leave. The sun had set*
> *Some minutes since, and now behold!"*

She pointed to a long red ray that streamed through the porthole when the waves had the ship momentarily at the right angle—

> *"The sea*
> *Grows wild all at once. I do not say*
> *That all is lost—but something's sore amiss.*
> *I think you're needed yonder more than here."*

Still groggy, Chuck half rolled out of the bunk and into his clothes. He couldn't quite remember what Ida was talking about, but long habit and good muscular reflexes made short work of dressing, even with the ship tossing in some kind of thunderless storm. He considered giving his bride another kiss, but she was already arranging her wimple.

> *"What? Still here? Is't privacy you seek?*
> *Or is your means of transport in your clothes?*
> *Then see you have them all, and quickly go!"*

Frisking himself to make sure he was fully dressed, Chuck left the cabin, found the stairs, and gained the deck. The sea was whipping up and down in a crazy quilt of purples and ochres, as if someone had filled in one of those Old Earth paint-by-numbers waterspouts with the wrong colors. At first Chuck thought the waves were arcing clear around the ship, but then, by the almost artificial red glow of the sun and a subtle difference in the color scheme, he saw that the sky was filled with clouds whose tag ends churned together with the waves at the horizons, leaving a few windows to show the sunset patches of aquamarine sky. The ship, despite the bustle of pirates reefing sails and battening down hatches, seemed about to melt like a Salvador Dali painting. The wind was almost visible.

"Dr. Falcon!" It was Daly, clinging to the rail. "Hadn't you better be getting back to your own world?"

Chuck butted his way to the Vicar of Ploverleigh. "What's going on?"

"I'd hoped you might know." Daly pointed to the waves off the poop deck. "Miss Margaret fell in. I think Sir Ruthven dived after her. Whether as cause or effect of this turmoil…" He shrugged helplessly. "I thought perhaps something in your outer universe… by returning you might be able to trace the trouble, quiet the storm…only a thought."

Chuck frowned and poked at his head. He remembered that Sir Ruthven's survival was vital to the existence of this world, and he remembered swimming—several times—through much such a psychedelic sea to reach here. At this point the man of action took over from the man of intellect, and Chuck dived overboard before he had decided his aim—whether to rescue the baronet or to swim back home to his own universe.

Drowning was not the principal problem—not for Chuck, anyway—or, rather, if he drowned or did not drown, that fact would be unrelated to his swimming prowess, because air and water had about the same consistency for him, which varied with some elusive pattern of the surge and undertow, the sea being sometimes almost pure, gaseous oxygen and the air sometimes liqueous syrup, like tar. Fortunately, the liquid states never lasted longer than Chuck's lung capacity, and during the gaseous intervals he made good headway, as if he were weightlessly swimming through air in a dream, though what he was making headway towards, whether up, down, north, or south, he had little idea. He tried to orient himself by the ship and the sun, heading away from both with some half-formed notion of separating and fanning out in a search party.

For what seemed a long time he saw nothing but clouds and waves in the direction he was more or less aimed. Then a headland loomed up ahead—a phosphorescent purple cliff towering above the tideline. A giant comber started carrying him towards this headland. He rode the wave until it dashed against the cliff face. Whilst the wall of water shattered on the rocks and slowly drained off in rivulets of glowing peach and orange, he continued swimming upward through the atmosphere. He had overshot the summit by a yard or so when the air turned back again from a liquid to a gassy state. He stopped breast-stroking and let himself tumble to the grass and rocks on the cliff top. He found a seat among the boulders, tried to wring himself out—unsuccessfully, because he was not wet—and stared at the rioting weather.

"I really would advise you to make for your own world in all haste, Dr. Falcon," said a voice behind him. He looked around and saw Sir Ruthven…who reached out to place his palms, one on either side of his friend's head, and…somehow…lift… "This tune," was the last thing Chuck heard Sir Ruthven say, then sing, "To a garden full of posies…"

CHAPTER 28

AND LAST.

The virtual helmet fell from Chandra's head and clattered to the floor. Instantly she thought, Oh, Lord, if it's damaged!

Quickly, she stared around. Where were Sister Harriet and Deuces Osborne? Misaki—over there, concentrating furiously at the keyboard and shipnet screen.

"Misaki!" cried Chandra.

The nurse spun around. "Dr. Falcon! Oh, thank God!"

"What is it? What's happened this time? Where are—"

"We don't know! Harriet and Deuces—they're trying to find out. What we had back of shipnet—there was a *zist!* and a few minutes later, it started sputtering…then Papa Gadore himself came on, told everyone to just stay calm, a piece of space debris hit—"

"Oh, *GOD!*" Chandra couldn't help crying out. It was all their worst nightmare—it was what the ship's shielding was supposed to prevent from ever, ever happening.

The doctor's upset seemed, a little, to steady the nurse. "Captain Papa Gadore was assuring us it wasn't a hit to the core, or any of the living pylons—neither of the neighborhoods, neither of the Order pylons—nothing we can't get through, he was saying—then it just zatted out, and I haven't been able to get it back… We've got our own pylon's power back—it blipped but just for a second, then it came back…but…"

Every pylon had two generators of its own. The core had five. For exactly this kind of emergency. That they'd all hoped they'd never be facing. "Well…" Chandra said shakily, and thought about Bob…looked at him, lying there patient in his virtual suit…looked down at the rest of her own virtual suit…picked up her helmet, hummed over to herself the last song he'd been singing to her.

Clearly for a signal. To get her back to the right time and place "in there." If her helmet still worked, that'd been quite a bump...

"We can't do anything else right now," she said. "Let's check this helmet out, see how soon I can get back 'in there.'"

As she'd feared, a number of the delicate little wires and components had been jarred loose. While they were fixing them, first Sister Harriet and then Deuteronomy Osborne came back into the room. Sister Harriet had been able to learn nothing from anyone in the outer labs and hospital units but rumors and speculations. Deuteronomy had combined the medical pylon's power with his own security manual override authority—now that shipnet had come back, if only temporarily, he could get that to work again—and made it to the core and back.

His news was grim. The chunk of space debris had crashed through the shielding into the middle of one of the hydroponics pylons.

"Oh, my *God!*" breathed Sister Harriet.

Chandra's mind spun with thoughts of the devastation—five klicks' worth of air...and how much else? sucked in an instant into the outer vacuum... "How many people were in that pylon?" she asked weakly.

"Can't be sure yet," Osborne replied. "Maybe a dozen, maybe as many as thirty, thirty-five. *Numbers,* ship's population's already made up. Two thousand colonists at Liftaway, already over twenty-five hundred this year. Probably woulda been up to three thousand colonists by now, 'f so many uv us hadn't been still just kids at Liftaway."

"But *individuals!*" said Sister Harriet. "A dozen to thirty-five of us...just...*gone!* In an instant. Oh, God, *who?* Which ones of us?"

"Gonna be hungry times ahead for the rest uv us," Osborne remarked fatalistically, "till they can get that pylon back in food production. Guess this puts paid, all right, t' whether or not they decide capital punishment's too good f'r our virus-creating sphincter."

"What do you mean?" said Misaki.

"I mean the damn shielding wouldn'ta failed if the ship's computer system'd been runnin' at full, like designed."

Chandra Falcon suppressed a shudder, thinking of capital punishment. "This makes it all the more important to be sure whether they were all four in on it, or Oshita alone." With a last double-check, not forgetting the one modification she'd been adding just as Deuteronomy Osborne got back to them, she lifted the virtual helmet back to her head. "Sister Harriet. Misaki. Can we try this one? 'To a garden full of roses...'"

Sister Harried nodded at once. "I know the song."

Shipnet didn't need to be back for the medical computer to play the right song. Chandra settled the helmet and let herself drift back "in there."

* * * *

Sir Ruthven had eight or nine plainly visible silver hairs now, a definite crease in his forehead, and a few small wrinkles at the corners of his eyes and mouth.

"It's all right," he explained, settling himself beside his friend on the boulders. "I'm no longer, as it were, the vessel of an In-carnation. I—that is, we—or perhaps I should say *he*—came to a realization in there." He nodded at the waves. "It was a rather remarkable experience. I don't recall anything of the sort during the initial possession, whenever it took place."

"How did you get out of that mess down there?"

"Instantaneously. Bob—having been on such close, albeit un-conscious, terms with him for so long, I suppose I can take the liberty of the nickname—put me ashore on this headland at the same time he brought it forward for your benefit."

"But he's still in there? Or..."

"I believe he is. Trying, as I comprehend matters, to complete the exorcism by separating himself from Margaret. She was his... is the expression 'back-up'? incarnation, you see. In case any-thing—er, fatal—had befallen me."

"I'm glad it didn't."

"Margaret...I cannot feel at all confident on this point, but I think...I believe that in my case it was some species of direct pos-session, but in Margaret's... Bob may have...somehow...and for some reason...gathered up lingering impressions into a...mask... leaving the real Margaret—insofar as any of us can be called 'real'—pursuing her independent existence elsewere."

Chuck studied the sky. The clouds skudding over the sea seemed a bit lighter, and somewhere on the mainland behind them the sun, now overhead, was breaking through. "Can you fill me in on any more of the details?"

"The moment of shared memory, complete as it seemed at the time, was scarcely more than a flash, but I'll do my best before it fades completely. First, in my own person, I have no idea whatsoever what all this business may be with a 'computational epidemic,' if that is the correct term. Murder, alas! I do understand, although—so far—myself guiltless of it. That was surely why the danger Bob perceived in the computational epidemic translated, as it seems, into the murder of one seeking to close an opium den.

"I believe I glimpsed them as four housemates: Bob, Mr. Schultz, Miss Cripps, and Miss Oshita. I seem still to have a recollection, obviously Bob's, of Miss Oshita dropping the idea of infecting... your outer universe?...with this epidemic. When the others didn't nibble, she seems to have attempted passing it off as a joke, but they were put on their guard.

"I gather that...it cannot actually have been Don Alhambra—someone the inquisitor represents in Bob's imagination...positioned...not Dick Deadeye, but whoever *he* represented...to play the spy on these four. By now the two men at least, Bob and Mr. Schultz, had determined that, whether Miss Oshita had been joking or not, the matter ought to be brought to some authority's attention. Miss Cripps may have wanted to cast her lot with the informants, as well. But they are...were..." Sir Ruthven blushed, but bravely went on, "lovers...in some sort of *ménage à* quatre...and to betray a lover, even though the betrayal be mere suspicion... But Miss Oshita's own suspicions of whoever Deadeye represented...is the name David Stevens? had been awakened, and the falling of a ladder in some area...theatrical, I think...gave her the opportunity to bang his head...more fatally than might otherwise have been the case...in the confusion. Bob witnessed enough to drive him to retreat into...well, into me." The baronet gave an awkward smile. "And Bob's knowledge, as it seems, put Miss Oshita into first the small opium den attendant, then eventually the lady Pitti-Sing and at last the princess Ida, who, being a woman of greater force and presence than most of us men, succeeded in exorcising the murderous presence from her own person. Now, once restored to consciousness 'out there,' Bob means to make a full confession of all he knows." Sir Ruthven tapped his chin reflectively. "Would I have been able to tell you all this otherwise?"

"You might have been. You seem to be individuals in your own right. All of you, here in your own world."

Sir Ruthven sighed. "And, if I understand matters correctly, we are all of us mirrored in a myriad other worlds—other minds. I suppose that's immortality of a sort."

"Hello, out there!" a voice hailed from the mainland. "You amid the boulders?"

They looked. The sun was shining over the mainland again, dispelling a wall of mist between them and a figure in black. It was the vicar of Ploverleigh, waving his folded umbrella like a signal flag.

"Dr. Daly!" called Sir Ruthven, standing.

"One moment." The cleric made his way out to them, prodding his bumbershoot like a cane through the lingering patches of mist. "Good heavens, it is you!" he exclaimed with a few blinks on reaching them. "Sir Ruthven? Dr. Falcon? Accept my congratulations on a very successful job of hiding yourselves this past twelvemonth."

"A *year?*" Sir Ruthven sat again. "An entire year has gone on around us while we've sat here? It's…it's like one of those faery enchantments…"

"Not a bad sign, though," said Chuck, "if things have been going more or less normally on the mainland for a year. Dr. Daly?"

The vicar nodded. "Indeed they have, aside from your inexplicable disappearance. It quite defused the international situation. His excellency the lord high ambassador and his charming wife departed for their own country almost as soon as the *Divine Emollient* made shore. The government of Japan has dropped the charge of flirting, and on the apprehension of Deadeye's true murderer, your sentence was overturned in that case also."

"It was the opium den attendant, then?" asked Sir Ruthven.

"It was, though I forget the name. Bunthorne has moved back into his castle and published two new volumes of verse. The first of them sold very well, due, I believe, less to its contents than to the notoriety attached to the circumstances of the princess Ida's late occupation of Castle Bunthorne."

"And…er…Margaret?" said the baronet.

"Oh, dear, forgive me. I should have told you the news of her at once. Yes, she and your brother seem more or less adjusted to wedded domesticity as headmaster and headmistress of a national school. Curiously enough, neither he nor she evinces the least awareness of her last little escapade, as we saw it. It almost resembles a case of bilocation."

Sir Ruthven nodded at Chuck.

"Though rumor has it," the vicar went on, " that he is ticking off the days until you can be declared legally dead, thereby throwing the title back to him."

"And in the meantime...the duties in the meantime..." Sir Ruthven's face lit up. "Why, in effect, I've been committing suicide every day for the past year!"

"And no reason why that state of things shouldn't continue indefinitely," Chuck finished the thought. "What about the princess? Ida?"

"Oh, my, yes—your wife! Dear, dear, I have displayed a positive genius for leaving till last those matters which would naturally most concern you." The vicar sighed. "When it became obvious that your marriage had indeed been consummated, Prince Hilarion lost interest in her highness, had their infant marriage annulled, and is currently trying to choose a bride from between the twin daughters of a South Sea island king. No, I fear he is not ticking off the days until *you* can be declared legally dead, my dear Dr. Falcon. The princess has taken her daughter and yours back home to her original castle in her own country. I had the christening of the child," he added, wiping his eye. "Her little highness Hypatia. A beautiful babe, doctor, a beautiful babe. My sincerest congratulations.... Princess Ida's father has, of course, been released by Hilarion's royal parent, and at last report was instigating an investigation into some Central European income-tax scandal. Cyril and Florian took to wife the fair ladies Psyche and Melissa—I officiated at that double ceremony also. Lady Blanche set up shop here in England as headmistress of her own school for young women. Most of the other scholars returned home with their princess. Shall I furnish you their direction? I believe her highness would further relax some of her already modified rules in favor of little Hypatia's paternal parent."

Chuck hesitated. So his virtual inner male even came equipped with virtually viable sperm. The idea of seeing the child, his child...was tempting, very tempting. But, "No...no thanks," he finally said with a rueful shake of his head. "Send them my love, but it'll be better for all of us if I just return straight to my own universe. Ida will understand. We both knew what the terms would have to be."

They were turned away from the sea for their talk, and had not noticed how the waves and clouds were quietly forming another long slope up to the headland, as they had done a while ago for Chuck. Another man, a young one, had swum up and gained footing on the rock. Now, as the sun broke completely free of all clouds and bathed the headland, he cleared his throat and got their attention with a cough.

"Bob!" Chuck exclaimed. "Bob Lozinski. Welcome ashore."

"Thanks, Doc...Dr. Falcon?" Bob grinned apologetically. "I'm ready to wake up, now."

Chuck reached for his right ear. If the new little gadget worked... But was it really necessary? Didn't it depend on how much Bob had really understood, even in his comatose condition? "Dr. Daly, Sir Ruthven, I think...I'd like a little privacy, getting Bob back 'out there.' If you wouldn't mind saying goodbye now?"

"Dr. Falcon," said Sir Ruthven, "before you leave us...suppose that you, and Bob, and all the people of your world are, like us, the mental creations of some still larger intelligence? And so on and on into infinity?"

"Or until the Greatest Mind of all is reached," said the vicar. "And with that thought," he added, bowing to Bob Lozinski, "I trust you'll forgive me, young sir, if I refrain from setting up an altar to you."

"Oh, no!—I mean, I don't want any altars. Of course not." Bob shook his head. "Well, just...just carry on, then, huh?"

A few more good wishes; then vicar and baronet were on their way. As they disappeared over a hillock, Chuck twisted a sideburn and shimmered into Chandra.

Bob looked at her, looked again, and grinned in a very Ruthven-like way. "What would Princess Ida have said if she had known?"

"Never mind that," said Chandra Falcon. "What does Bob Lozinski say now that he knows?"

And, without either of them being aware quite how and when it happened, they were in each other's arms.

"Bob Lozinski says, it might be about time to set up a new household arrangement completely," he whispered just before the long, long kiss that began on the coastline of his virtual Cornwall and ended in the medical lab room of pylon 19.

AFTERWORD, BY CLEA ORTIZ NEWCOME

More than three decades have passed since first I entered this little fantasy into shipnet. To my knowledge, at least three ship-mates have thought highly enough of it to spend luxury chips on precious paper and other materials for bound printouts. Alicia Lang, Dave Tolstoy, and Cassandra Torelli the younger have at once time or another illustrated scenes from it, which can be seen from time to time gracing our gallery walls, most recently in the Old Earth Theater of pylon 9.

It is only fair to acknowledge that there have been complaints about the text. The most frequent: that I spend so little wordage on the story unfolding outside the virtual fantasy. But shipnet already held nineteen historical novels about Chuck Wang's computer virus and/or the Hunger Year at the time I wrote my *Bloody Herring*. The last three decades have added fourteen more to the bibliography; and this is in addition to the serious nonfictional studies.

The second most frequent complaint is that in fact the accident to pylon 5 happened months *after* Wang's execution by freezing. But even before that execution, some voices had already begun to prophesy some such catastrophe thanks to his virus, and almost all students and analysts have agreed ever since that it happened due to a fatal weakening still not isolated and corrected in time. In any case, it all but ended the controversy as to whether the death penalty should have been applied. As we all know, Chuck Wang himself was the only person to suffer that ultimate penalty; and, indeed, as far as we know, he acted completely alone, no one else so much as suspecting his "practical joke" until it was accomplished. Bob Lozinski, Pete Schultz, Barbara Cripps, and Steve Davis are as completely fictional as Misaki Lang, Sister Harriet, and my protagonist Chandra Falcon—whom I can freely acknowledge, now, to have been a youthful daydream of myself. Chuck Wang having been so heavily fictionalized as Judi Oshita, the single one of all my characters (excluding, of course, the barely-glimpsed Papa Gadore himself) who can justly be said to have been based on life is, of course, Deuteronomy Osborne, fictional alter ego of the famous Leviticus Osgood, whom in early childhood I myself had the privilege of calling "Uncle Leo" in more than a casual social sense: in fact, he was to me a sort of honorary godfather.

The third most frequent complaint concerns nomenclature: that the name "Chuck" constitutes a false red herring. But Charles used to be a completely legitimate and not uncommon first name, and I for one have always regretted that it got soiled and fell out of popular use. It seems equally melancholy that all this man's descendants adopted the surnames of housemates and lovers, so that today the family name "Wang" appears nowhere in the living roster of the ship's population. Neither nationality nor personal name in itself signals criminality, which is why I carefully gave one of the good guys as Oriental a name as my fictionalized version of Chuck Wang.

One last objection is that I failed to actually spell out a happy shipboard ending for Chandra and Bob. I had not, at the time, felt it necessary. It had seemed to me that the cues were there in place for readers to assume Bob, Pete, and Barbara would all be quickly cleared of suspicion and freed to live their lives within bounds of the whole ship. In this, I seem to have mistaken. Three people have done me the honor of sequelizing my *Bloody Herring*, at the rate of one sequel making its shipnet appearance about every decade. Each sequel is independent of the others, and only the latest, *Herring Wine*, by whoever lies cleverly concealed under the pen name "Xandra Hapgood," carries on more or less as I had envisaged, with Judi's three housemates cleared and set free after a short investigation. *The Herring on the Wheel*, by Brother Luke Kasmierski, O.C.C., has all four housemates executed by freezing and Chandra withdrawing into the virtual fantasy—becoming, in effect, herself Mad Margaret as she relives the old dreams sometimes blissfully, more often in nightmare. The bitterly anti-Committee tone of Brother Luke's work should be taken into account; he seems at times less interested in telling a story than in making his points. And the earliest of the sequels, *The Herring Vindicated*, by Pat Chin, climaxes with a long trial before the ship judiciary as it existed—at least in Chin's reconstruction—a decade after Liftaway: after exciting legal maneuvers which occupy the bulk of the novel, Bob, Pete, and Barbara are finally acquitted and move in together with Chandra and Misaki to form a new, very genmoralistic household. Pat Chin being as pro-Committee and pro-genetic morality as Brother Luke against, *The Herring on the Wheel* might be seen as less a sequel to *The Bloody Herring* than a reaction to *The Herring Vindicated*.

It has also been suggested that Princess Ida's views on gender have been grotesquely exaggerated. But (a) they come straight from the Old Earth opera bearing her name and (b) not one of us in *Papa's Pride* today can ever fully understand the pressures of this historical Old Earth "problem" or the forces such a woman as Princess Ida must have felt demanded her vehement protest. It is thanks to women like her that we enjoy our own free society.

In sum, although this little novel would have been very different had I written it in maturity rather than youth, I do not today feel either the need or—more important—the artistic desire to revise it.

—C. O. N.,

Gormenghast Cottage, ship year 95.

A POSTSCRIPT FROM THE ACTUAL AUTHOR

The greater part of this novel was written 1978-1980 as a sort of double piece of fan fiction: a Gilbert and Sullivan fantasy within another creator's fictional universe. While snowbound in the spring of 2013, I transferred it into a framework drawn from my own fictional universe, that of the great exploration-colony starship *Papa's Pride*, which I started developing in 2011.

I feel confident that in this new version *The Bloody Herring* violates no one's copyright, the Savoy Operas themselves having been safe in Public Domain since the appropriately "upside-down" (at least in Arabic numerals) year of 1961.

—Phyllis Ann Karr Hoyt
"The Hobbitat," May, 2013

www.ingramcontent.com/pod-product-compliance
Lightning Source LLC
Chambersburg PA
CBHW051250250626
47155CB00009B/3235